ARNALDUR INDRIDASON

Arnaldur Indridason worked for many years as a journalist and critic before he began writing novels. His books have since sold over 13 million copies worldwide. Outside Iceland, he is best known for his crime novels featuring Erlendur and Sigurdur Óli, which are consistent bestsellers across Europe. The series has won numerous awards, including the Nordic Glass Key and the CWA Gold Dagger. *The Shadow District* won the Premio RBA de Novela Negra, the world's most lucrative crime fiction prize.

ALSO BY ARNALDUR INDRIDASON

ARNALDUR INDRIDASON

The Shadow District

TRANSLATED FROM THE ICELANDIC BY
Victoria Cribb

VINTAGE

1 3 5 7 9 10 8 6 4 2

Vintage
20 Vauxhall Bridge Road,
London SW1V 2SA

Vintage is part of the Penguin Random House group of companies
whose addresses can be found at global.penguinrandomhouse.com

Penguin
Random House
UK

First published in Vintage in 2018
First published in hardback by Harvill Secker in 2017
First published with the title *Skuggasund* in Iceland by
Vaka-Helgafell in 2013
Published by agreement with Forlagid www.forlagid.is

penguin.co.uk/vintage

A CIP catalogue record for this book is available from the British Library

ISBN 9781784704414 (B format)
ISBN 9781784704421 (A format)

This book has been translated with financial support from:

 MIÐSTÖÐ ÍSLENSKRA BÓKMENNTA
ICELANDIC LITERATURE CENTER

Printed and bound by Clays Ltd, St Ives plc

Penguin Random House is committed to a sustainable future
for our business, our readers and our planet. This book is
made from Forest Stewardship Council® certified paper.

MIX
Paper from
responsible sources
FSC® C018179

THE SHADOW DISTRICT

1

The police decided to enter the flat, but rather than break down the door they called a locksmith, figuring that a few minutes either way were unlikely to make a difference.

A neighbour had raised the alarm. She didn't dial the police emergency number but instead rang the main switchboard and informed the officer who took her call that she was a little worried as she hadn't seen her next-door neighbour for several days.

'He tends to drop in before he goes shopping,' she said. 'And I usually hear him coming and going, or spot him from my window walking to the shop, but I haven't seen him or heard him at all in the last few days.'

'Could he have gone out of town?'

'Out of town? He never leaves town.'

'Or to visit friends or relatives?'

'I don't think he has many friends, and he's never mentioned any relatives.'

'How old is he?'

'About ninety. But fit. He looks after himself, runs all his own errands.'

'Could he be in hospital?'

'No, I ... I'd have noticed. I live right across the landing from him.'

'Or could he have moved into a home? Sounds like it wouldn't be before time.'

'I ... goodness, what a lot of questions. I can't answer them all. But not everyone wants to just shuffle off into a home, you know. He's in very good health.'

'All right, thank you for ringing, dear. We'd better send someone round.'

Now there were two police officers standing outside the old man's door, waiting for the locksmith. The neighbour, whose name was Birgitta, was there as well. One of the officers had a prominent paunch; the other was much younger and so thin his uniform hung off him. They looked almost comical as they stood there chatting on the landing. The fat man, who was older, was the more experienced of the pair. This wouldn't be the first time he'd had to enter the home of a vulnerable elderly person who lived alone. Several times a year the police received requests to check up on people who had fallen through the gaps in the welfare system. The locksmith, Ómar, was one of his cousins and could pick a lock in seconds.

Ómar appeared on the landing and they exchanged cousinly greetings. All it took was a quick tinker with the lock and the door opened without a hitch.

'Hello!' the fat cop called into the flat.

There was no answer. Telling his cousin and the woman from

next door to wait outside, he beckoned his partner to follow him in.

'Hello!' he called again. Still no reply.

The policemen made their way cautiously into the flat. The fat cop sniffed the air. The smell that greeted them was bad enough for both men to clamp their hands over their noses. All the curtains were drawn and the lights were on in the hall, kitchen and sitting room.

'Hello!' called the thin officer, a little shrilly. 'Anybody home?'

No answer. The locksmith and Birgitta waited obediently outside the door.

The kitchen was small but tidy. There was a table with two chairs drawn up to it, and a coffee maker on the counter by the sink, its jug half full. It was switched off. In the sink were a bowl and two cups. There was a small fridge at one end of the room, and an old electric cooker with three hobs. A glance into the sitting room revealed a sofa and matching chairs, a coffee table and a desk by the south-facing window. There were books on the shelves but few ornaments. The sitting room was as neat and tidy as the kitchen.

The flat was carpeted throughout, with the exception of the lavatory and kitchen, and the wear and tear on the paths between the rooms was obvious. In one place the carpet was worn right through to the white threads that held it together. Next, the policemen opened the door to the bedroom and there, stretched out on top of a single bed, lay a man with eyes half closed, his arms down by his sides. He was dressed in shirt, trousers and socks, and looked for all the world as if he had decided to take a nap in the middle of the day and never got up again. Flat on his back like that, he didn't look ninety. The older officer went over to

3

the bed and felt for a pulse in his neck and wrist. You could hardly imagine a more polite death, was the first thought that crossed his mind.

'Is he dead?' asked the skinny cop.

'Looks like it,' said his partner.

Birgitta, unable to restrain herself any longer, tiptoed inside and peered into the bedroom where her neighbour was lying in tranquil solitude.

'Is he . . . dead?'

'I think we can be confident of that,' said the older officer.

'The poor, dear man, he must be glad to be at peace,' she said quietly.

Later that day the body was transferred to the National Hospital morgue where it was received and duly registered by the pathologist. According to procedure, the district physician had been called to the flat and pronounced the man dead at the scene. His death was not being treated as suspicious and no police inquiry would be judged necessary unless something untoward came to light during the post-mortem. In the meantime the flat was secured and the door would remain sealed until the pathologist's report was available.

The pathologist, whose name was Svanhildur, put off the post-mortem until later in the week. The matter wasn't urgent, and she had more than enough to do as it was before her upcoming three-week holiday to an attractive Florida golf course.

Two days later she slid the body out of the refrigeration unit and transferred it to the dissection table. A small group of medical students was there to observe the post-mortem and she went over the examination with them point by point. She filled them in on the circumstances: the body had been found after a neighbour notified the police; everything indicated that the man had died of natural causes. Nevertheless, she managed to engage the students' interest to the extent that one even briefly stopped listening to his iPod while she was talking.

Svanhildur was working on the assumption that the cause of death was cardiac arrest, and it turned out that she was right. The man had died of a heart attack. The problem was that she couldn't see any reason for it.

She examined his eyes.

Took a look down his throat.

'Aha,' she murmured, and the students leaned in closer over the table.

2

They hurried past the sandbagged sentry post in front of the National Theatre. She tried not to make it obvious that they were together, at least not while they were walking down the busier streets. Her parents had been furious when they learnt of the relationship and demanded that she break it off immediately. Her father had actually threatened to throw her out of the house, and she knew he would be as good as his word. She had been unprepared for such a violent reaction. Yet, unwilling as she was to defy her parents, she stubbornly resisted ending the relationship. Instead, she stopped talking about him and let them think it was over, but she carried on meeting him in secret.

There were few places to go if they wanted to be together. Back in late autumn, when they had first started courting, they had gone to Öskjuhlíd hill when the weather was fine. But now, in the depths of winter, their options were very limited. Checking into a hotel was out of the question, and so were the barracks. Once before they had resorted to the back of the National Theatre after nightfall. The building loomed darkly over Hverfisgata like the huge outcrop of columnar basalt it was designed to resemble, though it was in fact no more than a hollow shell. Work had halted on the ambitious project ten years ago with the onset of the Depression, and when the British occupied Iceland in 1940 they had requisitioned it as a supply depot, a role it had retained when the Americans took over in 1941. Now it was a popular meeting place for illicit lovers.

'You're never to see that man again!' her father had roared, beside himself with rage, and for the first time in her life he would have raised his hand to her if her mother hadn't intervened.

She had given him her word, only to go back on it straight away. Her lover's name was Frank, he came from Illinois, and he was always clean and neat and smelt nice, and he had beautiful white teeth. And such gentlemanly, polite manners. They had talked of moving to the States together when the war was over. She was convinced her father would approve of him, if only the old man could be persuaded to meet him.

It wasn't as though she was the only one, as though their relationship was unique. At the beginning of the war Reykjavík had had a population of forty thousand, but since then tens of thousands of servicemen had poured into the town. Liaisons between soldiers and Icelandic women were inevitable with the arrival of the Tommies, and they rapidly increased in number when the Tommies were succeeded by the Yanks who, with smarter uniforms, more money and better manners, were almost like film stars to the locals. Language was no barrier – the language of romance was universal. But such was the resulting moral panic that a committee was set up to deal with this scandalous state of affairs which came to be known, in all its manifestations, as the Situation.

She didn't give two hoots about committees and the Situation as she dashed across Hverfisgata with Frank from Illinois. It was a chilly evening in the middle of February. The wind whistled around the manmade castle of rock designed to resemble the elf palaces of Icelandic folklore. On entering the imposing theatre building, audiences were supposed to imagine that they were stepping inside a mountain, being transported to the gleaming halls of fairy tale. But for now, the sentries, huddled behind their barricade of sandbags, paid little attention to the pair who hastened round the corner, taking refuge from the street lights. She was wearing the warm coat she had been given for Christmas; he wore his army greatcoat over the uniform she found so glamorous. He was a sergeant with men under his command, though she didn't know exactly what this entailed. Her knowledge of English didn't go much beyond 'yes', 'no' and 'darling', and his Icelandic was no better. Yet in spite of this they managed to understand each other quite well, and right now she needed to talk to him about a matter that was weighing heavily on her mind.

The instant they were out of the wind, Frank began kissing her hungrily. She felt his hands fumbling under her coat and her thoughts flew to her father. If he could see her now. She heard Frank whispering endearments in her ear: 'Oh, my darling.' Felt his icy hands through the blouse that she had bought from Jacobsen after New Year. He stroked her breasts through the thin material, then unbuttoned her blouse, touching bare flesh. She remained passive, inexperienced in the ways of lovemaking, though she usually enjoyed kissing him and felt a hot frisson run through her body when he touched her. Now, though, it was

8

freezing cold and she wasn't in the mood; her father's fury loomed over her, and the thing she had to say to Frank was preying on her mind.

'Frank, there's something I have to tell you . . .'

'*My darling.*'

He was so ardent that she lost her balance, stumbled and almost fell. He caught her and made to carry on but she insisted he stop. They were sheltering in a small doorway and something had tripped her up. She saw that it was a large, broken-up cardboard box and some other rubbish that she assumed must have come from the depot. She hadn't noticed it when they slipped hand in hand into the doorway. And only now did she realise that sticking out from the debris were two slender legs.

'*Jesus,*' groaned Frank.

'What is it?' she asked. 'Who is it?'

They stared down at the legs: at the shoes with a strap over the instep, the ankle socks and above them the bare, blue-white skin. Nothing else was visible. Frank hesitated a second, then bent down and tugged at the cardboard.

'What are you doing?' she whispered.

He dragged the broken box out of the doorway, uncovering a young woman of no more than twenty, who lay on her side against the wall. It was immediately obvious to both of them that she was dead.

'Oh my God!' she gasped, clutching at Frank, who couldn't take his eyes off the body.

'*What the hell?*' he muttered under his breath as he squatted down beside the girl. He took hold of her wrist but couldn't feel a pulse, then put his fingers to her neck, though he knew it was futile. A shudder ran through him. He had not yet seen combat

9

and was unused to dead bodies, but he could tell at once that nothing could be done for the young woman. He searched quickly for signs of how she had died, but couldn't immediately see any.

'What are we going to do?'

Frank rose to his feet, putting his arm round his Icelandic girl. He liked her fine and understood only too well why she had never invited him home to meet her family. A lot of doors were closed to soldiers.

'*Let's get the hell out of here*,' he said, peering round to see if the coast was clear.

'Shouldn't we fetch the police?' she asked. '*Get police.*'

He couldn't spot anyone nearby. Sneaking a look round the corner, he saw that the sentries were still at their post behind the sandbags.

'*No police. No. Let's go. Go!*'

'*Yes, police.*' She said, struggling to resist him.

Pulling her by the arm, he hustled her in the direction of Lindargata, then along the road towards the grassy mound of Arnarhóll. As he was quicker on his feet, he almost dragged her along, and their progress attracted the attention of an older woman who was walking down Lindargata. She was on her way to Hverfisgata, on a route that would take her past the National Theatre. They didn't notice her, but she had seen them fleeing from a dark recess behind the building. The way these girls carried on, she thought. Why, she had a feeling she recognised this one, used to teach her at one time. Didn't realise *she* was caught up in the Situation.

As the woman passed the theatre, she peered into the doorway from which the couple had emerged and spotted the rubbish from the depot. She paused, then caught sight of the legs. Moving closer, she saw the girl's body, which somebody had obviously tried to conceal among the scraps of old cardboard and other refuse. What immediately drew her attention was how inadequately the girl was dressed for the time of year, in nothing but a thin slip of a dress.

The wind howled around the building.

The girl was beautiful, even in death, staring up with glazed eyes at the forbidding edifice above her, as if her spirit had departed into the elf castle evoked by the theatre walls.

3

Rivulets of sweat were pouring down Marta's cheeks. She had ordered number seven, the pork curry, described as the hottest dish on the menu. Konráð, who had tried a little of hers and could taste nothing but chilli, was frantically gulping down lemon water to soothe his scorched mouth and lips. He had ordered a chicken dish that actually tasted of something; in fact, it was pretty good.

The restaurant, a Thai place situated in an industrial zone on the outskirts of Reykjavík, looked rather uninviting at first glance, its frontage more like a garage than an eatery. It was the kind of place Marta liked: cheap, with fast service, good food, and no danger of any yuppies wandering in off the street.

When Marta had rung Konráð from the police station to ask if he felt like coming out for a meal, he had jumped at the chance. It was a while since he'd heard from her, and, besides, he had nothing better to do now that he was retired. Despite the age gap they had worked well together in CID, but since Konráð left their relationship had changed and lost its easy intimacy. Meeting up felt different somehow, as if they were no longer on the same team: Konrád had clocked off for good; Marta was still immersed in police work, her caseload heavier than ever.

'Bit hot for you, is it?' asked Konrád, watching the streams of sweat coursing down Marta's cheeks.

'I wouldn't say that. It's good, and I've eaten hotter.'

'I'm sure you have.' Konrád let it drop. It was too easy to get a rise out of Marta. She could never let anyone get the better of her, never admit she was in the wrong; she always had to have the final word.

'How are things with you?' she asked.

'Not bad. You?'

'Surviving.'

Marta finished her curry and mopped her face. She was on the plump side, with thick fingers, a large double chin and heavy eyelids that had a tendency to droop, especially after a big meal. Her hair was usually a mess and she wore an unvarying costume of baggy shirts and trousers. She didn't see the point in tarting herself up – didn't know who it would be for. She was known in the force, with typical irony, as Smart Marta. She had shacked up with a woman from the Westman Islands for a while, but the woman had eventually taken the boat home. Since then Marta had lived alone.

'Heard from Svanhildur at all?' Marta asked, picking her teeth, a habit that got on Konrád's nerves, especially when she started sucking air through them and blowing it out with loud smacking sounds.

'No,' said Konrád. It was a while since he had caught up with his old friend from the National Hospital.

'She's just been on the phone to us about a man who was found

13

dead in his flat. A pensioner who lived alone. We assumed he'd died in his sleep. His name was Stefán Thórdarson. Maybe you heard about it?'

Konrád nodded. He recalled a report in the newspaper several days earlier. A pensioner had been found dead in his bed. He had lived by himself and appeared to have passed away alone and neglected. A neighbour had alerted the police after she hadn't seen him for several days.

'What about him?'

'Doesn't Svanhildur keep you posted on the interesting stuff?'

'I don't know where people get that idea.'

'Well, she discovered something that had completely escaped the doctor we called to the scene.'

'Not much gets by her,' said Konrád.

'She thinks this Stefán was smothered. With his own pillow, probably.'

'Really?'

'She reckons he was murdered.'

'Why, for Christ's sake? He was ancient, wasn't he?'

'What do you mean?' countered Marta. 'Why was he murdered or why does Svanhildur think he was?'

She regarded Konrád with heavy-lidded, sated eyes, jabbing at her teeth with the toothpick. Konrád smiled, regretting that he had passed up the chance to needle her earlier.

'All right,' he said. 'Let's start with the first question: why was he murdered?'

'We don't know.'

'Then what makes Svanhildur think he was murdered?'

'Traces in his throat and upper respiratory tract,' recited Marta. 'Tiny broken blood vessels in his eyes. The usual.'

'What sort of traces? Fibres from his pillow?'

'Yeah. Svanhildur says someone must have held the pillow over his face until he breathed his last. Quite literally. He wasn't capable of putting up much of a fight. The poor old boy was over ninety, after all. It would have been over in no time, but even so those telltale fibres remained.'

'That old, was he?'

'Yes, it wouldn't have taken much to smother him. The officers who found the body didn't suspect a thing. There were two pillows, one under his head, the other beside it. He . . . It looked like he'd died in his sleep.'

'In other words, someone wanted it to look like that. Like he'd died of old age?'

'So it seems.'

'And it had you lot fooled?' Konrád couldn't resist a little dig. 'Were you there?'

Marta sucked her teeth. 'The medic who was called in to examine him didn't notice anything suspicious. And we're not doctors – it wasn't our job to go poking around in his throat.'

'So what made Svanhildur check?'

'Why don't you talk to her?'

'Maybe I will.'

'You do that.'

'Who was he? Anyone you know?'

'You mean was he an old friend of the police? No, he wasn't. He lived alone, like I said. Not a single brush with the law, at least not in the last twenty years. We still haven't managed to track down anyone who knew him, apart from the woman next door.'

'No friends or family?'

'None that we know of. Not yet. No one's laid claim to him.

Though maybe that'll change now. The news'll break online this evening. It'll be in the papers by morning. We'll see if that has any effect.'

'Was it a burglary? Any sign of a forced entry?'

'None. We've carried out a thorough investigation of the flat. Forensics have been there all day.'

'So he knew the guy who did it? Opened the door to him? Invited him in?'

'I thought you'd retired?'

'I have,' said Konrád. 'Thank God.'

4

When Konrád got home that evening he put on a record of Icelandic pop hits from the sixties, uncorked a bottle of red wine – Dead Arm, a favourite of his – and sat down at the kitchen table. The window faced west and the room was bathed in a soft pink glow. He loved to listen to golden oldies, knew all the lyrics by heart. They would run through his head at odd moments, reawakening memories warm with nostalgia. He had only to hear Ingimar Eydal's band playing the opening bars of 'Spring in Vaglaskógur' for his mind to fly back to the summer of 1966 when he had first heard the song.

His reverie was interrupted by the ringing of the phone in the sitting room and he got up to answer the call. It was past 11 p.m., so it could only be Marta. She would pick up the phone at any hour of the day or night for the most trivial of excuses. Often just for a chat. She'd been lonely since her girlfriend moved back to the Westman Islands.

'Were you asleep?' asked Marta, not sounding in the least concerned.

'No.'

'What are you up to?'

'Nothing. Any developments in the dead pensioner case?'

'We've finished searching his flat.'

'And?'

'We didn't find much. He lived alone and we still haven't established whether he had any living relatives. There were no family photos on the walls, no albums. Though he did keep a photo of a young man in a drawer by his bed. He had a few books, but apart from that hardly any personal possessions. The only items of interest were some old newspaper cuttings he must have hung on to for years.'

'Oh?'

'Yes. Not that there's much to be gained from them. I don't remember ever hearing about the case.'

'The case?'

'The one in the cuttings. There are three of them, probably from the same paper, but they're not dated or anything. There's no indication that the case was ever solved or taken over by the Americans. The last article says the investigation's ongoing but the police are reporting little progress.'

'What are you talking about? The Americans?'

'I'm talking about a murder inquiry,' said Marta. 'During the Second World War. A girl found strangled behind the National Theatre in 1944. Wasn't that the year you were born?'

'Yes.'

'The case seems to have sunk without trace. I can't find any record of it in the police files. We had to track it down in the newspaper archives.'

'The body of a girl, found behind the National Theatre?'

'Yes. What?'

'Nothing . . .'

'Does it ring a bell?'

Konrád hesitated. 'No, I don't know.'

'What?'

'Nothing.'

'Why are you being so mysterious?'

'I'm just sleepy,' said Konrád distractedly. 'It's rude to ring people this late. Let's talk tomorrow.'

He said goodbye, drained his glass and got ready for bed. But sleep eluded him. Thoughts about his father and the dead girl behind the theatre kept him awake into the early hours. Although he had been reluctant to share the fact with Marta, he was actually familiar with the case because of his father's rather bizarre connection to it. Konrád didn't much like talking about his dad, who had at one time dabbled in spiritualism, in partnership with a variety of psychics whose reputations didn't bear close scrutiny. A few months after her death, the murdered girl's parents had contacted one of these mediums and asked him to hold a seance for them. Konrád's father had assisted. What happened at the seance had subsequently ended up in the papers.

Konrád stroked his left arm absently, wondering whether he should pay Marta a visit or let sleeping dogs lie. He had been born with a slightly withered limb, a defect that seldom bothered him; after all, no one would really notice that his left arm and hand were weaker than his right. Unable to get comfortable, he went on tossing and turning until somewhere in the no-man's-land between waking and dreaming the notes of 'Spring in Vaglaskógur' stole into his mind and he drifted off to sleep at last, accompanied by a fair memory of yellow sand at Nauthólsvík Cove, children playing by the water's edge, and a flower-scented kiss.

5

She nearly jumped out of her skin when she heard someone knocking at the front door. It was late and she instinctively knew it must be the police, and that they had come for her.

She and Frank had fled over Arnarhóll in the teeth of a vicious north wind, down onto Kalkofnsvegur, and from there had walked towards Lækjargata and the centre of town, trying to act as if nothing had happened. In her mind's eye she could still see the girl lying in the doorway behind the theatre, and knew she would never be able to wipe the image from her mind. She couldn't understand Frank's reaction, their idiotic flight from the scene. His decision to run had been spontaneous; she had wanted to fetch the police. When they finally slowed down he had tried to communicate his reasons. It was none of their business. The girl was dead. They couldn't help her now. Someone else was bound to find her soon and then the problem would go away.

People were scurrying out of the icy wind into cinemas, into cafes or off to visit friends. Jeeps full of troops roared past along Lækjargata and up Bankastræti. Frank thought they had better split up right away. They could meet again in a few days' time, in their usual spot behind the cathedral. By then the fuss should have died down. He kissed her goodbye and she hurried home through the centre of town.

Although she knew it was wrong of them to run off and leave the girl like that, part of her was relieved. Perhaps Frank had done the sensible thing after all. She didn't relish the thought of having to explain to the police, or anyone else for that matter, just what she had been doing with him behind the theatre, why she had been sneaking off into dark corners with a GI. If the news ever got back to her father he would go berserk.

There was another round of knocking on the door downstairs, more insistent this time. Her parents had retired for the night and her two younger brothers were asleep. She had slipped into the house and up to her room as unobtrusively as possible, changed into her nightdress and climbed into bed, but sleep wouldn't come. She had tried to read a romance but couldn't tear her thoughts away from the dead girl and Frank.

Damn her, she caught herself thinking, as if it were all the poor girl's fault.

She heard her father moving about, then every step creaking as he went downstairs. She slid out of bed and pressed her ear to her bedroom door. Perhaps it wasn't the police after all. Perhaps it was somebody else.

No such luck. Hearing her father call her name, she shrank back and retreated across her room.

'Ingiborg!' she heard him shout again. Then a third time, his impatience growing.

22

Her door opened and her mother poked her head in.

'Your father's calling you, dear,' she said. 'Didn't you hear him? The police want to talk to you. What on earth have you been up to?'

'Nothing,' she said, aware how miserably unconvincing it sounded.

'Downstairs with you this minute,' snapped her mother. 'Come along. On the double. Goodness, what a to-do!'

She followed her mother out onto the landing and down the first few steps until she could see two men standing in the hall with her father, their faces turned expectantly towards the staircase.

'There you are,' said her father in an agitated voice. 'These gentlemen are from the police.' He turned to one of them. 'I'm sorry, I've forgotten your name.'

'Flóvent, sir,' replied the man. 'And this is Thorson,' he added, indicating his companion. 'He's here on behalf of the American military police, though strictly speaking he's Canadian Army. I daresay his Icelandic is better than mine.'

'I'm Canadian. From Manitoba,' explained Thorson. 'My parents emigrated from Iceland.'

Neither man was in uniform. The Icelandic policeman, who looked to be in his thirties, was tall, thin and wiry. Thorson, shorter and stockier, was about ten years his junior. They were both wearing heavy winter coats but had removed their hats when they entered the house.

'Ah, yes, Manitoba,' said her father. 'You don't say?' Then he rounded angrily on his daughter. 'They want to talk to you, Ingiborg, about an incident that took place behind the National Theatre. They won't tell me what it's about – they insist on speaking to you first. I want to know what happened. What in God's name were you doing there?'

She hardly dared look at her father, let alone answer him. The policemen apparently sensed her discomfort.

'If it's all the same to you, sir,' said Flóvent, 'we'd appreciate a word with your daughter in private.'

'In private?' barked her father. 'Why is that necessary?'

'If you wouldn't mind, sir. We can discuss it with you afterwards, if you'd like, together with the young lady.'

'What is the meaning of this, Ingiborg? Why won't you answer me?' Her father raised his voice. 'Would you mind explaining to me why a representative of the American military police is standing in my hall? Surely, you're not still carrying on with that soldier? Didn't I expressly forbid it?'

'Yes,' she admitted timidly, not knowing how else to answer.

'Yet you're still seeing him? In spite of . . . !'

For a moment it looked as though he was going to reach up and drag her the rest of the way down the stairs.

'Calm down, Ísleifur,' said his wife sharply from where she was standing beside their daughter. 'I'd rather you didn't speak like that in front of visitors.'

Her husband got hold of himself. He shot a look at his wife, then at the two policemen who were still standing there holding their hats, growing uncomfortably hot in their thick winter coats. It had been snowing outside and their shoulders were beaded with moisture.

'I beg your pardon,' he said.

'That's quite all right, sir,' said Thorson. 'It's never pleasant receiving a visit late at night like this. Especially not from the police.'

'I've strictly forbidden her to fraternise with soldiers but it seems she's determined to disobey me. Doesn't listen to a word I say. Her mother encourages it – this wilfulness.'

24

'If we might . . . if you would show us to a quiet place where we could have a word with Ingiborg, sir, we'd be very grateful,' said Flóvent. 'I assure you it won't take long. And please excuse us again for disturbing you at such a late hour. We felt it couldn't wait until morning.'

'You can use the drawing room,' said the girl's mother, coming down the stairs with Ingiborg following on her heels. She cast fearful glances at her father. The last thing she wanted was to anger him; in spite of everything she respected him. She knew she had put him in an awkward position by stubbornly persisting in meeting Frank, and now there were two policemen in their house and it was all her fault.

Her mother showed the men into the drawing room and pushed Ingiborg in after them. Ísleifur made to follow but she stopped him.

'We can talk to them afterwards,' she said firmly, closing the door.

'And her,' said her husband grimly. 'She'll have to answer for her actions, the silly little slut.'

'That's enough,' said his wife, now angry herself. 'I won't let you talk about our daughter like that.'

'But it's intolerable,' her husband snapped at her. 'Don't you understand? The girl's up to her neck in the Situation! The police here in our house! How could she do this to me? What do you think people will say? You know there'll be gossip. I have to think of my reputation. Do you have any idea what that means for a man in my position? It doesn't even cross your mind, does it? My reputation?'

25

6

Gratefully, they removed their heavy coats and hung them over the back of a chair in the drawing room. Having waited politely for Ingiborg to take a seat, Flóvent sat down himself, but Thorson remained standing behind him. The notification had reached Flóvent almost two hours earlier: a woman passing through the area known as the Shadow District had come across the body of a young woman behind the National Theatre building. On learning that the witness had seen two figures hurrying away from the scene in the direction of Arnarhóll, one of them unmistakably an American serviceman, Flóvent had put out a call for Thorson. The two men had worked together on other cases that fell within the jurisdictions of both the Icelandic police and the US Military Police Corps.

When war broke out Thorson had enlisted with the Canadian Army and, following the British occupation of Iceland, quickly found himself posted there as an interpreter. He had initially served with the British military police, then with the Americans when they took over the defence of the country. Born in Canada to Icelandic parents, he spoke the language fluently and was employed as a liaison officer between the occupying force and the Icelandic police. Although Thorson had never worked as a detective, he had taken a keen interest in the investigations right from the start, and he and Flóvent had come to collaborate on all the more serious cases involving servicemen and local civilians. The two men got on well and both preferred to solve cases with a minimum of red tape, sidestepping, where possible, the inevitable delays that would result from using the labyrinthine official channels.

When the report came in that a body had been found, Flóvent had been alone in the offices of Reykjavík's fledgling Criminal Investigation Department, which was housed in the large building at number 11 Fríkirkjuvegur. This property, which stood near the small lake in the centre of town and resembled an Italianate villa with its ornamental columns and balconies, had once belonged to the wealthiest family in Iceland. Before the war it had passed into the hands of the Temperance Movement, who now rented out office space to the Criminal Investigation Department, among others. Flóvent enjoyed working there, though the rest of the small plain-clothes team had been seconded to other assignments as part of the war effort, and detective work had been largely suspended.

When the phone rang he had just returned to the office after a conversation with his father and had been intending to dedicate a few hours to the fingerprint archive. Their conversation had revolved once again around the plot in the cemetery on Sudurgata. His father wanted him to look into the possibility of locating

27

and disinterring the remains of his mother and sister, and moving them to a new plot where father and son could also be buried in due course, but Flóvent was less than enthusiastic. He felt it would be better to leave well alone, but in the end he had half promised to find out who else shared the mass grave with his mother and sister and look into the possibility of opening it up. The grave had been dug at the height of the Spanish flu epidemic in 1918.

Flóvent strode briskly along Lækjargata in the blisteringly cold north wind, past the statue of the old poet laureate, Jónas Hallgrímsson. There was hardly anyone about. He had got into the habit of greeting Jónas whenever he walked by. Over time this had developed into a superstitious compulsion to raise a hand to him or silently recite a line of his verse, for fear it would call down bad luck if he neglected the ritual. 'No one mourns an Icelander / Lying in his lonely grave . . .'

A small knot of people had gathered by the National Theatre: the woman who had discovered the body, a couple of passers-by and the sentries who had now ventured out from behind their barricade of sandbags.

Thorson was over at the US naval air station at Nauthólsvík Cove when he belatedly received the summons. He jumped into the military jeep at his disposal and tore into town, reaching the theatre just as they were about to remove the body. After greeting Flóvent, he knelt down beside the girl.

'Injuries to the neck?' he asked.

'Yes, she appears to have been strangled.'

Judging by her clothes, the young woman must have been killed elsewhere, then dumped in the doorway. She could hardly have been outside wearing a flimsy dress and nothing else in that weather. It appeared that someone had tried to conceal her body under pieces of cardboard and other rubbish.

'Not a very good hiding place,' remarked Thorson, looking up at the gloomy building.

'No, indeed.'

'There are sentries out front.'

Flóvent shrugged. 'You can drive a vehicle right up to the back of the building. It would've taken next to no time to dispose of the body.'

'But why here, why the National Theatre?'

'Good question.'

'Perhaps the murderer was making a dramatic gesture,' said Thorson. 'By leaving her here.'

'What about the soldiers manning the depot?' asked Flóvent. 'Could she have been inside? Did she know someone here?'

'How come the witness is so sure the man she saw was American?' asked Thorson, glancing over at the older woman who had found the body. She was standing a little way off with two uniformed policemen, complaining that she didn't have time for all this and needed to be getting home.

'She's positive.'

'There are still some British troops around. Canadians too. And Norwegians.'

'She recognised the young woman with him as well.'

'Oh?'

'Says she used to teach her at Reykjavík College.'

'It's not exactly a tough job,' said Thorson, wrapping his great-coat more tightly around himself.

'What isn't?'

'Being a cop in Reykjavík.'

'Maybe not,' said Flóvent. 'Right, I'm going to get a photographer out here. We need pictures of the scene.'

Ingiborg looked mortified as she sat hunched in the chair, her thoughts focused on her father waiting out in the hall. Both men sensed they would have to go easy on her if they didn't want her to break down.

'You're not the only girl meeting soldiers in secret, miss,' said Thorson in a friendly voice. 'Not the first and you won't be the last either.'

She tried to smile.

'What's his name, miss?' asked Flóvent. 'The soldier you were with.'

'Please, there's no need to call me "miss".'

'All right,' said Flóvent.

'Frank,' she replied. 'His name's Frank. Have you spoken to him?'

'No. Frank what – do you know his surname?' asked Thorson.

'Of course I do. Frank Carroll. He's a sergeant. How did you know I was there? Did somebody see me?'

'It's a small town,' said Thorson drily.

'You were spotted by a woman who recognised you,' Flóvent elaborated. 'It doesn't matter who she is, but she saw you with a soldier, an American, and assumed you two must have hurt the girl, then made a run for it. Was she right?'

'No!' exclaimed Ingiborg vehemently. 'I've never seen the girl before. Never in my life. Frank and I were . . . we only went there to . . . you know . . .'

'Neck?' suggested Thorson.

'Daddy doesn't want me seeing him. You heard what he said. He's forbidden me to meet him. There are so few places we can go.

30

I don't like being around the other soldiers, and I don't want to ask my friends to lend us their rooms, so really all we can do is meet out of doors. We've been there once before.'

'What is he? Infantry? Artillery?'

'All I know is that he's a sergeant. We don't talk much about the army. He hates it and he's afraid of being sent to Europe.'

'Where did you two meet?'

'At Hótel Borg. Last autumn. He's ever such a nice man. So polite and considerate.'

'So you mainly meet at dances?'

'Yes. He's . . . he's a terrific dancer.'

'You like the jitterbug?' asked Thorson, trying to lighten the atmosphere a little.

'Yes.'

'What else do you know about Frank?'

'He's from Illinois. He's five years older than me. He's going to start a car dealership when he gets out of the army. Everyone owns a car in America. He likes going to the movies, but I haven't dared go with him since Daddy banned me from meeting him. He has two brothers and lives with his mother. His father's dead.'

'Did he strangle the girl in the doorway of the theatre?' asked Flóvent with sudden brutality.

Ingiborg recoiled in shock. 'No! He didn't lay a finger on her. I don't know who the girl was. Oh my goodness, you mustn't say things like that. Was she strangled?'

'Did you watch him do it?'

'Me? No, I . . . no, how could you say such a terrible thing?'

'Afterwards did you take her and dump her behind the theatre like a worthless piece of rubbish?'

'My goodness . . . how can you talk like that . . . ?' She began to whimper.

'Then why did you two run away?'

'Because he insisted. Frank did. He thought it was the most sensible thing to do. Said it was none of our business. And . . . he was right. We had nothing to do with it. Nothing at all. It's terrible. Absolutely terrible. Of course, I know we shouldn't have run off but . . .'

'Is Frank aware of your father's position at the ministry?'

'No.'

'That he's chief adviser to the government on the inauguration of the republic this summer?'

Ingiborg looked at Flóvent. 'All Frank knows about Daddy is that Daddy despises him and won't have anything to do with him.'

'Have you seen the girl before?'

'No, never. I've never seen her before and I don't have a clue who she is. Do you know who she is?'

'Why did Frank say that running off and leaving her was the most sensible thing to do?' asked Thorson, ignoring her question.

'Because it was none of our business,' said Ingiborg. 'And it's true. We only found her. We didn't do anything to harm her. Honestly. We never touched her.'

'How do you know that?'

'What?'

'That it was none of your business?'

'Because I don't know who she is. I've never seen her before.'

'What about your boyfriend, Frank?'

'What about him?'

32

'Had he seen her before?'

'Frank? No.'

'How can you be so sure of that?'

'Because . . . I just know. Why are you saying that? Why would you think he knew her?'

'Because he fled the scene,' said Thorson. 'That might be why he ran away. Because he knew her.'

Ingibjörg stared at him aghast as she realised what he was insinuating.

'But she was a complete stranger to him,' she said, with less conviction this time, because now she stopped to think about it, she didn't really know much at all about Sergeant Frank Carroll from Illinois.

'All right, Ingibjörg, I think that'll do for now,' said Flóvent.

'Are you going to arrest me?'

'No,' said Flóvent. 'We're not going to arrest you. But we may need to speak to you again, possibly even tomorrow. I hope that'll be convenient.'

She nodded.

'Perhaps you should fetch her parents now,' Flóvent said, turning to Thorson. He noticed a fresh look of dismay cross the young woman's features.

The following afternoon, once Thorson had combed through the lists of all the US servicemen in Iceland, made a few phone calls to confirm his suspicions, and also checked the lists of other nationals, he rang Flóvent at the Fríkirkjuvegur offices.

'She's lying to us,' he said, when Flóvent picked up.

'What makes you so sure?'

'We can't trace that sergeant of hers.'

33

'You can't find Frank?'

'We can't find any sergeant by the name of Frank Carroll stationed here. He doesn't exist.'

'Are you absolutely sure?'

'Yup. The guy doesn't exist.'

'Then what are the odds he's not from Illinois either?'

'I'm willing to bet that's a lie too,' said Thorson.

7

Marta was in the middle of trying to do ten things at once when Konrád dropped in to see her at the CID offices. He rarely went in now that he was retired, and he paid little attention to what was going on there, except for what he heard on the news.

'I wanted to ask if you could use any help with the murder inquiry into the old man's death,' he said when Marta had a momentary break between calls. They were sitting in her office, surrounded by piles of documents, folders, newspapers and other junk that Marta had accumulated over the years, much of it unrelated to work. Amid the clutter was a handsome sword that had belonged to a Danish lieutenant around the turn of the twentieth century. She had picked it up in an antiques shop, and now it lay in its scabbard atop a tide of paper on the windowsill. Konrád had never asked why she'd bought it but vaguely remembered hearing that her grandfather had been an officer in the Icelandic Coast Guard.

'You what?' said Marta.

'Aren't you permanently short-staffed?'

'I thought you'd retired.'

'Yes, and you can rest assured that I have absolutely no intention of coming back. But I'd like to help out with the case, if you'd let me.'

'Why?'

'Boredom, simple as that. You wouldn't even need to tell anyone. I'd report my findings to you and if I uncovered anything significant I'd let you know at once.'

'Konrád . . . I . . . you're supposed to be retired,' said Marta. 'Shouldn't we just keep things the way they are? You can't start trying to make private deals with me. It's out of the question. Honestly, what are you like?'

'Fair enough, you're the boss,' said Konrád.

'Yes, I am, and don't you forget it.'

'Fine.'

'Right, we'll be in touch.' Marta picked up her mobile phone.

'It's just that . . .'

'What?'

'I grew up in that neighbourhood,' he said. 'In the Shadow District. I remember hearing about the girl you mentioned, back when I lived there, so . . .'

'You're interested?'

'I want to know why the old man kept cuttings about her. I don't believe the case was ever solved.'

'Konrád –'

'You'd be doing me a big favour, Marta. All I need is access to his flat. I can take it from there. Anyway, you can hardly stop me gathering information about a seventy-year-old murder. And

36

Forensics have already been over the place. It's not like I'd be compromising any evidence.'

'We can always use more hands,' Marta admitted, after a long pause. 'Are you seriously intending to look into that old case anyway?'

'Yes.'

'Then you'll have to promise me something.'

'What?'

'The second you discover anything, you'll get on the phone to me. The very second.'

Two days later Konrád received the green light to enter the dead man's flat. Since Forensics had already conducted a thorough examination of the crime scene, there was no need for a seal on the door. Konrád opened it with the key he had picked up from Marta's office and closed it carefully behind him.

Exactly what he was looking for he didn't know. He had brought along photocopies of the three newspaper cuttings that Marta had handed over with the key. He'd read them in the car. According to Marta, they'd been found inside a book on the man's desk. The cuttings contained three separate reports about the girl whose body had turned up in a doorway behind the National Theatre. They were undated but all appeared to have come from the same paper, *Tíminn*. The first reported that a young woman had been found murdered; she was thought to have been strangled, and then moved to the spot behind the theatre. The detective leading the inquiry, a man called Flóvent, was quoted as saying that it was a heinous crime, a deliberate act intentionally concealed. The second story reported that the inquiry was making good progress. A post-mortem had revealed death by asphyxiation; pressure had been applied to the victim's neck until she died and the injuries indicated that the killer had strangled her with his bare hands. But the motive was unknown and the girl had yet to be identified, so anyone who could provide information about the case, however insignificant, was urged to contact the police. The third article reported that the police were searching for an American soldier calling himself Frank Carroll and claiming to be a sergeant in the US Army, though the occupying force had no record of anyone by that name. It was further stated that the soldier had been in the vicinity of the National Theatre with his Icelandic girlfriend, the daughter of a senior civil servant. The young lady in question had provided the police with her full cooperation and did not appear to be otherwise implicated in the crime.

Konrád wandered around the flat, taking his time, wondering why the dead man had hung on to cuttings about a murder committed a lifetime ago. From what he saw in the flat, he tried to form a picture of the pensioner's solitary existence. The last meal the man had cooked himself was porridge. That was easy – he hadn't washed up the pan. And he had eaten liver sausage with the porridge. The other half of the sausage was in the fridge, and the bowl in the sink contained traces of this meal. Judging by the contents of the fridge, he had subsisted largely on traditional Icelandic fare. The bread bin contained flatbread and a loaf of rye that was going mouldy. There wasn't much in the kitchen cupboards, just a few plates and cups. The radio on the table was tuned to the National Broadcasting Service.

In the bedroom was the old single bed where the man had been lying when he was found. On the small bedside table Konrád saw a lamp and a novel in English, *The Grapes of Wrath*. The wardrobe contained everyday clothes – trousers, shirts – and a lone black suit that scarcely seemed to have been worn. There was a small washing machine in the bathroom, a basket of dirty laundry, and a toothbrush in a glass.

The sitting room was neat and tidy. There were shelves of books, both Icelandic and foreign, none published recently. Several proved to be about the construction of bridges. A TV in one corner. Two cheap prints on the wall. An old sofa and two chairs grouped around a small coffee table, and a desk that turned out to contain various bills in the dead man's name.

Konrád sat down at the desk. Everything suggested that the man had led a simple, monotonous life in his last years, as one might expect of someone his age. The most unexpected thing, Konrád thought, was that there was no evidence of contact with family or friends: no letters, no family photos, no computer that would allow him to access email or social media. An aura of quiet solitude emanated from every object in the flat, an impression only enhanced by those that were missing.

Konrád could see no clues to help him resolve the questions in his mind. Why had the man's life ended in such a senseless manner, and why had he been holding on to three newspaper cuttings about a long-forgotten murder? But he did find the book where the cuttings had been gathered. Marta had told him it was still lying on the man's desk just as they'd found it. The book turned out to be an anthology of Icelandic folk tales and legends.

Konrád had got quite a shock when Marta told him about the cuttings. He had grown up in the Shadow District, on Skuggasund, only a stone's throw from the theatre, and as a child had heard the tale of the murdered girl from his father, who had been adamant that American soldiers were responsible for the deed. He had known plenty, he said, and they would have been more than

39

capable of treating an Icelandic girl like that. Of having their way with her, then dumping her body. According to him, the matter had been hushed up because a senior American officer had been involved and the military authorities had protected him by posting him abroad. Konrád never discovered what grounds his father had for believing this, and it was not until shortly before he died that he let his son in on the secret of what had happened at the seance requested by the parents of the murdered girl. It wasn't something his dad was proud of, but characteristically he had no regrets either. Konrád's dad wasn't a spiritualist himself; his sole purpose in attending seances had been to con people into parting with their money, which he had done on numerous occasions. All the same, he did have a link of sorts to the otherworld through his sister, who believed in everything normally dismissed as superstition. She had complete faith in spells and curses, in the afterlife, in ghosts and monsters, and the *huldufólk* or 'hidden people', as the elves were known, and possessed a fund of stories that her brother drew on for his deceptions. She was convinced that there was always a good reason why the dead haunted the living, and that reason had to be discovered and solved before the departed spirit could find peace. This sister, who at the time still lived on the family farm up north, had rather eccentric, old-fashioned beliefs and claimed to have more than a touch of the second sight herself. She used to insist that Konrád's withered arm was the result of a curse that had been laid on the family.

Konrád made another circuit of the flat, browsed the bookshelves, wandered back into the kitchen, then into the bedroom. He pulled out a drawer in the little bedside table and found a large photograph lying on top of an ancient, dog-eared copy of the Bible. The picture showed a handsome man aged around thirty, taken, at a guess, in the 1950s. It was black and white, unmarked and unframed. The back had yellowed with time, but otherwise the picture was very well preserved apart from a few stains in one corner. The man, who was lean and dark-haired, with strongly marked eyebrows, was staring straight at the camera, a faint, inscrutable smile playing on his lips.

Taking the picture into the sitting room, Konrád sat down again in the old man's chair at the desk, holding the newspaper cuttings in his other hand, his gaze wandering from them to the photograph and then to the book lying open in front of him. A succession of thoughts passed through his head: thoughts of his father, the murdered girl, the military occupation, seances, the tormented souls of the dead, and an old man who lived alone and was found lying on his bed as if asleep – but had in fact been murdered.

8

Konrád was startled out of his reverie by the sound of someone knocking three times on the door. Rising from the desk, he went rather hesitantly into the hall, uncertain how to act. There was another round of knocking, more determined this time.

'Hello,' he heard a voice call, 'is there somebody in there?'

Realising he had to do something, Konrád opened the door. Outside on the landing stood a tallish, middle-aged woman with a cloud of dark hair.

'I saw someone go inside,' she said. 'Are you related to Stefán, by any chance?'

'No, I'm with the police.'

'Oh, I see. I haven't noticed you here before.'

'No, I was just on my way out,' said Konrád, without elaborating on the reason for his presence.

'I'm Thorbjörg,' said the woman. 'I live upstairs, in the flat directly above Stefán's. I've spoken to the police, to someone called Marta.'

'Yes, I know her.'

'Are you any closer to finding out what happened?' asked Thorbjörg, not unnaturally curious about her neighbour's shocking fate. News of his murder had been splashed all over the media.

'No, not yet,' said Konrád.

'Who would do such a thing – attack an old-age pensioner like that? He can't have had long to live anyway.'

'Did you know each other well?'

'No, I can't say we did – he kept himself to himself. We've been here for, what, eight years, but I wouldn't say we knew him well.'

'Who lives opposite him?'

'Birgitta. She's a widow. I suppose she knew him best of all – she's been here the longest.' The woman leaned towards Konrád, lowering her voice. 'You should talk to her. There was something going on between them – especially, I'd imagine, after her husband died three years ago'

'Something going on?'

'Yes, I wouldn't be surprised if they were more than just friends. Not that I want to spread gossip, you understand. It's none of my business.'

'Did you notice if Stefán had any visitors recently?'

'No, the police have already asked me that. He didn't have many visitors. Although it's not like I kept track or anything.'

A few minutes later Konrád knocked on Birgitta's door. She was short with silver hair, a calm demeanour and a kindly face, though just now she appeared to be in low spirits and was reluctant to talk to Konrád. She had already spoken to the police, she said, and had little to add.

'I'm sorry to bother you like this,' Konrád said, hoping to change her mind. 'It'll only take a few minutes.'

'Oh, well,' she said at last, not wishing to seem unhelpful. 'Would you like to come in?'

They took a seat in her sitting room and Konrád asked if she had known Stefán long.

'Ever since he first came here, which must have been about twenty-five years ago,' she said. 'He moved here from Hveragerdi where he'd lived for a long time. They got to know each other a bit, my husband Eyjólfur and him, used to pass the time of day on the landing, that sort of thing. After Eyjólfur died, Stefán kindly offered to help me out with odd jobs here and there, and he always used to drop in for coffee when he was going out to our local shop. He never shopped anywhere else.'

'Didn't he have any family?'

'No, he never married and preferred not to discuss it. We had so much else to talk about.'

'He was able to look after himself, was he? In spite of his age?'

'Oh, yes, he was very active, and strong as a horse, despite being ninety. He used to say he had no intention of being put in a home.'

'Did you happen to notice if he had any visitors recently or went out to see anyone? I get the impression he was a bit of a recluse.'

'That's right. He kept himself to himself, talked very little about friends or relatives. I don't remember anyone visiting him recently, though it's possible I just didn't notice.'

'What did he do for a living?' asked Konrád. 'Before he retired, I mean.'

44

'He was an engineer. He built bridges all over the country. Though of course he retired years ago. What do the police think happened?'

'Hard to say.'

'They said on the news that he was smothered. That a pillow was held over his face and he was too weak to fight back.'

'I'm guessing it was something like that.'

'What a monster,' said Birgitta quietly, as if to herself.

'What about the other neighbours? Any tensions there?'

'The neighbours? No. Why do you say that?'

'Just a thought.'

'No, I believe the police interviewed everyone in the building and ruled out the idea that any of them could have done it. They're all decent people. They'd never do a dreadful thing like that.'

CID had indeed questioned all the occupants of the three-storey building. The flats, eight in all, were on the small side and most of the residents were elderly people who had downsized after their children left home. The police had also knocked on the doors of the neighbouring houses, but hardly anyone they spoke to had even been aware of Stefán's existence.

'Did he ever talk to you or your husband about the National Theatre?' asked Konrád.

'The National Theatre? I don't think he was a theatregoer.'

'I was actually referring to incidents linked to the National Theatre, rather than plays.'

'What kind of incident?'

'During the war, for instance.'

'The war?'

'The Second World War,' Konrád said, anxious not to give away too much, not least because he knew so little himself.

45

'What kind of incidents during the war?' Birgitta asked, puzzled.

'Was he religious, would you say?' asked Konrád, changing the subject.

'He never discussed it. So, no, I shouldn't think so. I shouldn't think he was particularly religious.'

'Interested in the supernatural, then?'

'No, I very much doubt it. Again, he never mentioned it. Do you mean . . . What exactly do you mean?'

'Did he believe in life after death, visit psychics?'

Birgitta stared at Konrád. 'What *did* you find in his flat?'

'Not much.' He smiled. 'I just happened to notice that he'd been reading a book of Icelandic folk tales. Were you aware of his interest in them?'

'No.'

'Or in Icelandic folklore generally?'

'He never brought up the subject with me. But . . .'

'Yes?'

'You were talking about the war and asked if he'd received or paid any visits. Well, he did tell me he'd gone round to a nursing home in the neighbourhood. He wanted to refresh his memory of something that happened during the war. When I asked him about it, he cut the conversation short as if he didn't want to discuss it. I didn't press him – I knew he'd fill me in later if he felt like it.'

'So you don't know what it was about?'

'No.'

'Did you get on well?'

'Yes, very well. We were good friends.'

'Do you know if he had any other friends, any acquaintances I could talk to?' asked Konrád, thinking of the photograph in the bedside drawer.

'No, I'm afraid I can't help you there.'

'Where was Stefán from originally? The south?' Marta had given him only the most basic facts about the dead man. 'You said he moved here from Hveragerdi.'

'No, actually. He was Canadian,' said Birgitta. 'His parents emigrated. He was born in Manitoba. Came over during the war.'

'With an Icelandic name like that – Stefán Thórdarson?'

'No, well, that was later. He used his Canadian name for the first few years, then adapted it to Icelandic.'

'His Canadian name?'

'First he went by the name he'd had at home in Canada,' Birgitta explained patiently. 'Then he changed it when he took citizenship here. He used the Icelandic version, Stefán Thórdarson.'

'So what was he called back in Canada?'

'Thorson. Stephan Thorson.'

9

A quick inquiry revealed that the Association of Chartered Engineers had very little information about Stefán Thórdarson, or Stephan Thorson. It was a good many years since he had retired, and he had been receiving regular payouts from the engineers' pension fund, but the staff there knew nothing else about him. It was news to Marta that the dead man was Canadian. Birgitta hadn't shared that information with the police when they spoke to her. It appeared that Stefán had never married and had no known children. And since no one had come to view his body at the mortuary or enquired after him, it was hard to establish anything else about him. The lack of progress was making Marta irritable.

'Nobody can be that alone in the world,' she complained to Konrád over the phone.

'Why not?' asked Konrád. He had just left Birgitta and was about to head over to the nursing home the old man had apparently visited. 'Presumably his family were all in Canada, and anyway his closest relatives would be long dead by now. He chose to begin a new life here and never started a family of his own. All the same, he must have had a few other friends like Birgitta, so maybe you'll manage to track some of them down.'

'Let's hope so,' said Marta. 'It's bound to have been someone close to him.'

'Who killed him, you mean?'

'Yes, the poor old boy opens the door to someone he knows and invites him in. Or there'd be signs of a break-in or a struggle. Nothing was stolen. So it looks as though his visitor intended to do away with him, but even so –'

'I don't agree,' said Konrád. 'We can't assume he knew the person who came to the door. That was my first reaction too, but when you stop and think about it, we open our doors to anyone who knocks or rings the bell. You'd have to be unusually distrustful not to. So the old man didn't necessarily know the person or people who did this. You can't make that leap.'

'All the same, the chances are he did. I'll get in touch with the Manitoba police and find out if they can dig anything up on this . . . Stephen Thorson, was that what you said?'

'Stephan. Not Stephen.'

'Anything else? Anything in connection with the newspaper cuttings?'

'No, nothing except . . .'

'What?'

'Well, it was a strangely quiet death, but . . .'

'What? What are you trying to say? Spit it out.'

'But it's oddly consistent with the way he lived. He was so

self-effacing. No one's aware of his existence. He simply lived. And died.'

The manager of the nursing home was rushed off his feet and could scarcely spare a moment for Konrád. He was a big man and loud with it. Konrád tracked him down by following the noise from the other end of the corridor. The man was thundering down the phone – at a supplier, apparently. There were two other men in his office. The manager ended his conversation with a few choice expletives, barked at the two men, who scurried out, then swung round to Konrád.

'And what can I do for you?' The phone on his desk started ringing. He picked up the receiver, said no three times, at equally spaced intervals, then banged it down.

Konrád introduced himself. 'I'm enquiring about a man who came here recently, presumably to visit one of the residents.'

'Oh yes? Who was that?'

'His name was Stefán Thórdarson. He was very old, over ninety.'

'That's no age nowadays,' said the manager. 'It's like the old have stopped dying altogether.'

'Quite. Anyway, it occurred to me that he might have asked you or your staff for assistance.'

'Stefán Thórdarson?'

'Yes.'

'I recognise the name. Isn't that the man who was found murdered in his bed? I remember him. He was round here a few days before that. Asking after our Vigga.'

'Vigga?'

'She's a patient of ours. Spends most of her time in bed, completely out of it. Used to live in the Shadow District.'

Konrád stared at the man. 'Do you know why he wanted to see her?'

'No, though I seem to recall him saying he was an old friend of hers.'

'I used to know a woman called Vigga from that neighbourhood,' said Konrád. 'She'd be very long in the tooth by now. I wonder if she's the one he came to visit?'

'We've only got the one Vigga here. Do you want to see her? Who did you say you were again? Are you with the police?'

The phone started ringing again and the man snatched up the receiver.

'Thank you,' said Konrád. 'I'll find my own way.'

He left the office smartly. Walking along the corridor, he remembered how, as a child in the Shadow District, life had held no greater terror for him than a woman called Vigga, who lived on Lindargata. Years later he had discovered to his surprise that she was born in 1915. In those days people used to age much faster, ground down by hardship and back-breaking work, so although he had always thought of her as ancient, she couldn't have been forty yet in his earliest memories.

She had lived alone and was the target of the local children because of her eccentric clothing and habits. They used to call her Vigga Pig and were petrified of her, giving her a wide berth except when they ganged up in sufficient numbers to torment her. Once in a while she would lose her rag, which only increased the thrill. If the kids saw her coming to the door as if to chase them, they would run away shrieking. Occasionally she would take on her persecutors, catching a couple and laying into them, all the while producing a stream of the most terrible curses they had ever heard. Boiling lead was a favourite threat of hers; she used to exclaim that she'd pour it all over the little swine. Once, when Konrád was six years old, she had caught him throwing snowballs at her house. She came storming out in her peculiar get-up of woollen vest, three ragged jumpers, several layers of skirts and a large pair of rubber galoshes that reached almost up to the knee. Konrád would have got away, silly little fool that he was, if he hadn't slipped and fallen on his bottom. She had grabbed hold of him, slapped his cheek, already raw with the cold, so hard it brought tears to his eyes, then hurled him to the ground and said if he didn't bugger off home she'd lock him in her cellar.

Konrád had never been inside her cellar but knew of its existence from the blood-curdling tales of children who had gone missing in the Shadow District or neighbouring Thingholt and never been heard of again. It was rumoured that they had come to a sticky end in Vigga Pig's cellar. She had always lived alone on the edge of the district, in a small house clad in corrugated iron that gave a satisfying boom when you threw stones at it. The single-glazed windows used to ice up in freezing weather. She seemed to have few friends; at least she had few regular visitors, apart from the man in the coal lorry who used to come once a fortnight until Vigga relented in her hatred of inevitable progress and allowed the Reykjavík District Heating Authority into her home to install the new geothermal radiators. She made her living as a washerwoman, according to Konrád's mother, who used to forbid him to tease Vigga as her life was tough enough without a pack of naughty children giving her grief.

Konrád entered the room where Vigga was asleep under a white duvet. He reflected that the Shadow District had a strange, roundabout way of seeking him out. There was the girl murdered during the war, the cuttings the old man had kept, his dad's seance, and now Vigga, lying under the covers, invisible apart from her grey hair and wrinkled forehead. He wondered what business Stefán could have had with his childhood bogeywoman, this indomitable old lady whom even death had not yet managed to defeat.

10

The doctor, Baldur, was a big-boned, craggy man of around sixty, with a booming bass voice, who hailed from the Hornstrandir Peninsula in the remote north-west of the country. When Flóvent entered the mortuary, Baldur was standing over the young woman's corpse, pouring out a thick line of snuff on the back of his hand. He snorted it first up one nostril, then the other, then took a red handkerchief from the pocket of his white coat and wiped his nose.

'Morning, Flóvent.' He returned the snuff rag to his pocket. 'This is a nasty business you've been landed with. Such a young girl. What a waste.'

'Have you had a chance to examine her yet?'

'Briefly. Looks to me like a case of manual strangulation.' The doctor ran a finger down the girl's long, elegant neck. Bruises were visible under the skin, patches of discoloration encircling her neck like thick fingers. 'I'm working on the assumption that it was a man, based on these marks. They were inflicted by a strong pair of hands. He wouldn't have had any problem obstructing her windpipe. The girl would have tried to fight him off. Tried to defend herself. He must have punched her in the face – see the contusion here? Her nails are broken too. Look.' Baldur lifted one of the young woman's hands to show Flóvent.

'Was she attacked behind the theatre?'

'No, I doubt it happened outdoors. If it had, we would have found marks from the sharp gravel, but I can't see any cuts or abrasions. So I really don't believe she was assaulted outside.'

'You think her body was disposed of behind the theatre after she was killed?'

'That's plausible. And, yes, she was probably dead already. There's another fact you ought to be aware of, though I stress I've only carried out a preliminary examination so far. The girl appears to have had an abortion.'

'Really?'

'Yes, fairly recently. Not a professional job either. A bloody mess, in fact.'

'Meaning?'

'I find it hard to believe it was the handiwork of a qualified medic. Though I suppose it's not impossible. There are incompetent fools in my profession, like in any other. Did the girl have a boyfriend?'

'We still haven't identified her,' said Flóvent. 'So it's possible.'

'A soldier, maybe?'

'We're currently searching for the man who found her body. An American soldier who fled the scene as soon as he realised what was up. He had an Icelandic girl in tow. We've spoken to her, but she couldn't help us much. We believe it's possible the soldier was acquainted with the victim. Do you know of anyone she could have gone to about her . . . her predicament?'

'You mean for an abortion? No, I don't. The law was changed a few years ago to allow them in strictly limited circumstances. If the mother's life's in danger, for example, or in cases of rape or incest. But one of those specific conditions would have to have been present for a doctor to perform an abortion. Getting pregnant by a soldier wouldn't qualify.'

'Naturally, it's a sensitive subject for many people,' said Flóvent.

'I imagine it's not too hard to come by a backstreet job in the present situation,' said the doctor. 'But of course it's all done behind closed doors. There's a black market in that sort of thing just like anything else in these strange times we're living through.'

The hunt for a Sergeant Frank Carroll among the American troops had yielded nothing so far. Thorson was convinced the man had lied to Ingiborg. After all, it wouldn't be the first time a soldier looking for some fun had exaggerated his rank and strung a girl along with promises that when the war was over he would take her home and introduce her to a brave new world in America. In an attempt to find out more about the man calling himself Frank Carroll, Flóvent and Thorson paid another visit to Ingiborg, though they saw no reason at this stage to arrest her and bring her in for a formal interview.

The identity of the murder victim was still a mystery. No one had reported her missing, as far as the police could ascertain, but news of her fate had spread following reports in the morning papers and on the radio, and Flóvent was confident that sooner or later someone who knew the girl would realise she was missing and get in touch. He broke the news to Thorson that she had undergone an abortion not long before she died.

This time, when the two detectives turned up to question Ingiborg further about her American boyfriend, she was alone in the house with her mother. Her father had torn a strip off her after their first visit, but now that he wasn't home she seemed a little more relaxed. They wouldn't permit her mother to listen to the interview, politely showing her out of the same drawing room they had used last time.

'The fact is, Ingiborg,' said Flóvent, 'we can't find any record of a Frank Carroll in the US Army.'

'Which means,' said Thorson, 'that one of you is lying. Either you're lying to us or he lied to you.'

'If we find out that you've lied to us, Ingiborg,' Flóvent went on, 'we'll take you down to the police station and from there to the prison on Skólavördustígur. We've given you the benefit of the doubt so far and been very considerate, but if it turns out you've been spinning us a yarn, all that will change.'

'I'm not lying,' protested Ingiborg. 'I'd never lie to you. I've done nothing wrong. We just found the body and . . .'

'And what, Ingiborg?' asked Thorson.

'He must have been lying to me,' she said in a small voice. 'He told me his name was Frank Carroll. That's all I know.'

'Have you been with a soldier before?' asked Flóvent.

'No, I'm not a slut.'

'Did he promise to take you to America?'

Ingiborg didn't answer.

'Did he say he was going to marry you?'

'We discussed it.'

'Was the wedding going to take place soon or after the war?'

'After the war. He was terrified of being sent to Europe, to the front. So he said we'd have to wait until the war was over. It sounded perfectly reasonable to me.'

'Going to come back for you, was he?' asked Thorson.

Ingiborg nodded. 'I'm not an idiot, whatever you may think. I'm no soldier's tart. Frank's always behaved honourably towards me. He knew Daddy was opposed to our relationship and he was sorry about it. He knew we'd never be accepted by my family. That we'd always have to stand on our own two feet.'

'And you were reconciled to that?'

'You have no idea what it's like living with my father,' she said coldly.

'What else do you know about Frank?' asked Flóvent. 'Did you notice any stripes or insignia on his uniform? Did he ever mention what regiment he belonged to? Or mention any of his friends?'

'No, I have no idea. I never met any of his friends except at Hótel Borg, and I didn't pay that much attention to his uniform.'

'Do you remember any of their names?'

'No.'

'Do you have any letters from him? Any photographs?'

'No.'

'Has it occurred to you,' said Thorson, 'that since you found the dead girl everything he's told you about himself has turned out to be a lie?'

It had most definitely occurred to her as she lay wide awake in the dark watches of the night, racked with anxiety. Frank had not been particularly forthcoming about his circumstances, and their conversations had been necessarily limited in scope due to the language barrier. She was aware that he was interested in cars but knew next to nothing about his family. But then they'd only been together a matter of months, and she had imagined that as her English improved – because he was certainly making no effort to learn Icelandic – they would become better acquainted.

'I'm sure his name's Frank because they called him that at Hótel Borg. Other men he bumped into. His friends.'

'All right, that'll do for now,' said Flóvent. 'If you remember anything else, please get in touch.'

'Do you know who the girl was?' asked Ingiborg.

'No, not yet,' said Thorson.

'Could she have gone there with a soldier, like I did?'

'It's possible.'

'Someone like Frank, who took her behind the theatre?'

'We have yet to establish that,' said Thorson, anxious to avoid hurting her. 'Was there any particular reason why you and Frank chose that spot?'

'It was his idea. He said they sometimes go there. The soldiers.'

'With their girls?'

'Yes.'

The sentries in their sandbagged post in front of the National Theatre were unable to help the police as none of them had noticed the girl. And if anyone else apart from the schoolmistress had been in the Shadow District that evening and knew something, they weren't coming forward. It seemed no one had witnessed the girl's arrival in the doorway, by whatever means and in whatever company. The police had scoured the area around the theatre for clues that could shed light on her fate but had found no leads.

Thorson took charge of questioning the soldiers who worked in the supply depot. Inside, the place could hardly have looked less like a theatre. The stage had yet to be built and the auditorium was piled to the rafters with stores and munitions. At Flóvent's suggestion, they established themselves in the coal cellar. Although originally intended as a boiler room, the cellar was now to become a banqueting hall since coal heating was being phased out in favour of natural hot water. At present there was a fair amount of commotion in the building as the depot was moving to a new location: the decision had been taken to resume work on the theatre at long last.

None of the servicemen they spoke to said they knew the victim, though two privates admitted to being on friendly terms with Icelandic girls.

'Turns out there are any number of soldiers in the Reykjavík area called Frank,' Thorson told Flóvent as they left. 'I checked that while I was looking for a Sergeant Carroll. He's fed her a pack of lies. Though that's nothing new.'

They strode rapidly down Hverfisgata in the raw weather, hands dug deep in their pockets; Flóvent in hat and long winter coat – the only one he owned – Thorson in his cap and wearing his military greatcoat over his uniform. The cathedral bell struck two.

'No, that's nothing new.'

'As long as he wasn't lying about his Christian name, we ought to be able to track him down,' said Thorson.

'Round up the men who match Ingiborg's description, or come close,' said Flóvent, 'and we'll see if she can pick out her man. It wouldn't hurt if they came from Illinois as well.'

'None of them are sergeants.'

'No, I never thought they would be.'

They parted ways, Thorson continuing to the military police

headquarters at the camp in Laugarnes, Flóvent heading down to the CID offices on Fríkirkjuvegur. When he arrived, he found an elderly couple sitting on a bench in the lobby. He marched straight past without giving them a second glance, but they stood up and looked after him as he entered the office. A secretary grabbed his arm as he went by.

'They want to talk to you,' she said, nodding towards the couple.

'Who?'

'That couple. About *their daughter*.'

She gave him a meaningful look as she said the last two words, and Flóvent immediately cottoned on. He glanced out into the lobby where the couple stood huddled together, eyes fixed on him and the secretary.

'But they're so old,' he whispered.

'She was adopted,' the secretary replied in an undertone. 'They're hoping it's not her they heard about on the news but they haven't seen their daughter for a couple of days and don't know where she's got to.'

Flóvent went back out and greeted the couple. The man shook him by the hand and introduced himself and his wife. Their manner was restrained, though their eyes were anxious. Flóvent guessed they were in their late sixties. Both wore thick overcoats. The woman looked good-natured; the man was thin with gaunt cheeks, and accustomed to hard labour if his hands were anything to go by.

'We didn't want to bother you unnecessarily, sir,' he said. 'But we heard about the girl behind the theatre, that she was around twenty, and –'

'I told him to talk to the police but he wanted to wait and see if she turned up,' his wife broke in. 'Do you know who she is, sir? The girl you found?'

'No, not yet,' said Flóvent. 'No one's enquired after her.'

'This isn't the first time she's disappeared like this,' said the woman.

'Oh?'

'No, but last time she turned up again.'

'I can take you over to the mortuary, if you feel up to it.'

The couple exchanged glances.

'You'd have to identify her,' explained Flóvent. 'It's the only way we can be sure.'

'I've never been there before,' said the woman.

'No,' said Flóvent. 'It's not a place you want to have to visit.'

He rang Baldur at the National Hospital and asked him to make himself available, then escorted the couple out to the CID car and drove them the short stretch to the hospital. It was one of the largest buildings in the country. The doctor greeted them at the door of the mortuary. He had brought out the girl's body, which lay on a table under a thin, white sheet. The couple stood close together, hand in hand, as the doctor lifted the sheet from the girl's face.

Flóvent saw the instant recognition. Saw from the way the hope died in their eyes that she was their missing daughter.

11

Baldur replaced the sheet.

'Who could have done this to her?' gasped the woman, looking at her husband. 'Our poor little girl.'

'I'm afraid we'll have to take a statement from you,' said Flóvent. 'I'd be grateful if you could come back to Fríkirkjuvegur with me.'

'Would it be possible . . . ?' The woman turned to Flóvent. 'Could we possibly stay with her a little longer? Just for a few minutes?'

'Of course.' Flóvent gave the doctor a sign to leave the room with him.

'Any luck tracking down that Yank?' asked Baldur once they were alone.

'At present he's only a witness who fled the scene. I don't think we should read any more into it. Thorson's helping us. Have you met him?'

'I don't recall.'

'He's a good lad. Icelandic-Canadian. He's proved very helpful in liaising with the troops in the past.'

'Well, you're bound to get the odd troublemaker. I expect the majority are decent enough,' said the doctor.

'Indeed. Look, I think it would be best if a doctor filled them in on the facts – how she came to die, the abortion.'

'I can do it if you like.'

'Thank you, it might sound better coming from you.'

Baldur nodded and went back to join the couple. Flóvent waited outside in the corridor, trying but failing to imagine how the girl's parents must feel.

After a considerable length of time, the door opened and the couple came out again, accompanied by the doctor. The woman was wiping her eyes with a handkerchief she had taken from her bag. Her husband had his arm around her. After saying goodbye to the doctor, Flóvent gave the couple a lift back to Fríkirkjuvegur where he showed them into his office. He offered them some genuine coffee that Thorson had rustled up from US Army stores, and gave them a chance to recover from their initial shock. He didn't want to come across as overbearing or intrusive in their hour of grief.

'Do you have any idea who could have done this to her?' the woman asked eventually.

'I'm afraid we have nothing to go on yet. We very much hope you'll be able to help us get the investigation off the ground, now that we know who she is.'

'I just can't imagine who would have wanted to do this,' said the man. 'It's so . . . so unreal somehow. That something so horrible should happen to our little girl.'

'I understand she was your adopted daughter?'

'That's right,' said the man. 'Our Rósamunda came to us when she was one and a half. We didn't have any children of our own. We'd always wanted them, but it wasn't meant to be.'

'Where was she from?'

'From up north in Húnavatn County,' said the woman. 'My sister worked on a farm there. A local woman died leaving behind a large family of young children and, thanks to my sister's efforts, the father gave us his daughter to bring up.'

The man explained to Flóvent how in the end they had gone out looking for children to adopt. They weren't getting any younger, and when his sister-in-law wrote to tell them of a poor family in her area who needed help they didn't hesitate. Three of the children were to be farmed out to neighbours, but the father wasn't averse to the idea of one of them going to a nice couple in Reykjavík. The sister had told him about them, and he had nothing against meeting them. So the couple had travelled north over the moors to talk to the girl's father, who turned out to be a crofter living in very straitened circumstances. And there they took the little girl in their arms for the first time. A happy, healthy child in her second year. Her mother had died four months earlier while giving birth to her eighth and last baby.

'Life can be very unfair,' said the woman, raising red-rimmed eyes to Flóvent.

So they took little Rósamunda home with them, her husband continued. She was happy in town with them, went to Austurbær School and passed her school certificate. Though she wasn't especially good at her books, she had always been hard-working and clever with her hands. They had talked to her about going to college but she was bored of schoolwork and at the beginning of the war she had taken a job at a dressmaker's near Austurvöllur

Square. Rósamunda enjoyed sewing and had been over the moon to get a position with such a good seamstress. She was desperate to learn how to make dresses and soon started creating her own pieces. She'd made a very pretty frock for her mother.

'She used to talk about setting up her own shop one day,' said the woman, her pride shining through.

'No chance of that now,' added her husband.

'It was ever such a nice dress,' said his wife. 'Ever so pretty and exquisitely made. I must say, I've never owned a dress that suited me so well. She was always good with a needle, so it came easily to her.'

'You mentioned that she'd disappeared once before,' Flóvent prompted gently.

'Yes,' said the man. 'About three months ago.'

'What happened?'

The man glanced at his wife, suddenly unsure of himself. 'She didn't come home for two days.'

'She never really told us what happened,' said his wife.

'Oh?'

'Yes, the poor dear. I expect she must have been with a young man. But she didn't want to talk about it and we didn't press her. Though, I don't know, perhaps it would have been better if we'd insisted. In hindsight.'

'What did she say?' Flóvent searched their faces in turn.

'She said she'd needed a little time to herself. That was it really. Didn't come home for two days and that's all she would say.'

'Was she in some sort of trouble?'

'Not that we could tell.'

'And she gave no further explanation?'

The couple exchanged glances again without answering.

'Had she ever done anything like that before?' asked Flóvent.

'No, never,' said the husband. 'It was just that one time. We didn't want to press her. If something had happened and she didn't want to tell us, that was her business. We thought maybe she'd tell us later. Once it had all blown over.'

'And did she?'

'No, she hadn't by the time she . . .'

The man trailed off. Flóvent looked at them sitting dejectedly before him. It was plain that they bitterly regretted not doing more when their daughter disappeared the first time. They couldn't turn back the clock now.

'She told us not to worry,' said the woman. 'That it was nothing to worry about.'

'Was she seeing a young man at the time?'

'Not as far as we know,' said her mother.

'What about her friends? Did they know anything?'

'She didn't have that many friends,' said the woman. 'She'd never had a boyfriend, though she easily could have found one, a pretty thing like her. But she did get on well with another girl who worked at the dressmaker's.'

'Did she have any contact with her birth family?' asked Flóvent.

'No, very little,' said the man. 'It was only recently that she began to take an interest in her background. She exchanged letters with her . . . her father, I suppose I should call him, and was thinking of taking a trip up north sometime soon.'

'Had she known for long that she had family up there?'

'She knew from the very start,' said the woman. 'It was never a secret, if that's what you're asking. We never kept anything from her. Our relationship wasn't like that. She was our daughter.'

'Yet she never told you why she didn't come home for two days?'

67

They were silent.

'She must have had her reasons,' the man said finally.

'Did she associate with American soldiers at all?'

'Soldiers?' said the woman, surprised. 'No. Not at all. No. Impossible.'

'Why do you say that?'

'Because she didn't want anything to do with them. You can be sure of that – she didn't know any Americans. Personally, I mean. Of course soldiers may have come into the shop where she worked, but that was all. She definitely didn't have any other occasion to meet them. She never mentioned it. Not once.'

'When did you last see her?'

'The day you found her,' said the man. 'She went to work and we never saw her again. We went out of town to stay with friends in Selfoss.'

'It was only a short trip and we assumed she was fine,' said his wife. 'We heard on the wireless about the girl behind the theatre but of course it never crossed our minds that it could be our Rósamunda. Then, when we got home yesterday evening she wasn't there, and she didn't come back in the night, so early this morning we spoke to the woman who owns the dressmaker's but she didn't know where Rósamunda was, only that she hadn't turned up to work yesterday, so she'd assumed she was ill. Then we began to suspect –'

'What makes you think she might have been involved with an American?' the husband cut in, leaning forwards in his chair.

'The doctor must have told you what he discovered during the post-mortem,' said Flóvent. 'How your daughter lost her life and how she'd used the services of –'

'He said she'd had an abortion recently,' interrupted the woman.

68

'That's right. Were you aware of that?'

'No, we had no idea.' The woman struggled to control her voice. 'The poor child. It breaks my heart to think about it. She never told us and I . . . I didn't notice anything. No doubt I should have done but . . . she hid it so well.'

'Was it an American soldier who did this to her?' asked her husband.

'I really don't know,' said Flóvent. 'But it's a possibility we have to consider, given the current situation in Reykjavík.'

'Was it the same man who got her in the family way?'

'We can't rule it out,' said Flóvent. 'But we don't know for sure. We know nothing of the circumstances that led to Rósamunda losing her life.'

The couple sat in silence, their hands in their laps, and Flóvent was deeply moved by their plight, by their wordless grief, their bewilderment in the face of such an incomprehensible tragedy.

'She was so beautiful and such a good girl,' said the woman, her voice thick with tears. 'I just don't understand how something like this could happen to her. Just can't begin to understand it.'

12

As Konrád sat beside Vigga's bed waiting for her to wake up, his thoughts drifted back to the little street where he grew up: Skuggasund. Even in his earliest memories, the war had been over for several years, though the prosperity that it brought was still very much in evidence. But the years that followed had been tough. The Shadow District used to be its own little world, with its shops and businesses, large and small. It was intersected from west to east by Lindargata, bracketed by high culture at one end and the meat-packing trade at the other. At the western end, the National Theatre turned its back to the street as if it were too grand for the neighbourhood. It was flanked by the National Library, for those who thirsted after knowledge, and the High Court, for those who had strayed from the path of virtue. At the eastern end, the autumn lambs would fall eerily silent at the gates of the abattoir. Between these poles, the properties ranged from shacks clad in corrugated iron to modern houses built of concrete, with two or even three storeys; some well maintained, others dilapidated, their small back gardens facing south into the sun. It was here, in one of the poorest basement slums, that Konrád had grown up.

The inhabitants, an assortment of labourers, artisans and toffs, got on with their lives in relative harmony. There were drinkers and teetotallers. Those who went to church on Sundays a little the worse for wear and celebrated the word of God with a twinge of conscience, chiming in wholeheartedly when the minister intoned: '. . . and forgive us our trespasses'. And those who donned their fedoras and strolled through town with their lady wives – showing off a new coat perhaps – removing their hats and decorously greeting others of their kind. While their wives gazed into shop windows, exclaiming over a beautiful dress or tasteful hat direct from Copenhagen or London, the men would squint out to sea with narrowed eyes, keeping track of the ships, or they would follow the progress of a magnificent new automobile, gliding down Austurstræti like a glittering dream. At noon the savoury smell of roasting meat would waft into every corner of the house, and the afternoon would pass in a satisfied doze until coffee time. That was how Sundays used to be. And there was always some hungover bloke standing at a window wearing nothing but a vest, trying to recruit a boy to run down to the shop and fetch him a cold Pilsner, yelling after him 'Keep the change!'

It was all so vivid to Konrád that he would often revisit it in his mind. Unusually for the time, his mother had worked outside the home and been the one to put food on the table. His father, on the other hand, rarely held down a job, and was involved in all kinds of dodgy schemes, most of them illegal. As Konrád got older he discovered that petty crimes and lawbreaking were his father's daily bread. His parents didn't have a large family to provide for, just him and his sister Elísabet. Konrád recalled the visitors who used to come to their home: relatives from the north, friends of his mother, his father's more dubious associates. The heyday of the fraudulent seances had been before he was born, but he remembered his dad's tales about the meetings held in their little flat. His father never adopted the role of medium himself, freely admitting that he was a lousy actor. The psychics, sometimes male, sometimes female, used to warm up by asking if the names Gudrún or Sigurdur – some of the most common in the country – meant anything to those present; if anyone was familiar with a painting of Mount Esja or knew why a smell of mothballs should suddenly assail the medium's senses.

At the height of these seances, the sitting-room tables would levitate and the chairs shift as if by magic; a rumbling would be heard, and the most extraordinary details would surface from the past. The sitters latched on to these purported connections to the deceased, their hearts gladdened that life had conquered death and that death was only a door to another, better world. Of course, the entire thing was a hoax cooked up by Konrád's father and his associates. They used to toy with the feelings of the bereaved, merely for the sake of swindling a few krónur out of them. When, years later, these shameless deceptions came up in conversation, Konrád's father showed no sign of contrition. He'd spotting an opening, he said, when the Icelandic Society for Psychical Research was at the height of its popularity in the late thirties and forties. The society had gained particular fame as a result of two incidents. One was the disinterment and reburial in Skagafjördur of the remains of Solveig of Miklabær, an eighteenth-century woman, the subject of a celebrated ghost story; the other was the extraordinary peregrinations undertaken by the bones of the beloved nineteenth-century poet Jónas Hallgrímsson, all the way from the Danish capital Copenhagen to his birthplace of Hraun in Öxnadalur, before finally coming to rest at the ancient assembly site of Thingvellir. Their spirits had allegedly made contact at seances organised by the society, and it seemed only right to comply with their desire for reburial. In such a heady atmosphere, Konrád's father's psychic agency had prospered. Some of the mediums he worked with genuinely believed they had the gift but just needed a little leg-up to get things going. Others were simply good actors, sensitive to the reactions and body language of the credulous, and ingenious at extracting information from them.

Hearing a faint moan from Vigga, Konrád took the liberty of lifting the duvet from her face. There she lay, all sunken cheeks and toothless jaw, her wrinkled skin as dry as parchment, grey tufts of hair plastered to her skull. Her eyes opened a fraction.

'Vigga?' whispered Konrád. 'Can you hear me?'

No reaction.

'Vigga?' he said again, louder this time.

The old woman didn't move a muscle, merely stared dimly into space.

'I don't know if you remember me. My name's Konrád and I used to live near you in the Shadow District.'

She didn't stir, and he lapsed into silence. The girl who looked after Vigga had told him she was only occasionally compos mentis. The girl didn't think she had long to live, but admitted that she would have said the same several years ago too, adding that she was an amazingly tough old bird.

'I wanted to know if a man came to see you recently. His name was Stefán, Stefán Thórdarson.'

Vigga blinked.

'Do you remember him at all?' Konrád waited for a reaction but none came. 'He may have been calling himself Thorson,' he added, in the faint hope that the old woman could hear him.

This seemed to do the trick. Slowly Vigga turned her head and regarded him with colourless eyes.

'Thorson,' repeated Konrád. 'Do you know him?'

The old woman stared at him without speaking.

'Did he come here to see you a week or two ago?'

Vigga didn't respond but nor did she take her eyes off Konrád.

'Thorson's dead,' he continued. 'I thought you'd want to know that if you were friends with him. You may have heard already. I gather he came here to visit you recently.'

Vigga's gaze was unwavering.

'I don't know if you remember me. I grew up in the Shadow District, not far from where you lived. My name's Konrád.'

'H . . . ?' Vigga tried to whisper, but it came out so quietly that Konrád couldn't catch it.

'What did you say?'

'H . . . ow?'

'How? Do you mean how did he die? Well, it was rather a bad business actually. He was smothered. Very probably murdered.'

Vigga grimaced. 'Mur . . . dered?' she whispered weakly, almost voicelessly.

'We don't know who did it,' said Konrád. 'He lived alone, and he was found dead. I understand he came here shortly before he died, so I wanted to ask how you knew him.'

'He . . . came . . .' Vigga's eyes closed.

'I found some cuttings in his flat – newspaper cuttings about a girl who was found dead behind the National Theatre during the war,' Konrád continued. 'The girl had been strangled. Do you know

74

why he kept those cuttings? Did he come to see you about the case? Or for a completely different reason? How did you two know each other anyway? How did you know Stefán Thórdarson?'

Konrád kept up a flow of questions but Vigga no longer seemed able to hear him.

'Why did he visit you, Vigga? Why did he visit you just before he died?'

The old woman had fallen asleep again. Konrád restrained the urge to try to wake her and instead sat quietly and patiently by her bed, remembering that Vigga hadn't always been in a foul mood, cursing the local children. Once, when Konrád was seven, he had plucked up the courage to knock on her door early one Sunday morning. He was selling stamps for the Scouts and had knocked on almost all the doors in the neighbourhood except hers. He'd had scant success – had in fact only sold one measly stamp – but then perhaps he had set off a little too early in his excitement and woken his prospective customers, who didn't hesitate to let him know what they thought about that. He hadn't intended to risk approaching Vigga's lair, as he had always avoided her like the plague, but for some reason he forgot his cowardice and before he knew it he had rapped on her door. A long time seemed to pass and he was on the point of running away while he still could when the door opened and there stood Vigga, glaring down at him.

'What do you want, boy?' she had asked, scanning the street for more little pests waiting to torment her. There were none to be seen.

'I . . . I . . . I'm selling stamps,' Konrád stammered.

'Stamps? What are you on about?'

'Scout . . . Scout stamps.'

'After my money are you? A little scamp like you? Want to come in?'

75

Konrád hesitated, then told the truth: 'No.'

Vigga regarded him stormily for a moment and Konrád thought he should perhaps have said 'no, thank you' and was about to correct himself when she began to emit a rumbling noise which became a full-blown guffaw. She laughed so hard she had to lean against the door.

Konrád had turned, ready to flee down the steps, when her laughter subsided.

'There, there, I'll buy some stamps from you, boy,' said Vigga. 'Wait a minute while I fetch my purse.'

She bought three Scout stamps on the understanding that he would never knock on her door or show his face there again, for any reason whatsoever.

Konrád studied the old woman under the duvet, still hearing the echo of her laughter on that long-ago Sunday morning. Without warning she opened her eyes and looked at him.

'Th . . . orson?' Her whisper was barely audible.

'Do you remember him?'

'Is it . . . you . . . Thorson?'

Konrád didn't know what to say. Did she really think he was Thorson? 'I'm not him if . . .'

Vigga closed her eyes again.

'Do you know if he was asking questions about that girl who was found behind the National Theatre?'

No response.

'Do you have any idea why Thorson held on to cuttings about the case for all these years?'

There was no point asking. Vigga had dozed off again. After sitting beside her for a while longer, Konrád rose to leave. He stroked the old woman's cheek gently. Once she had terrified him, but no longer. There was an air of tranquillity about her. He was on his way out of the room when he thought he heard her voice behind him.

Konrád turned. 'Did you say something?'

Vigga opened her mouth but barely had the strength to articulate the words. 'Thorson? Is that . . . you . . . back again?'

'Is everything all right, Vigga?'

'Have you come . . . about that girl?'

'Yes,' said Konrád, thinking he might as well go along with it.

'. . . not . . . just her . . .'

'What did you say?'

'. . . there was . . . another one,' croaked Vigga from under the duvet, her voice hoarse and threadbare with age. 'Another one who disappeared . . . and the *huldufólk* . . . the *huldufólk* . . .'

'Another girl?' Konrád leaned closer to hear. 'Who do you mean?'

'. . . never . . . found her . . . never found her bones . . .'

13

The military police had their headquarters at the Laugarnes camp. There, standing in a huddle, were twelve GIs guarded by four armed men. They had been rounded up from various parts of Reykjavík and the surrounding area by the military police and brought there without any explanation. Nine were privates, one a lieutenant, two worked in the mess hall, and one was from the US naval base in Hvalfjördur. They still hadn't worked out that they were all called Frank when the door opened and Thorson greeted them. Flóvent had telephoned following his meeting with Rósamunda's parents to inform him that the body had been identified and the girl's parents were adamant that she hadn't known any American soldiers, let alone been walking out with one.

The men were made to line up in a row, facing forwards. Two or three demanded to know why they were being treated like this, but Thorson just asked for their patience, thanked them for assisting the police in a difficult case and assured them that they would soon be free to go. At that moment Flóvent entered the room, accompanied by Ingiborg, who recognised her Frank immediately.

She walked straight up to him, and he gave her a chilly, embarrassed smile. The other men watched, still unsure what the police wanted with them and what sort of drama they were witnessing.

Thorson went over to Ingiborg. 'Is that him?'

'Yes,' she said. 'This is Frank Carroll. If that is his name.'

The soldier met Thorson's eye and nodded. '*I'm Frank Carroll*,' he murmured in English.

'Why did you lie to me?' Ingiborg asked him, with a hurt expression. He may not have understood the words, but he couldn't fail to detect the pain in her voice. 'What's your real name? Who are you?'

'*Sorry*,' he said. '*I –*'

'Was everything you told me a lie?' she whispered. 'About us? Everything?'

Frank's gaze slid away from hers. Thorson turned to the other soldiers, thanked them again for their help and told them they were free to go. Exchanging bemused glances and muttering under their breath, the men filed out of the room. Ingiborg turned to Flóvent.

'May I go too?'

'Yes,' he said. 'But wouldn't you like a ride home?'

'No, thank you, I'll manage.' She hurried out without looking at Frank. He watched her leave, his expression hard to read, though Thorson couldn't detect even the slightest hint of remorse.

Once they were alone, the three of them sat down and Frank lit a cigarette, looking from Flóvent to Thorson in turn.

'Is this about the girl we found?'

'Yes,' said Thorson.

'I had nothing to do with it.'

'Then why did you run away?'

'Because it wasn't my problem. I know nothing about it. I didn't know the girl. I can't help you. I realised that right away and got the hell out of there. Did Ingiborg call you? Did she lose her nerve?'

'What's your real name?' asked Thorson, ignoring his questions.

'Frank Ruddy.'

'Why did you give a fake name?'

Frank shrugged as if it was self-evident.

'You're not a sergeant either,' continued Thorson. 'You lied to the girl about that as well. You didn't think being a private would impress her?'

'They like it better if you're an officer,' said Frank. 'They can't tell the uniforms apart. Don't understand the stripes.'

'And that makes it all right to feed them a pack of lies, does it?' asked Flóvent. He spoke good English with a slight Scots burr from a stint in Edinburgh.

Frank didn't answer.

'It says here that you're married, with two children,' said Thorson, leafing through some papers. 'Are you divorced?'

'No,' said Frank, seeing no reason to lie any more since he assumed they would check up on whatever he said. 'I didn't want Ingiborg to find out I was married. That's why I skedaddled.'

'You didn't want her to know that you were a husband and father of two back in Illinois?' said Flóvent.

'That's right,' said Frank. 'I thought if we were summoned as witnesses I'd be exposed, and I didn't want to hurt Ingiborg.'

'A true gentleman,' said Thorson. 'Are there other women in the picture?'

'Other women?'

'Other Icelandic women, I mean. Are you seeing other women? Apart from Ingiborg?'

Frank hesitated. 'OK, I'll tell you so you don't think I'm lying. This is the truth. I've been dating one other girl. That's all. There aren't any others.'

'Does Ingiborg know about her?' asked Flóvent.

'No. And she doesn't know about Ingiborg either.'

'So you had a few reasons for fleeing the scene,' said Thorson disgustedly.

'I didn't want any trouble.'

'And that's the only reason, eh? You'd been screwing around?'

'What are you driving at?'

'Sounds like more bullshit. Like the name you invented. Where did you get it from anyway? Who's Carroll?'

'He's a Hollywood actor. They were showing a movie of his when I met Ingiborg. *The Flying Tigers.*'

'With John Wayne,' Flóvent told Thorson in Icelandic. 'I saw it. The actor's called John Carroll. He's not making that part up.'

'Right,' said Frank, catching the name and looking rather shamefaced. 'John Carroll. We were standing by the movie theatre and she asked me what else I was called besides Frank and I saw the name John Carroll on a poster and . . . it just slipped out. I didn't even think, just told her my name was Frank Carroll.'

'Why did you run away from the theatre, Frank?' asked Thorson.

'I've already –'

'Was it because you recognised the girl the moment you clapped eyes on her?'

'No. I never saw her before.'

81

'Ever heard the name Rósamunda?'

'No. Who's that?'

'The murdered girl.'

'Never heard of her,' said Frank. 'I swear to you. I didn't know that girl. Didn't recognise her. I never saw her before. Did you talk to the guy who was standing on the corner?'

'What guy?' asked Thorson.

'The one who was standing on the corner behind the theatre.'

'Which corner?'

'Which one? I don't know the names of the streets around there. He was standing on the corner smoking when we first arrived, but when I looked back he was gone.'

'Who was he?'

'I don't know. He wasn't a soldier, I can tell you that. He was an Icelander – he was dressed like a civilian, wasn't in uniform. But I couldn't see that well. It was dark. I just happened to clock a man standing there and it looked to me like he had a cigarette, but when I checked to see if he was still there, he'd disappeared.'

'Was this to your right or left as you were facing away from the theatre?'

'The nearest corner on the right, the other side of the street,' said Frank, patting his right arm for emphasis.

'Which street is that?' asked Thorson, turning to Flóvent.

'Skuggasund,' said Flóvent. 'That'll be the corner of Lindargata and Skuggasund.'

'Ingiborg didn't mention a man.'

'Then she can't have noticed him. I only saw him for a second. But I'm not lying – he was standing there.'

'What was this man doing?'

'Nothing. Just standing on the corner, smoking. Then he was gone.'

Thorson wanted to head straight over to Skuggasund, even though a couple of days had passed since Frank had spotted the man. He and Flóvent parked on Lindargata, walked to the corner in question and looked around for evidence of the smoker. A faint illumination came from Skuggasund, but apart from that the place was shrouded in darkness; the street light on the corner was broken, and the next one was a fair way off. Thorson had a torch, which he shone carefully around them. They didn't know exactly what they were looking for, and all they found were the butts of two American cigarettes that had been ground into the street.

'What kind are they?' asked Flóvent.

'Lucky Strike.'

14

That evening Konrád's sister dropped in to see him. She was single, worked in a library and lived a life of fairly unrelieved monotony. Her workplace suited her down to the ground, as books had been her greatest passion since childhood. She was something of a collector too and had built up an enviable library of her own. Elísabet, or Beta as she was affectionately known, was an old-school communist and took a dismissive attitude to most things on the grounds that they were bourgeois. There was nothing she loathed more than capitalism, a term that covered a multitude of sins in her book.

'Is this a bad time?' she asked, perfunctorily as always. If it was, she pretended not to notice.

'No, come in,' said Konrád. 'Would you like a glass of wine?' He took out a bottle of Dead Arm.

'No, thanks. Drinking rather a lot, aren't you?'

'I don't think so. Anyway, red wine's good for you.'

'Good for you?'

'Yes.'

'Huh, don't tell me you swallow that crap from the red-wine capitalists,' said Beta, taking a seat in the kitchen. She noticed that her brother seemed rather distracted.

'What's wrong?' she asked.

'What do you mean?'

'Did I come at a bad time?'

'No. Actually, I was just thinking about Dad and the seances at our flat.'

'What on earth made you think of that?'

'A case I'm looking into. Remember the girl who was found strangled behind the National Theatre during the war?'

'All I remember is that Dad held that disastrous seance because of her. Why?' she added suspiciously. 'Was he involved in the case?'

'No, not directly,' said Konrád. 'It turns out that an old man called Thorson, who came over during the war, had hung on to some cuttings about the girl's murder, and it seems he went to see Vigga about it.'

'Old Vigga? Is she still alive?'

'Only just. I went to visit her, but she was pretty out of it – started rambling on about some other girl, not the one found by the theatre. You don't remember hearing about any similar incidents, do you?'

'No. But then it all happened before we were born. Was the other girl found in the Shadow District too?'

'I don't remember anyone mentioning another case when I was with the police. The question is whether it ever made it into the papers.'

'Well, it shouldn't be too hard to look it up.'

'The thing is, shortly after he visited Vigga, this man – Thorson – was murdered. He seems to have been digging around for information about the dead girl by the theatre. And possibly about a second girl too, given what Vigga said. I got the impression she mistook me for Thorson. She's a shadow of her former self, poor old thing.'

'What was her name again? Rósamunda, wasn't it? The girl behind the theatre?'

'That's right, Rósamunda. Why was he wondering about her now, seventy years later? Thorson was in his nineties. Why did he go and see Vigga? For that matter, how come he knew her in the first place and what could *she* have known about the case?'

'Well, the girl was found in the neighbourhood and Vigga used to keep her ear to the ground. She lived there almost all her life.'

'Yes, but he must have unearthed something directly connected to the case. God knows what that could have been and how he managed it.'

'Perhaps it had been nagging at him his whole life,' said Beta. 'Perhaps he stumbled across some new information. Who was he?'

'I haven't been able to find out much about him,' said Konrád. 'Incidentally, Vigga said something else about the other girl. It was very hard to hear but I thought she said her bones had never been found. But I don't know what she meant and I couldn't get any more out of her.'

'So some other girl must have suffered a similar fate, but her body was never found?'

'Actually, that fits with something Dad said about the seance, though it was all a bit vague.'

'What, that there were two girls? Rósamunda and a second girl you know nothing about?'

'Yes, a girl who was never found,' said Konrád. 'Assuming there's any point in trying to make sense of what Vigga said. I wonder if Thorson was still looking for her after all these years? Was that why he visited Vigga at the nursing home? Mind you, I've no idea what she was saying about the *huldufólk*.'

'The *huldufólk*?'

'Vigga mentioned this second girl and referred to the hidden people – the elves, presumably – in the same breath.'

'Meaning what?'

'I haven't a clue. But I was wondering if it could be the same girl the medium mentioned to Dad.'

'What are you on about?'

'The medium said there was another girl.'

'That was a hoax,' said Beta angrily. 'They were con men. You can't believe anything that came out of those seances. When are you going to wake up? Don't tell me you're still trying to . . . Dad was an absolute shit and no doubt deserved what happened to him. He was a nasty piece of work who swindled people and harmed people and treated Mum so badly she walked out on him, thank God.'

'Leaving me behind.'

'She didn't leave you behind, Konrád – he wouldn't let you go. He split us up. That's the kind of man he was. We've been over this again and again. How do you think Mum felt when she had to leave you behind? He was just using you to get back at her. He broke up the family. Mum couldn't live with him any longer and that was his way of punishing her. That's the kind of man he was and you're old enough to stop defending him. Our father was a feckless creep and a scumbag.'

'I remember what he was like,' said Konrád. 'There's no need to fly off the handle. I know how he treated Mum. I know all that and I don't need you to remind me every time we talk about him. But he wasn't completely worthless.'

'He was a total shit. That's all there is to it.'

'How can you say he deserved what happened to him? You know nothing about it. You come out with this crap but you have no idea what you're talking about.'

'He brought it on himself,' Beta snorted, and stood up to leave, as she did from time to time when she got really angry with Konrád. 'He brought it on himself.'

15

Following their interview with Frank Ruddy, Flóvent and Thorson took a table at a restaurant on Hafnarstræti called Hot and Cold. The place had opened after the outbreak of war and was popular with servicemen. It sold fish and chips alongside traditional Icelandic dishes such as breaded lamb chops, rhubarb pudding, and *skyr* with cream, which proved a hit with the soldiers. The worst of the crush was over by the time the two men arrived and the owner, a short, curly-haired man in shoes with noticeably built-up heels, was busy clearing the tables. As they tucked into their salt cod with boiled potatoes and dripping they fell to discussing Frank Ruddy.

Ruddy would remain in the custody of the military police until they had confirmed his statement and checked whether he had a criminal record in the States. He had given them the name of the other Icelandic girl he was seeing and Flóvent was planning to talk to her later that evening. Both men instinctively felt he was lying to them about the man he claimed to have seen on the corner of Skuggasund and Lindargata, deliberately misleading them to divert attention from himself. It seemed that had been his intention all along: he was as deceitful and slippery in his dealings with them as he was where Icelandic women were concerned.

'Luckily they're not all like him,' said Thorson.

'No, the girls deserve better than jackasses like that.'

'John Carroll?' mused Thorson. 'Didn't he play Zorro?'

'Yes, he was Zorro.' Flóvent blew on his hot dripping. He was a keen cinemagoer, and a particular fan of two stars, Clark Gable, and the new lead, Humphrey Bogart.

'Maybe Frank sees himself as some kind of Zorro,' said Thorson. 'A womanising adventurer.'

'Yes, some hero.'

'Do you think he had something to do with the girl's murder?'

'I can't picture it,' said Flóvent. 'He's a good-for-nothing fool but I don't believe he knew her. Why would he take his girlfriend to the scene of the crime? Seems a bit far-fetched to me.'

'Rósamunda stayed away from GIs according to her parents,' said Thorson.

'We shouldn't set too much store by what they say. After all, Ingiborg kept her relationship with Frank secret from her parents. It's a common problem with families who forbid fraternisation with soldiers. Many of the girls choose to keep quiet about the men they're seeing.'

'This dripping's pretty good, by the way.'

'Don't you have it in Canada?'

'No, isn't it uniquely Icelandic?'

'Probably. How are you enjoying life in the army?'

'It's fine. Though I'm counting the days till the war's over and I can head on home.'

'Anybody waiting for you there?' Flóvent had never touched on personal matters before in his conversations with Thorson and hoped he hadn't overstepped the mark.

'No.' Thorson smiled. 'Nobody.'

Since he hadn't seemed to take offence at the question, Flóvent decided to keep probing. He knew little about Thorson except that he was a good man to work with, shrewd, diligent and obliging. Didn't give himself airs either. 'What about here?' Flóvent ventured to ask.

'Nope, nobody here either.'

'Of course, you're only, what, twenty-something? Plenty of time to think about that later.'

'Twenty-four. I guess so. How about you?'

'Unmarried,' said Flóvent. 'Somehow I've never had time for . . . for that sort of thing.'

'But there must be someone –'

'Not at the moment,' said Flóvent and changed the subject. 'So you're planning to head home? Once the war's over?'

'Home to Manitoba, yes. Get an engineering degree. Do something useful.'

'Engineering?'

'I want to build bridges. I was minding my own business, studying structural engineering, when war broke out and I ended up over here.'

'What about the police? You don't feel you're doing anything useful as a cop?'

'I didn't mean it like that.' Thorson looked up from his salt cod. 'Of course the job's interesting, the crimes and investigations and all that, but I can't really see myself as a cop. I'll be glad to be free of police work when the war ends.'

'Have you visited any of your Icelandic relatives since you came here?'

'No, there aren't many left. Anyhow, what about you? What made you become a detective?'

'They were short of men – and know-how – when they set up the department ten years back,' said Flóvent. 'I'd been on the force for several years so they sent me to Scotland and Denmark to learn about criminal investigation. I wanted to go abroad. And the job suited me well. I learnt a great deal. We're building up the department from scratch really. Collecting fingerprints, photographs of convicts. It's all new to us. Mind you, operations have mostly been suspended since the war began. In fact, I'm the only one working on that side at present.'

He was devoting every spare moment to compiling the fingerprint archive, though in practice he had very little time. The archive had been started in 1935 when the police first began taking prints from criminals and cataloguing them. At around the same time they had introduced the practice of taking three-dimensional photographs of felons at the police headquarters on Pósthússtræti, using a large stereoscopic camera for the purpose. The collections were still in their infancy, however, like the department itself, which had been founded in Reykjavík about a decade earlier, employing a handful of plain-clothes detectives, including one to take care of the technical side. They carried special badges, a circular silver shield bearing the police star and the inscription *Criminal Investigation Department* instead of the regular police motto 'With laws shall the land be built'. The shield was attached to a silver chain and was to be carried in the pocket of the officer's trousers. Flóvent had never seen any reason to take his out.

'So what . . . what do you enjoy about it?' asked Thorson.

'Enjoy? I don't know if that's the right word. You have to be interested. And have faith in your ability to solve cases.'

'Is it that challenging in a society as simple as Iceland's?'

'It's getting more complicated by the day,' said Flóvent, smiling. 'When a poor farming community is torn up by its roots and dragged into the maelstrom of world events, who can say where it'll end? But it's not likely to end well.'

They finished their salt cod.

'So, what do you do in your free time?' asked Flóvent. 'Any particular hobbies?'

'No,' said Thorson. 'I go hiking in the mountains now and then. I like being alone, surrounded by nature. I've climbed Mount Esja a few times, and Keilir too. It's . . . this is a beautiful country. It's easy to find peace and quiet out there in the wilderness. Fill your lungs with fresh air. Lie in the grass and contemplate the cloudless sky.'

Flóvent smiled again. He had warmed to the young Canadian from their first meeting. 'If Frank Ruddy's telling the truth,' he said, returning to their case, 'and there really was a man standing on the corner, do you think he saw the girl being brought there? Or was he even the killer?'

'Maybe.'

'Can we track him down?'

'We can try.'

'Shouldn't he have come forward?'

'Maybe he didn't actually witness anything.'

'Or didn't exist,' said Flóvent. 'Frank Ruddy's an incorrigible liar.'

'He sure is. I don't think we should rule out the possibility that soldiers were involved.'

'Something occurred to me, though I don't know if it has any bearing on any of this,' Flóvent said after a pause.

'What's that?'

'The business of Rósamunda's disappearance three months ago. Could it be linked to her recent abortion?' said Flóvent. 'I should have asked her parents.'

'Are you thinking she might have been with the man who knocked her up?'

'It crossed my mind. It seems natural to connect the two events.'

'You mean she stayed over with some guy and didn't want to tell anyone?'

'Yes, conceivably.'

'Why? Because she was afraid her parents wouldn't approve? I thought you Icelanders were unusually relaxed about that kind of thing.'

'Well, not everyone is. Actually, I was thinking she might have had an assignation that turned nasty,' said Flóvent. 'Maybe with a soldier. Or an Icelander.'

'Why didn't she want to have the child? If the father was an Icelander?'

'Any number of reasons. She was unmarried, she wanted to learn dressmaking, set up her own shop.'

'A modern woman, in other words?'

'Yes, a modern woman.'

After their meal they paid a visit to Rósamunda's parents who agreed to let them see her bedroom. The couple enquired about the progress of the investigation and offered them coffee and doughnuts, but the two men begged them not to put themselves out. They asked if Rósamunda had ever mentioned the National

94

Theatre or shown any interest in it. Her parents couldn't remember that she had.

'We were going to try and get hold of a sewing machine for her,' the woman told them as they stood in Rósamunda's room, surrounded by pieces of needlework, foreign fashion magazines and drawings of skirts, blouses and dresses that would never now be made.

'A second-hand one,' added her husband. 'They're pricey.'

'She always used to say that a good sewing machine would soon pay for itself,' said his wife. 'The room's just as she left it. Please excuse the mess – she was never one for tidying, bless her, my poor darling girl,' she added in a choked voice.

'Lots of girls keep diaries,' said Flóvent. 'Do you know if she did?'

'No, no idea,' said the man, patting his wife's shoulder.

'Do you mind if we search for one?'

'Please, go ahead,' said the woman. 'Look, you can see she was making a dress out of velvet, with a lace trim. It was her Lana Turner dress. She saw a gown like that in a Lana Turner film.'

The room was like a little dressmaking workshop. There was a small kitchen table that Rósamunda had used for her sewing, a single bed against one wall and a wardrobe against another. A trunk lay open in the corner, spilling out fabric, ribbons, ruffles and a tin of buttons. As they looked around, they saw the room of a girl who knew what she wanted out of life and was happily immersed in her work.

Flóvent cleared his throat. 'When Rósamunda returned home three months ago, did everything go back to normal? Was she well? Did she seem like herself?'

'I didn't notice any difference,' the woman said. 'She worked very hard. She was seldom home. Used to leave early in the morning and come home late at night, only to snatch a few hours' sleep really.'

Flóvent surveyed the room again. They hadn't found any kind of diary detailing Rósamunda's day-to-day existence, dreams, wishes and desires, and nothing that could explain her tragic fate.

Later that evening Flóvent had a brief meeting with Frank Ruddy's other girlfriend, who was somewhat taken aback to hear that Frank had a wife back in Boston, though less surprised to learn that she wasn't the only girl he was seeing in Reykjavík.

'He's from Illinois,' said Flóvent.

'Yes, Boston,' said the girl.

'Boston's not in Illinois.'

'Oh? What's this "Illi" then? I've never heard of that.'

'Illinois is a state. Boston's a big city in a completely different state.'

Her parents exchanged glances.

The girl, who was nineteen, was sitting with her parents and younger brother in their basement flat in Skerjafjördur, at the address supplied by Frank. He had once escorted her home to her door. Her parents had watched furtively from the window as he kissed her goodbye and when he waved to them, they had waved back. They were from the east, from the countryside.

The girl couldn't tell Flóvent anything he didn't already know. She knew next to nothing about Frank except that he was a real gentleman, always had plenty of cigarettes and chewing gum, and used to invite her to dances, and although she didn't speak much English she had the distinct impression that he had once talked seriously about marrying her and taking her back with him to the States.

16

The next day, Flóvent and Thorson went to visit the dressmaker's where Rósamunda had been learning her trade. The owner said she'd been expecting a visit from the police about what she described as 'this tragic business with Rósamunda'. She was fortyish, thin and seemed a little flustered, her words coming out in a nervous gabble. She simply couldn't understand it; Rósamunda had been such a good girl. So clever with her hands too.

'A really gifted seamstress,' she went on. 'Dressmaking came naturally to her. She could mend garments so the repair was invisible. Quite invisible. And she made some absolutely ravishing dresses.'

'Do you know of anyone who might have wanted to harm her, ma'am?' asked Flóvent, glancing around him. 'Was she involved in any altercations that you're aware of?'

He was no judge of women's clothes: of the dresses, skirts, hats and underwear that had been sent to the shop for mending. The rest of the staff had left for the day. Four electric sewing machines were lined up on a row of tables, surrounded by lengths of material, by needles and pins. Opening off the main work floor was a small room containing two old treadle machines. Bolts of cloth, ribbons and other sewing paraphernalia littered the place, along with fashion magazines and dress patterns.

'No, not with anyone here,' said the woman.

'What about the customers?'

'She was such a sweet girl, I can't imagine anyone having anything against her.'

'I assume most of your customers are women?' said Flóvent.

'That's right.'

'Do you get any soldiers coming in?' asked Thorson.

'To my shop? No, no, I can't say I do.'

'So they wouldn't have any reason to come in here?'

'Well, I've seen one or two drop in with Icelandic girls, but they don't use our services, if that's what you mean. They just tend to tag along with their girlfriends.'

'Do you have any regular customers in town?'

'Do I? Good heavens, yes. Dozens. Some of my ladies have been coming here for years. We offer a first-class service – I've always set great store by quality and I can assure you that my company's the best of its kind here in Reykjavík.'

'Do you happen to know if Rósamunda was seeing a soldier?' asked Thorson.

'No, not that I'm aware.'

'What about other suitors?'

'Oh, no, I shouldn't think so. At least, she never mentioned it. But then I didn't know much about her private life. She's worked for me for several years now and has turned out awfully well, I have to say. I've got several experienced seamstresses working for me and another girl in training, but she's not a patch on Rósamunda. She's – she was – so much more talented. There's no comparing them.'

Flóvent noted down the other girl's name. The owner granted them permission to look around in the back room. Apparently Rósamunda had approached the woman about the possibility of working for her; they hadn't been acquainted beforehand. Another girl had left recently so the woman had decided to take Rósamunda on for a trial period. A fortuitous decision. On her last day at work she had been putting the finishing touches on an evening gown for one of their regular clients, the wife of a bank manager, who used to shop at Magasin du Nord on her visits to Copenhagen before this ghastly war began, and the bank manager's wife had declared that this shop was in no way inferior to the famous department store.

Is that so? Flóvent thought to himself, noting down the name of the bank manager's wife.

'Yes, I try to . . . well, you could say that my clientele are very discerning people. And I try to keep it that way.'

Flóvent nodded.

'These days, of course, with everything in such short supply,' the woman sighed, 'we're forced to make the most of what we have, even to make new clothes out of old ones. And everything's grey or black. I haven't laid eyes on a roll of silk in a month of Sundays.'

Looking around the room, they couldn't see any sign that Rósamunda had brought any personal possessions to work. She used to sit at one of the treadle sewing machines, and the evening gown for the bank manager's wife, a simple design in black, was draped over a hanger next to it.

'Do you know where she went after work on her last day here?' asked Flóvent.

'I assume she went home; she didn't mention any other plans.'

'Was that what she usually did?'

'Yes, or so I believe. Though I don't encourage that sort of familiarity from my staff – talking about personal matters, I mean. I prefer to keep things on a formal footing. I feel it's important to be professional, especially these days.'

'So you don't know much about her private life?'

'Very little.'

'Did she ever mention the National Theatre in your hearing?' asked Thorson.

'The National Theatre? No. Why do you ask? You mean because she was found there?'

'You never heard her talk about it?'

'No, never.'

'Do you remember an occasion three months ago when she failed to turn up to work for a couple of days?' asked Flóvent.

'No,' said the woman. 'No, I'm afraid I don't remember.'

Thorson was also in tow when Flóvent went along that evening to see the other girl who was training to be a seamstress. She was the same age as Rósamunda and knew her much better than the owner did. The girl was slim and pretty, with shoulder-length, raven-black hair and thick dark brows that almost met over her dark brown eyes. Her skin was chalk-white, which only enhanced the obsidian sheen of her hair. She rented a small room in a basement near the centre of town and was busy mending a ladder in a silk stocking when they knocked on the door. She and Rósamunda had been close confidantes, she told them, and she'd had the shock of her life when she heard that her friend had died, and in such horrible circumstances. She added that she'd been about to come to the police herself with some information about Rósamunda.

'It's so awful,' she said. 'I can't stop thinking about her. 'What . . . what she must have gone through. I can't stop wondering exactly how she died. Do you know what happened? How *could* something like that happen?'

'That's what we're trying to find out,' said Flóvent in a reassuring tone.

'Have you talked to the old bag at the shop?' asked the girl.

Flóvent said yes they had visited the owner.

'Honestly, the way she forced poor Rósamunda to slave for her, half the night sometimes, without paying her so much as a króna extra.'

'Is that so?' said Flóvent. 'We understand that Rósamunda was very good at her job.'

'She was. And the old cow knew it. Rósamunda wasn't planning to stay with her long. She meant to set up her own mending and dressmaking business, and I'm sure the old bag suspected it. She was worried about it. I'm sure she was.'

'Did this lead to any unpleasantness between them?'

'No, Rósamunda didn't breathe a word about it, not so far as I know. Or if she did, it must have been very recently. She dreamt of becoming a couture dressmaker like the lady who runs Haraldarbúd. She even had plans to go abroad after the war to train.'

'Do you know her parents at all?' asked Thorson.

'I met them once – they were like something out of the dark ages. But she always spoke well of them. You know she was adopted?'

'What do you mean about the dark ages?'

'Well, I got the feeling they were quite strict with Rósamunda when she was growing up, and they're spiritualists too, of course.'

'Spiritualists?' said Thorson.

'Yes, that's what Rósamunda said. That they were into all that spiritualist stuff. Went to seances and had a load of books about ghosts and life after death.'

'Was Rósamunda interested in that sort of thing?'

'God, no, not in the slightest. She didn't believe in it. Thought it was a load of old mumbo jumbo. And when he said that to her . . . the filthy sod . . .'

'What?'

'Like I said, I was going to come and see you about something that happened to Rósamunda. But she didn't like talking about it and begged me not to tell anyone.'

'Oh? What was it?'

'She refused to tell me who the man was or where it happened. Only that it did and that it was horrible. Disgusting. There was never any question of keeping the baby when she found out she was in the family way. I don't know . . .' The girl faltered, then made herself say it: 'He raped her. Rósamunda came round here afterwards and stayed with me for two days before she could face going home. She was in a terrible state . . .'

'Was this about three months ago?' asked Flóvent.

The girl nodded.

'Who raped her?'

'A "bloody bastard", she said. She couldn't go home so she stayed here with me until she'd recovered a bit.'

'Did she tell you who he was?' asked Thorson.

'No. She just said he was completely off his rocker. I found her waiting for me outside when I got home, her clothes all torn. She was a dreadful sight. He told her to blame it on the *huldufólk*. Told her to say she'd been on Öskjuhlíd hill and one of the hidden people had attacked her. So you can tell he was completely unhinged.'

'The *huldufólk*?'

'I wish she'd reported him. I wish she'd said who he was. She shouldn't have let him get away with it. She should have shouted his name from the rooftops, told everyone what he did to her, refused to leave him alone.'

'What's this about the *huldufólk*?' asked Flóvent. 'Are you sure she wasn't interested in the supernatural?'

'No.'

'Did she believe in stories about the elves?' asked Thorson.

'No, of course not.'

'Then what did she mean?' asked Flóvent.

'Search me. She wouldn't say any more. Only that the man was off his rocker.'

Flóvent and Thorson caught each other's eye.

'Do you know if she had any contact with her family up north?' asked Flóvent.

'No, very little. Some of her brothers had moved south – two of them, I think. She said something about them working for the army. In Hvalfjördur or somewhere like that.'

'What did she do in the evenings after work?' asked Thorson.

'Just went home, I think. She often worked late – far too often, if you ask me. We sometimes went to the pictures or dancing at Hótel Borg, but mostly she just slaved away for the old bag. Then, after she was raped, she stopped going out altogether.'

'Do you know if she was acquainted with anyone from the supply depot in the theatre building?'

'No, I very much doubt it.'

'Or if she knew a soldier called Frank Carroll?' asked Flóvent.

'She never mentioned a Frank.'

'He might have been calling himself Frank Ruddy.'

The girl shook her head again.

'She wasn't in the Situation?' asked Thorson.

'No. Definitely not.'

'Did she have a boyfriend?' asked Flóvent.

'No. Unless she met him very recently.'

'No boys she was interested in?'

'No. Rósamunda wasn't really the type.'

'You say she was determined to get rid of the baby. Do you know who performed the abortion?'

'She wouldn't tell me who it was. She was ashamed of what she'd done and didn't want to discuss it. So I avoided bringing it up.'

'But you spoke to her afterwards?'

'Yes. She was so crushed by the whole thing. Was feeling so terrible. Actually, I . . .'

'What?'

'I don't know who fixes that sort of thing here in town, but my mum knows a woman who makes all kinds of herbal cures. I told Rósamunda about her and I know for a fact she was going to pay her a visit.'

'And who is this woman?'

'Her name's Vigga and she lives in the Shadow District. I'm pretty sure Rósamunda did go and see her.'

Thorson jotted down the name.

'And she definitely didn't tell you who raped her?' asked Flóvent.

'No,' said the girl with the raven-black hair, frowning. 'I don't know why she protected the bastard. I just couldn't understand it.'

17

17

Konrád downloaded newspapers from the archives, a page at a time, reading reports of air raids on Berlin and a lull in the fighting in Italy. News of the war tended to dominate, interspersed with domestic reports of political infighting and shipping losses. 'The *Óðinn* Believed Lost with Five Men.' 'Preparations in Full Swing for Independence Celebrations at Thingvellir.' They were all freely available online and Konrád carefully scanned the papers from the time of the girl's death and a good while afterwards. However, he could find few articles about the case apart from the ones Thorson had kept, and those he did find told him nothing new. Censorship had been in operation during the war, Konrád reminded himself, to ensure that nothing would be printed that might be of advantage to the enemy, but that could hardly have applied to the case of the strangled girl.

He had also searched the CID archives for old files relating to the inquiry but found next to nothing. It seemed that almost everything relating to the case had been lost, and he could find no indication that it had ever gone to court. All he managed to turn up was part of an interview with a witness, the woman who had found the body. She claimed she had seen a girl running away from the theatre. In the margin of the witness statement someone had written a name. Konrád copied it down.

It was possible that the case had been handed over to the military authorities. At the time, the occupation forces had included servicemen from Norway, Canada, Britain and the United States, though the Americans were by far and away the largest group. If it had turned out that the girl's killer was subject to the jurisdiction of the occupying military powers, that might explain why there had been so little about the incident in the Icelandic press and police records.

Konrád searched for other stories from the first few months of 1944, the historic year Iceland had become an independent republic, the year he was born. According to his father, news of the notorious seance held at their flat had found its way into the papers. Konrád had never checked whether or not this was true, but he took the opportunity now, sifting carefully through the dailies in search of anything about a fraudulent medium and his accomplice.

The first he'd heard of the affair was when his Aunt Kristjana stormed into the flat like a whirlwind from the north and unleashed a tirade of recriminations against her brother, full of obscure accusations about 'that seance' and warning him to keep his nose out of matters he had no business meddling in. That had been almost a decade after the event. Her anger had been sparked by a newspaper obituary for Rósamunda's adoptive father who had died in hospital after a short illness. Aunt Kristjana had given her brother a crude tongue-lashing about honour and shame and what a good-for-nothing scoundrel he was to treat people like that, until he lost patience and told her if she didn't shut up she could just sod off back up north.

His father had held no further seances at their flat. He was no longer a member of the Society for Psychical Research, from which he had previously selected his victims, and had ceased all collaboration with mediums. Konrád's mother had divorced her husband by the time of Aunt Kristjana's visit, utterly sick of her life with him, of his duplicity, his swindling and the small-time crooks he associated with. Not only was he unreliable and incapable of holding down a job, but he drank heavily in the company of riff-raff, had dared to raise his fist to her and repeatedly humiliated her in front of his friends. One day she announced that she'd had enough, she was leaving him and taking the kids. 'Do what you like,' Konrád's father had yelled at her, 'you can bugger off and take the girl with you, but you're not having my boy!' She hadn't let this stop her, though she had hoped against hope that he would relent and let her have Konrád. It was not to be, however, and the matter remained a source of bitter conflict between them.

Following Aunt Kristjana's visit, Konrád had asked his father what she meant about a seance.

'Don't you start,' he said, ruffling his son's hair. 'It's nothing to worry your head about. My sister's always been half-cracked.'

Konrád went on downloading newspaper pages from 1944 until at last his attention was caught by a headline: 'Stir at Seance'. It turned out to be a fairly detailed account of a seance recently held in the Shadow District, which had been exposed as a hoax, much to the disgust of those in attendance, especially an older couple who had recently suffered a tragic loss. No names were given, but the article referred to a veteran psychic and his accomplice, a family man whose home was used for the meeting, who had conspired to elicit information from the sitters, then pretended it had been channelled through the medium from beyond the grave. An ugly trick, the newspaper called it, adding that the couple who had sought their services had been distressed in light of their bereavement and . . .

Konrád had read enough. He closed the page and didn't search for any other references to the incident. Suddenly he didn't want to know what the papers had to say. Rising from his chair, he went into the kitchen and put on some coffee. Then he fished out a scrap of paper from his pocket: he had jotted down the name from the margin of the witness statement. It was a woman's name he'd not heard before and thought was probably uncommon in Iceland. It was almost certainly borrowed from Danish. Settling in front of his computer again, he clicked on the telephone directory and entered the name. There was only one result.

'No harm in trying,' he told himself, picking up his phone and tapping in the number.

It rang for a while.

'Hello?' he heard a voice that was elderly but clear answer at last.

'Is that Ingiborg?'

'Speaking.'

'Ingiborg Ísleifsdóttir?'

'Yes, speaking,' said the woman. 'Who's calling, please?'

18

It didn't take Flóvent long to find the right address, a small house clad in corrugated iron, with a cellar and a tiny attic, which stood on the edge of the Shadow District. He climbed the short flight of steps and rapped on the door. No one answered. There was a small yard behind the house and, rounding the corner, Flóvent saw that the owner had converted it into a vegetable garden. He was turning to go back to the street when the cellar door opened and out stepped a woman in a ragged jumper, dirty linen trousers and a pair of waders, with long woollen socks showing over the tops. Her thick shock of hair made her head seem huge. She was carrying an empty bucket.

'Who are you?' she asked, slamming the cellar door behind her and securing it with a padlock.

'Excuse me, are you Vigga?' asked Flóvent.

'What's it to you?'

'I'm from the Reykjavík police. I'm investigating the death of the girl whose body was found behind the National Theatre. You may have heard about it. Her name was Rósamunda.'

'Nothing to do with me.'

'Is your name Vigga?'

'Yes, that's what they call me.'

'I wondered if I might have a word with you.'

'I've nothing to say to you,' said Vigga and stumped off up the steps. She obviously had no intention of letting Flóvent interrupt her chores.

'I hear you know a lot about Icelandic herbs.'

'What business is that of yours?'

'And understand their healing properties.'

'I wouldn't say that.'

'And destructive powers.'

'Look, I haven't got time for this,' said Vigga. 'Please get out of my garden.'

She went into the house, shutting the door behind her and leaving Flóvent standing there like an idiot. Determined not to admit defeat so easily, he climbed back up the steps and banged on the door. A long interval elapsed before Vigga appeared again.

'I thought I asked you to leave.'

'I understand Rósamunda may have come to you for help. I wanted to know if she had, and, if so, what passed between you.'

He pulled out a photograph of Rósamunda that her parents had given him and showed it to the woman. 'This is the girl.'

Vigga studied the picture for a while, then regarded Flóvent impassively with small, catlike eyes. Her brow was high under the wild mop of hair, her face narrow with thin, almost invisible lips, her sour expression hinting at a life of hardship.

'She did come here.'

'What did she want from you?'

'She was in a wretched state, poor thing. At her wits' end.' Vigga gave Flóvent a searching look. 'Come in, then.' She opened the door wider and went back inside. 'I don't suppose I'll be able to get rid of you. But I'm not offering you anything. I don't have any coffee and it's no good asking me for booze.'

'I don't want anything,' Flóvent assured her, following her inside.

Vigga led the way through a small hall to the kitchen and gestured to Flóvent to take a seat at the table. He didn't get a glimpse into any of the other rooms. He sat down and Vigga positioned herself by the old coal range. She appeared to be making a concoction involving dried Iceland moss, reindeer lichen and wild thyme. The kitchen window faced the street and he saw a woman walk past in the gathering dusk, pushing a pram.

'I'm experimenting with dyes,' Vigga explained, when Flóvent expressed curiosity about the plants. 'For an artist here in town. You won't have heard of him. He's nothing special.'

'Do you make herbal cures? Mountain plants have strong medicinal powers, don't they?'

'Sometimes. If I'm asked to.'

'Did Rósamunda ask you to help her?'

'She told me her problem. Took her forever to spit it out. I told her straight off there was nothing I could do for her. She was almost hysterical, poor child, when she first arrived, but she soon calmed down. Sat where you're sitting now. I gave her a tea that I brew myself. Felt sorry for her. I get visits like that from time to time because they think I'm some kind of witch who can sort out their problem. It's to do with the soldiers, if you get my meaning. I directed her to a woman I know, but I've no idea if she ever went to see her.'

112

'Which woman is that?'

'I'm no snitch. You won't get her name out of me so don't bother asking.'

'All right. Then what did you and Rósamunda talk about?'

'The *huldufólk*, mostly. She started rabbiting on about the elves for some reason, so I told her about that girl up north in Öxarfjördur.'

'What girl up north?'

'The one who went missing.'

'Who was she?'

'A girl from the countryside. I met her once when I was working as a cook for the road-building crew. Hrund, her name was, if I remember right.'

'What happened to her?'

Vigga stuck a sprig of wild thyme in her mouth and tipped the reindeer lichen into the concoction in the saucepan. Then she began to relate the story of a girl who had grown up on a poor croft in a rural farming community up north, one of a large brood of children; she'd received a good Christian upbringing and had just started walking out with a boy from the same district. One day, when she was twenty, she was sent to see her eldest sister, who was married and lived on a nearby farm. The girl arrived on foot at the appointed time, completed her business and set off home. But she didn't turn up until twenty-four hours later, and when she did she was in a state of shock, weeping uncontrollably one minute, unable to speak the next, and proved incapable of explaining where she'd been, how she'd come to lose some of her underwear, why one of the sleeves on her jumper was torn, and how she had come by the injuries to her face and neck. She was terrified of being left alone and refused to leave the house. When questioned, all she would say was that she'd got lost and couldn't really remember what had happened. She'd been out all night and only found her way home in the morning.

After two days she was a little calmer but still refused to describe what had happened in any detail. And she was in such a fragile state that no one had the heart to coax or scold her into revealing the truth. It would all come out in time, but no one could fail to see that she had gone through some terrible ordeal.

'They should have kept a better watch on the poor child,' said Vigga, 'because one morning they found her bed empty. She'd run away in the night and was never seen again. They'd been keeping a close eye on her, but not close enough. They checked all the neighbouring farms but nobody had seen her. Later a big search party was sent out but they never found anything.'

'Was this after the British occupation?'

'Yes.'

'Were there troops in the area, do you happen to know?' asked Flóvent.

'There were soldiers around – at Kópasker, for example. You used to see them from time to time.'

'Was the girl involved with one of them?'

'I don't think so. But you never know.'

'So it's not impossible?'

'I really couldn't say.'

'What did people think had happened?'

'There were rumours doing the rounds that she wasn't right in the head. That she may even have lied about the incident, invented it to cover up something else, something she didn't want people to know about.'

'Like what?'

114

'Haven't a clue.' Vigga stirred the contents of the pan. 'Nobody knew for sure.'

'What do you think happened to her?'

'How should I know? Some people thought she'd thrown herself into the waterfall at Dettifoss. But that's just a guess. Nobody knows what became of her.'

'Did it occur to anyone that the soldiers might have played some part in her disappearance?'

'Nobody even considered that angle, as far as I know. The poor girl was assumed to have killed herself and that was that. But I expect people had their suspicions. Of course it was seen as a tragedy, but there was never an investigation or anything like that. That's why I'm a little surprised by your interest.'

'What did you say the girl was called?'

'Hrund.'

'Had she been having problems before the incident?'

'No. Apparently not. I . . . well, I gather she was the gullible type: believed in the elves, used to lap up folk tales about the *huldufólk* as if they were the gospel truth. A bit simple, poor dear. Or so it was said.'

'So the whole thing took everyone completely by surprise?'

'Yes, I believe so. The only thing she ever said . . .'

Vigga's herbs were in danger of boiling over, and she turned back to them, stirring them vigorously with a large wooden spoon.

'Yes?' prompted Flóvent.

'This is too damned hot,' said Vigga, blowing into the saucepan. 'The only thing the poor girl said about it was something her younger sister reported later on.'

'Which was?'

'They were very close and Hrund had told her a bit about what happened to her that night – some nonsense about being waylaid by one of the *huldufólk*.'

'The *huldufólk*?'

'Yes. She insisted that an elf man had attacked and beaten her. Even had his way with her. I had to repeat this three times for Rósamunda. She couldn't believe her ears. Then suddenly she was off. Ran out of the house without stopping to say goodbye, poor girl.'

When Flóvent didn't respond, Vigga stopped stirring and turned to find that he had risen to his feet and was staring at her in disbelief.

19

'What's the matter? You look like you've seen a ghost.' Vigga stood over her saucepan, observing Flóvent's reaction with curiosity. The coal crackled in the range. The woman with the pram walked back past the window on her way home.

'She mentioned the hidden people?' said Flóvent after a moment. 'That she'd been attacked by an elf man?'

'That's what her sister said. She claimed she'd run into a man from the other side. It was all very muddled and ridiculous, unless you happen to believe in those sorts of old wives' tales, which I don't. Don't believe in the elves or any other invisible creatures.'

Flóvent didn't know what to think. Two girls, on opposite sides of the country, with identical stories; one found dead behind the theatre, the other missing, possibly a suicide. Both had mentioned the hidden people. Could it be a coincidence? No one but himself and Thorson and the young seamstress knew that a man had raped Rósamunda and told her to blame it on the *huldufólk*. And neither he nor Thorson had breathed a word about it to anyone else.

'When was all this?'

'Three years ago.'

'And how did people react to the girl's explanation?'

'Some thought she'd gone round the bend. Others started repeating all kinds of stories about ghosts and elves, and found nothing odd about it. The old beliefs die hard.'

'Which ones?'

'Folk beliefs, of course. You know the kind of thing – supernatural beings and cursed ground and people vanishing into elf palaces hidden in rocks or mountains. I gather the girl was a sucker for fairy tales like that, though I don't believe for a minute that it was a supernatural being who attacked her.'

'But she believed it, you say? Believed in the *huldufólk* and spirits?'

'Yes, so they say. She knew all the local elf rocks and tales of the hidden people. Of course they tell these stories on every farm up there, whether they believe them or not.'

'What do you think happened?'

'It's not for me to say.'

'But from what you've heard.'

'You can't go asking me that. I don't know what went on,' said Vigga testily. 'But some of the locals thought maybe the girl had been messing about with a soldier and it'd gone wrong, so she felt she had to lie and blame it on the elves. You know how people are about the Situation. But if she was seeing a soldier, he never came forward. And the local boy she was supposed to be sweet on flatly denied having anything to do with it. He swore blind he hadn't touched her.'

'You talked of an elf man having his way with her. Are you talk-ing about rape?'

'That's what they said, but I don't know whether there was any truth in it.'

'And Rósamunda was shaken when she heard this?'

'Knocked sideways. I told her in my opinion the girl must have been raped and the bastard who did it told her to lie and blame it on the hidden people. It wouldn't be the first time that had hap-pened. She turned white as a sheet and rushed out of the door.'

Flóvent pondered this news. If the incident in Öxarfjördur had taken place three years ago, might the man who raped Rósa-munda have got wind of it? Surely the only possible conclusion was that the two cases were linked? Didn't Rósamunda's reaction suggest as much? Flóvent didn't for a moment believe Hrund's explanation. It must have been a man. It had nothing to do with the elves. Could the same man have raped both girls, and found the girl up north easier to fob off with this ridiculous lie than Rósamunda?

'Isn't it obvious that the poor girl was raped, beaten and had her clothes torn off?' said Flóvent.

'Yes, you'd have thought so,' said Vigga. 'But they never had a chance to get to the bottom of what really happened.'

'You said there were British soldiers in the area. Were you aware of any other visitors to the district, anyone passing through, anyone – ?'

'Why do you assume it was an outsider?'

'I don't,' said Flóvent. 'But it seems natural to consider that angle.'

'There were British soldiers around. I didn't come into contact with any of them, though I can't answer for the people on the farms – whether they had any dealings with the Tommies. Then there was the road crew, quite a crowd, all men, apart from us cooks. Must have been about thirty, forty men altogether. I don't know who else was passing through, though I expect there were the usual summer visitors on the farms.'

'Including the farm where the girl lived?'

'Of course.'

'Anyone from Reykjavík around at the time?'

'Other than me, you mean? Our foreman, he was from town. And two or three others, but most of the crew were locals, boys from Húsavík, Kópasker and the other villages, and two or three cocky little sods from Akureyri.'

Flóvent stopped off at Fríkirkjuvegur on the way home to make notes on the information he had gathered that day. He telephoned Thorson's office, only to learn that he had been called out and no one knew when he would be back. So Flóvent walked home across the bridge over the lake, calling in at the cemetery on Sudurgata as was his custom. Pausing by the grave, he said a brief prayer, then carried on through the west end of town to Framnesvegur.

Flóvent lived with his father in a small flat in a wooden house that had been converted into two apartments. It looked out over Faxaflói Bay, and from its windows Flóvent had watched the British invasion force sailing into Reykjavík harbour early one May morning in 1940. The occupation hadn't come as a surprise to him, and since occupation by one side or the other was inevitable, he preferred the Tommies to the Nazis of the Third Reich.

His father had worked on the docks for many years, and was still employed there as caretaker for a small tool shed. He could have earned more working for the armed forces but refused to take part in any profiteering from the war. He was asleep on the couch in the kitchen but woke up when Flóvent came in.

'That you, son?' he said, sitting up. 'I must have dozed off. Have you eaten? I've made rice pudding and there are some slices of liver sausage to go with it.'

They sat down to eat. Knowing just how much the cases that landed on his desk interested his father, Flóvent filled him in on the latest about Rósamunda. He knew his father would keep it to himself, trusted fully in his discretion as he trusted him in everything.

'The *huldufólk*?' said the old man. 'Odd that the girl up north should mention them too.'

'There may be a connection,' said Flóvent. 'It's highly unlikely that two girls, on opposite sides of the country, would come up with an outlandish story like that unless there was a link. In fact, it's out of the question.'

'Have there been other stories about attacks of that kind?'

'I wouldn't know,' said Flóvent. 'Maybe in a folk tale. Or even in old court records. I could check. See if anyone's peddled that kind of nonsense before.'

'You'd be wise not to rule it out. Supposed to have thrown herself into Dettifoss, is she?'

'Nobody knows what became of her.'

'Remember, just because you and I don't believe in them, that doesn't mean she didn't genuinely believe she saw one of the hidden people. There must be a reason why we have all these folk tales about light elves and dark elves and trolls and ghosts. I wouldn't dismiss it out of hand or condemn her as being soft in the head.'

'I'm not.'

'No, I know, son. Your dear mother had a lot of time for the old beliefs. She'd have given the girl the benefit of the doubt, I expect. By the way, did you drop in at the graveyard?'

'Yes, I did.'

'God bless them,' his father said, not for the first time when the subject of the cemetery came up.

They had been living in a small, draughty basement room in one of the houses set back from Hverfisgata. It had been the coldest winter in living memory. People called it the Big Freeze. The pack ice had come right in to shore, the harbours froze over, you could walk out to the island of Videy without getting your feet wet, and the temperature kept plummeting below −30°C. Day after day, Flóvent had huddled around the coal range with his parents and little sister, bundled up in all the clothes they owned, while his father used anything he could lay hands on for kindling.

And that was only the beginning of that fateful year, 1918. After a fleeting summer, autumn had set in, bringing with it the sickness that was said to have killed millions of people around the world. Their basement had provided some shelter from the cold, however inadequate, but it couldn't keep out the Spanish flu. Flóvent's mother and sister had both succumbed after a short illness. Flóvent had fallen ill too but recovered, while his father had escaped it entirely, which he put down to having contracted the influenza that ravaged the country in 1894.

The majority of the fatalities occurred in Reykjavík. The town's mortuaries were soon overflowing and the authorities resorted to digging mass graves in the cemetery. On one terrible day at the height of the epidemic, almost twenty bodies had been interred in two graves, Flóvent's mother and sister among them. Flóvent had been too ill to attend their funeral. In some cases as many as six coffins at a time were placed before the altar in the cathedral.

Emergency measures were put in place. The town was divided into thirteen districts, medical students were given temporary licences to practise, and house-to-house visits were organised to help those in need. The situation was desperate. People died in their beds a few days after being infected. Children were found standing alone over their parents' bodies. Others lay gravely ill, unable to move.

Although Flóvent's father had lost his wife and young daughter, or perhaps because of this, he did his bit for the relief effort. Once he had nursed his son through the flu, he worked day and night to support the doctors and nurses, accompanied all the while by church bells ringing the death knells of loved ones and the echo of weeping, carried from house to house by the bitter wind.

'God bless them,' his father said again, his eyes resting on his son. 'God bless them and keep them, now and for ever.'

20

Konrád pulled up in front of an imposing detached house in the west end. It consisted of two storeys and a basement flat and had been built shortly after the war when the prosperity brought by the changing times had started to make its presence felt. It was clad in pebble-dash, like so many buildings of that era, and had a large back garden, bordered with tall rowan trees and a handsome sycamore.

Ingiborg had given him directions over the phone. The house belonged to her son, she told him, and she lived in a small flat in the basement that he had fitted out especially for her. She was alone there at the moment because her son had taken his family to Europe on holiday. She hadn't felt up to going with them; she was too old and tired for travelling.

She greeted him at the door and invited him in, explaining that she'd been listening to an audiobook as these days it was difficult for her to read. She indicated the large reading lamp on the kitchen table with a magnifying glass and newspaper lying beneath it. Her hair was white and she moved slowly with the aid of a stick, stooping slightly as she walked. There was a Zimmer frame in the hall. When she asked if he'd like a coffee, he accepted gratefully. It was stiflingly hot in the flat. The sitting-room window looked out over the garden.

'I was so astonished when you rang,' she said. 'When you said you were with the police. I haven't received a visit from the police since I was young, and that was in connection with the very same case you were asking about. The strangled girl.'

'It can't have been much fun for you, being caught up in an inquiry like that.'

'The worst part was stumbling on the poor girl's body. That was an unpleasant experience, believe you me.'

'I can imagine.'

'I did completely the wrong thing: ran away like an idiot, let myself be taken in. But I learnt my lesson. You have to learn from your mistakes or what would be the point of them?'

Ingiborg put down her stick to free up her hands for the coffee jug.

'Can I help you at all?' asked Konrád.

'No, thank you,' said Ingiborg. 'I can still make coffee.'

Konrád was careful not to charge straight in and took his time with the old lady, chatting to her about the weather and politics and her favourite TV programmes. Ingiborg said she watched a great deal of television; she was particularly fond of daytime soaps. She struck him as talkative and sunny by nature, well informed about current affairs and pleased to receive a visitor who showed an interest in everything she had to say. Nevertheless, he sensed an underlying tension and wariness. Her past was catching up with her, and she was understandably cautious. When he spoke to her on the phone it had quickly become apparent that she was indeed the girl referred to in the newspaper article, the civil servant's daughter who had found the body by the theatre.

'Do you remember it well?' asked Konrád, when he had finished his first cup of coffee and she was urging him to have a second.

'I've never been able to go to a play at the National without thinking about it,' Ingiborg said. 'For as long as I live I'll never forget the moment we found her. Of course that sort of thing stays with you always. The way she was lying on the ground with her eyes open. The biting cold. But what's prompted you to ask about her now, after all these years?'

'As I mentioned on the phone, I'm looking into the case in connection with a recent murder,' said Konrád. 'You may have read about it in the papers, about a man a little older than yourself who was found dead in his home.'

'Yes, that sounds familiar.'

'When we examined his flat it turned out he'd kept some old newspaper cuttings about the murdered girl, and he seems to have been looking for information about her just before he died. I wanted to know why. Your name cropped up in an old police report –'

'I'm sure it did.'

'Do you know if they ever solved the case?' Konrád asked. 'If they ever caught her killer?'

'I'd have thought you would know that.'

'Unfortunately there's nothing in our archives. We can hardly find a scrap of paper relating to the case. It's as if it never went to court.'

'No, I didn't ever try to find out what happened. Shortly afterwards, only a few weeks later, I was . . . I moved to another part of the country and stayed away for a couple of years. Then I came home and got engaged to my husband.'

Ingiborg smiled at Konrád. She had been thrown by his phone call, having never expected to hear Rósamunda's name again. Konrád had been very polite, though, and his manner had reminded her of those other policemen, Flóvent and Thorson, who had come round to her house long ago and been so kind and understanding once their initial suspicions had been allayed. She only hoped he wouldn't expect her to go into details, or she would be forced to reveal to him, a complete stranger, why her father Ísleifur had taken the decision to pack her off to the countryside after her relationship with Frank Ruddy. No amount of persuasion, tears or curses had succeeded in changing his mind. Even her mother had been powerless in the face of his tyranny. He had got it into his head that she would recover best with her relatives in the East Fjords, and that it would minimise the gossip if she simply vanished. His brother was a wealthy farmer out east, so although it was in the middle of nowhere, she would at least be tolerably comfortable. By the time she came back to Reykjavík the occupation was over and most of the soldiers had left. Her father, who had acted in the belief that he was averting disaster, made it up to her by introducing her to a highly promising young man who had worked with him on the independence celebrations. The young man in question had influential backers within the civil service who had secured him a valuable import licence and access to credit, and his wholesale business in American goods was really starting to take off. 'A secure future,' her father had said. 'At least consider it, dear.'

'He built this house,' Ingiborg told Konrád. 'My husband. He died several years ago. He was a wholesaler.'

'It's quite a house,' said Konrád, for the sake of saying something.

'Yes, far too big for the three of us to rattle around in. My husband and I only had the one child. My son takes very good care of me down here, so I really can't complain. I lack for nothing. Never have lacked for any of the things that are supposed to matter in life.'

Konrád sensed a certain underlying bitterness, as if her words held a deeper, quite different meaning. He wondered how happy her life had actually been since that fateful day when she chanced upon the body.

'You weren't alone?' he said. 'When you found the girl?'

For the first time Ingiborg didn't answer.

'Obviously, it must be painful to talk about after all this time,' Konrád added after a pause.

'I was . . . no, it's not very nice having to talk about it.'

A silence developed, which Konrád refrained from breaking.

'He was a soldier,' Ingiborg said all of a sudden.

'Who?'

'You're right, I wasn't alone when I found her. He said his name was Frank Carroll but that was a lie, like everything else he told me. His real name was Frank Ruddy – the American soldier I was friendly with for a while – and he wasn't a very admirable character. A real cad, in fact. He lied to me. Not just about his name. He turned out to have a wife back in America. And children. He was even two-timing me with another girl here in Reykjavík.'

The words came in spurts, she almost spat them out, and again Konrád sensed bitterness mingled with an old anger.

'An absolute snake,' Ingiborg continued. 'It was the police who told me what sort of person he was. Lovely men, both of them. They knew I'd been taken for a . . .' She broke off, then continued apologetically: 'I wasn't going to tell you any of this. When you rang and wanted to dredge the whole thing up. I wasn't going to talk about it at all.'

'Don't worry,' said Konrád. 'You can say as much or as little as you like. It's up to you.'

'I was . . . I was dreadfully upset when I learnt the truth about Frank, what sort of person he was. Flóvent, the detective, came to see me specially to tell me everything. Please excuse me but I . . . I don't feel comfortable digging all this up. Perhaps it would be best if you left now. I don't think I can help you any further.'

'All right,' said Konrád. 'Of course. I didn't mean to upset you.'

Ingiborg stood up with some difficulty to see him out.

'What can you tell me about Flóvent?' asked Konrád, rising to his feet as well. He remembered the name from one of Stefán's newspaper cuttings. 'Was he in charge of the investigation?'

'Yes, he led the inquiry into the girl's death. There was another policeman too, representing the army. Thorson, his name was. An unusually nice, charming young man.'

'Thorson?'

'Yes.'

'Did you say Thorson?' Konrád couldn't hide his astonishment.

'Yes. Thorson.'

'Was he investigating the girl's death as well?'

'Yes. There were two of them. Flóvent and Thorson.'

'Do you have any idea what became of him?'

'No. He was from Canada. I expect he went back there after the war.'

'He was a policeman here?'

'Yes, with the military police.'

'And he investigated Rósamunda's death?'

129

'Yes.'

It took Konrád a while to digest what Ingiborg had told him.

Finally she lost patience. 'Why are you so astonished?'

'You mean you don't know?'

'Know what?'

'Thorson died a couple of weeks ago. He was the pensioner found murdered in his flat. He went by the name of Stefán Thórdarson in later life. He was the man who kept the cuttings about the girl and had recently started asking questions about her, after all this time.'

It was Ingiborg's turn to be stunned. 'You mean that was Thorson?'

'Yes.'

'Who on earth would have wanted to harm him?'

'We don't know. I thought you might be able to help us answer that.'

The old woman sank back into her chair.

'Can you tell me anything about him?' asked Konrád, copying her example and sitting down again.

'I shouldn't . . . my son . . . I can hardly tell you – a complete stranger.'

'It needn't go any further.'

'No, it's probably best if you leave now. I . . . I've had enough. I'm tired. Would you please go?'

'All right.' But Konrád showed no signs of moving. He could see that the old lady was troubled and sensed that in spite of what she said, she hadn't finished.

'It's . . . it's one of those things that happens, and then you're left facing it all alone, powerless,' she said. 'And it never leaves you, however many years go by. It stays with you for ever.'

'Perhaps you'd like to know how Thorson died,' said Konrád. 'He was suffocated. At home in his bed. His pillow was held over his face and –'

'Please, spare me the details.'

'Tell me something: did you ever hear about another girl who suffered the same or a similar fate to Rósamunda?'

'Another girl?'

'There's a chance Thorson was asking questions about her before he died. Another girl from those days. A girl who disappeared. I gather they never found her remains.'

'And she was supposed to have suffered the same fate?'

'Yes, does that ring any bells?'

'No,' said Ingiborg pensively. 'Thorson told me the girl from the theatre had mentioned the *huldufólk*, but I can't remember exactly what it was she had said.'

'Really? The *huldufólk*?'

'Yes, just like the woman I went to see. Mind you . . . I didn't know whether to take it seriously or if it had any bearing . . .'

'What?'

Ingiborg heaved a sigh of resignation. 'If I tell you, it's only for Thorson's sake, in case it helps you find out the truth about his death. He was so very kind to me.' She fell silent. 'Maybe I should . . . I've never told anyone else.'

'What?'

'I told Thorson about her and what she did, and I know he and Flóvent went to see her. Thorson believed Rósamunda had gone to her for the same reason. To the woman on the hill. It's an experience I'll . . . I'll never forget as long as I live . . .'

21

One cold February day, not long after Ingiborg had identified Frank at the military police headquarters, she put on her best coat and a fetching hat, and went down to number 11 Fríkirkjuvegur where she asked to speak to Flóvent. It was the first time she had been inside the grand building that housed Reykjavík's Criminal Investigation Department. A secretary greeted her at reception and asked her to wait.

Shortly afterwards Flóvent appeared and showed Ingiborg into his office.

'I didn't know where else to turn,' said Ingiborg, once she was seated in front of his desk. She took in her surroundings with interest. The office wasn't large. One window looked out over the dusk-filled back garden where the stables used to be. The only source of illumination in the room was a desk lamp, which cast a pool of light on Flóvent's papers, a card with fingerprints, and some photographs of Rósamunda's body at the scene of the crime.

Frank was still being detained by the American military police; Ingiborg hadn't met her former lover since his arrest. Flóvent told her that he would remain in custody until they had verified his story.

'What can I do for you?' he asked now.

'What'll happen to Frank, do you know?'

'I can't say for sure. If he turns out not to have played any part in Rósamunda's death and they find no other reason for him to remain in custody, he'll be released.'

'And allowed to stay in the army?'

'I expect so.'

'Here in Reykjavík?'

'I really couldn't say. He may be a cheat and a liar but I'm afraid that's not a criminal offence. There's talk of troop movements to Britain, an imminent invasion of the Continent. He may well be sent over there with his regiment.'

'I need to speak to him,' said Ingiborg. 'I'm afraid it's unavoidable.'

Flóvent's face registered surprise. 'I'd have thought you wouldn't want anything more to do with him.'

'I don't, I never want to see him again, but I *have* to talk to him. I thought you might be able to arrange it. If they're going to keep him in jail for a while.'

'Well, I could have a word with Thorson. May I ask what it is that you need to discuss with Frank?'

'It's . . . it's private.'

'Nothing that has any bearing on the case under investigation, then?'

'No, not at all. It's . . . it's personal.'

Ingiborg didn't dare meet Flóvent's eye. Instead she lowered her gaze to the photographs of the girl on the desk. She didn't want to tell him why she urgently needed to speak to Frank Ruddy even though the mere thought of seeing him made her feel sick to her stomach. She'd been a bit under the weather in the mornings lately: queasy, weak and lethargic, and she had begun to suspect the reason. It wasn't simply that she'd been let down by a GI who'd stooped to assuming the name of a film star to deceive her, although admittedly that had sapped her energy and made her feel very depressed. There were undeniable physical symptoms. They had started earlier and had been making her increasingly anxious for weeks. She wished she could have confided in her mother but that was out of the question in the circumstances. Her parents had been put through enough. She'd been intending to share her fears with Frank on the terrible evening they took refuge behind the theatre, but fate had intervened. Now, in spite of all that had happened, she felt he ought to know.

Flóvent had arranged a meeting with Ingib, g a couple of days earlier to bring her up to date with what the police had found out about Frank. He needn't have bothered but she got the impression that he was well disposed towards her, and she had come close to sharing her concerns with him then. He had gone out of his way to be tactful, understanding and sympathetic. She knew he wanted to soften the blow she'd suffered as a result of Frank's behaviour. When they parted, Flóvent had told her she could come to him about anything; if it was in his power he would assist her.

'All right,' he said now. 'I'll have a word with Thorson and see what he says.'

Two hours later Thorson himself received her at the camp and escorted her to the military jail. He was just as mystified as Flóvent about why she wanted to see Frank. All Flóvent had told him over the phone was that it was personal and unrelated to the investigation. Thorson didn't query this. He asked Ingiborg if she would like him to interpret, but she hastily assured him that there was no need.

Thorson showed her into a small room and told her to wait. The jail was housed in a prefab hut in the Laugarnes camp, one of the largest in the country, which contained not only barracks but also offices, a mess hall, a post exchange, a sick bay and the military police headquarters. A number of such camps had risen within the city limits, each like a village of Quonset huts huddling in the bleak terrain, here at the ends of the earth.

Frank was led into the room and looked astonished when the identity of his visitor was revealed.

'*You?*' he said in English, sounding as if he'd never expected to set eyes on Ingiborg again.

The door closed behind him and he took a seat.

'*Look, I never meant to lie to you. It was just . . . I just . . .*'

'*No matter,*' Ingiborg said in her halting English. She didn't want to listen to any more of his lies. She needed to go ahead and say what she'd come here to say, because she felt he had a right to know. How she acted afterwards would depend on his response. During the long, sleepless nights she had considered not telling him at all, but she didn't feel this was fair.

'*I have . . . baby,*' she said, placing a hand on her belly so there would be no mistaking her meaning.

Frank didn't react.

'*Your . . . your,*' she added.

'*My what?*'

'*Baby.*'

Frank stared at her. *'No way,'* he said. *'Hell, no.'*

'Yes.'

'Oh, no. No, you don't . . .'

'What do you mean?' She looked puzzled.

'You come to me with that shit . . . It isn't mine. That's a lie. A goddamn lie.'

'It's yours,' Ingiborg said in Icelandic, patting her belly for emphasis.

'That's a lie,' repeated Frank angrily.

'No.'

'I'm not doing this. This is not my problem.' Frank leapt out of his chair and banged on the door. The guard opened it and let him out. Thorson appeared behind them and came into the room as Frank was led away.

'Is everything OK?' he asked.

'Yes, I should be going.' Ingiborg stood up.

'What did he say to you?'

'Nothing. It's all right.'

She had been afraid of Frank's reaction, and her suspicions had now been confirmed; she couldn't expect any help from him. Part of her was relieved. When they made love he had promised to be careful. She had found it painful both times.

'Let me drive you home,' said Thorson. 'I have a car at my disposal.'

'No, thank you, I can walk. Thank you for letting me see him. I won't need to visit him again.'

She was fighting back tears and Thorson took her hand in an attempt to comfort her.

'You're not the first girl to be taken in by a soldier. You were unlucky. Frank's a no-good liar. Fortunately they're not all like him.'

'No.'

'Why are you so upset?'

'I don't know what to do. He . . .'

'Why did you want to see that jackass? I'd have thought he was the last person you'd want to see.'

'I needed to talk to him . . .'

'Why? About the investigation?'

Ingiborg shook her head. 'About something else.'

'What? Why are you so unhappy?'

'I can't say. I have to go home.'

'Can't you . . . are you . . . ?'

Ingiborg burst into tears.

'You're not expecting his child?'

She nodded. 'I . . . I think so . . . I know I . . .'

She hadn't meant to say anything, had meant to go home with her secret intact and lock herself in her room. She had no idea what to do, no one to advise her. In the end she would have to tell her mother, but she was dreading it. Though that would be nothing to the storm that would break when her father discovered that she was expecting and that the father was an American soldier. She raised her eyes to Thorson. She had blurted out her secret inadvertently, but afterwards it was a relief to have got it off her chest.

'Have you been examined by a doctor?'

'No, I don't need to be. I just know.'

'Are your parents aware?'

'God, no.'

'You should confide in them.'

'I daren't. I don't know what to do.'

'You should at least see a doctor,' said Thorson. 'Get confirmation.

Then you must talk to someone you trust. I'm guessing Frank didn't take the news too well?'

'He thought I was lying about it being his. But I'm not. He's the only man who . . . the only man in the picture.'

'I expect you've already considered your options.'

'I'm not going to get rid of it,' Ingiborg said. 'I'm not doing that.'

22

As Konrád listened to Ingiborg describe her encounter with Thorson, he wondered if he dare ask whether she had stuck to her guns. But he didn't know her at all and realised that he himself would take offence at this kind of prying.

'Thorson was good to you,' he said instead.

'He was a lovely man,' said Ingiborg. 'A genuinely kind man.'

'He settled in this country, as I said. Did you have any contact with him after the war?'

'No, none. I left town. And never ran into him again after I came back. I assumed he'd returned to Canada.'

'Actually, I understand he lived in Hveragerdi for many years before moving to Reykjavík about twenty-five years ago.'

'Did he have a family? Children?'

'No, I don't think so.'

'What about Flóvent?'

'I have almost no information about him,' said Konrád. 'All I know is that he was one of the pioneers of the Reykjavík CID. His name crops up in accounts of the history of the department. Never met him myself – he was rather before my time.'

'I was pregnant and had no idea where to turn. I'd heard of people who could help out – some girls I knew were talking about it. Then I got a message from Frank that just goes to show what kind of man he was. A friend of his came to see me and told me about a woman I could visit. Frank knew what he wanted. He swore the child had nothing to do with him, but in spite of that he directed me to a woman I could talk to if I wanted to go down that road. I don't know how he knew about her. I just hoped it wasn't from experience.'

'And did you go and see her?' asked Konrád hesitantly.

'I did,' Ingiborg replied, after a little pause.

'So you changed your mind?'

'I couldn't see any other way out. And I didn't have much time if I was going to . . .'

'But you wanted to keep the child?'

Ingiborg looked at him, offended.

'Forgive me, I didn't mean . . .'

'What do you think?' she snapped.

The woman Frank sent her to see lived in a low, concrete farmhouse set among the small hills east of the Ellidaár rivers, just outside the city limits. It was quite a trek from Ingiborg's home and it took her a long time to get there. She hadn't spoken to her parents about her dilemma, her fear, dread and confusion, or to any of her friends or relatives. She felt so ashamed of what had happened to her that she couldn't bear the thought of people knowing, especially after the way Frank had behaved – lying and making a fool of her like that.

When she reached the bridge spanning the rivers, she sat down briefly on a rock to catch her breath. She had a bad taste in her mouth. How did he know about the woman on the hill? Had he sent another girl there before her? Did the soldiers know about her for obvious reasons? Was she herself really going to follow his advice? Advice from Frank, of all people! Could she really stoop that low?'

She stood up and forced herself to go on, her reluctance growing with every step as she struggled up the final stretch to the farmhouse. The concrete building had an air of neglect: flaking patches of paint here and there bore witness to the fact that it had once been whitewashed. Adjoining the main house, and enclosed by a chicken run, was a tumbledown disused cowshed with a turf roof. Hens wandered in and out under the watchful eye of an alert cockerel. Two children, playing on the grassy roof, paused and subjected Ingiborg to a silent stare. It was a mild, windless day and there was a beautiful view north to the snow-covered form of Mount Esja.

Avoiding the children's gaze, Ingiborg knocked at the door. It was opened a crack by a woman in her forties.

'Good afternoon,' Ingiborg began.

'What do you want?' asked the woman.

'I was told I should talk to you, ma'am.'

'"Ma'am?" Well, aren't you posh? I don't call anyone "ma'am" and you shouldn't either.'

'No, sorry . . . I . . . don't know how to put it . . . I was told you could help women like . . . in my position.'

The woman studied her through the narrow gap.

'Gone and got yourself knocked up, have you?'

She asked the question bluntly, but without any trace of

accusation or disapproval, and before Ingiborg knew it she was nodding and confessing to this unknown woman both her fall from grace and the crime she had come here to commit.

'How did you find me?' asked the woman.

'I was referred by someone.'

'Yes, I expect you were. Who by? Who told you about me? Your parents? It can hardly have been a doctor. Your gentleman friend, maybe?'

Ingiborg nodded.

'Soldier, is he?'

'Yes,' she whispered.

'Come in, then.' The woman opened the door wider. 'Let's have a look at you.'

The woman ushered Ingiborg into her kitchen and asked if she wanted anything to drink. Ingiborg shook her head. The kitchen was primitive and very cramped, with a larder off to one side. The woman had been rinsing eggs in the sink and packing them into boxes.

'How far along are you?' she asked. She was short and wore her hair in a bun. What drew Ingiborg's attention most were her hands, which were unusually large. Arthritis had twisted the little fingers and ring fingers into her palms, rendering them almost useless. The long, dirty nails resembled talons. Ingiborg averted her eyes.

'I don't know, not exactly.'

'More than twelve weeks, you reckon?'

'No, not that long. More like eight or nine.'

'I see,' said the woman, turning to her and drying her hands. 'That's all right, then.'

Ingiborg didn't move.

'No need to look so terrified,' said the woman. 'It's a very simple operation. I know what I'm doing.'

Ingiborg found herself staring at the woman's fingers again and wishing that she had never entered this house.

'I . . . I didn't know what you charge for . . . how much money I should bring.'

'Does it look like I do this for the money?' asked the woman, glancing around her humble kitchen.

'No. I don't know.'

The woman studied her for a while. 'Maybe you need more time to think.'

Ingiborg nodded. 'I think I'm making a mistake.'

'It's up to you. You shouldn't be here unless you're sure this is what you want to do. You can't allow yourself any doubts. There was a girl here a while ago who was like you, scared out of her wits, with the oddest excuse for her condition, though I've heard worse.'

'Excuse?'

'Claimed she was a respectable seamstress. That she didn't know any soldiers. She was hardly in her right mind after I'd dealt with her – kept rambling on about some bastard who'd forced himself on her; apparently he said some strange stuff about the *huldufólk*.'

Ingiborg struggled to keep her gaze from straying back to those hands with their twisted fingers.

'You should go home,' said the woman, resuming her washing of the eggs. 'Go home and think about it, and if you want you can come back and we'll see what I can do for you. You've still got a bit of time on your side.'

* * *

Ingiborg fell silent. Neither of them spoke for a while as she lost herself in her memories of the concrete farmhouse on the hill and the woman with the twisted fingers.

'Did you go back?' asked Konrád, finally venturing to break the silence.

'No, I didn't, and I never saw the woman again. My parents found out once I began to show, and I had to confess to having sinned with Frank. They banished me to the countryside. I had the child, but it was taken away for adoption. Where, I don't know. I never asked.'

'You must have had some say in the matter?'

'I agreed to it. I let them decide. Let them push me around instead of doing what I wanted. The worst part was that I didn't know what I wanted. I couldn't make up my own mind. Somehow it was easier to let other people take over, hope that it would all fade over time. Perhaps it was even worse than an abortion. I don't know. I've tried not to think about it. My father insisted, and I obeyed. I had no choice. But at least the woman in the farmhouse was honest. The alternative has involved living a lie for the rest of my life. My husband never knew. My son still doesn't. I hope I can trust you to keep it to yourself?'

'That goes without saying,' said Konrád. 'But your story's hardly unique.'

'No, naturally I wasn't the only one.'

'Did you ever see Frank again?'

'No. Never.'

'What did that woman mean about the *huldufólk*?'

'I haven't the faintest idea. But Thorson happened to mention to me that Rósamunda had worked as a seamstress and made beautiful dresses, so I put two and two together. I thought I'd better let him know and rang him. It turned out that the police were already aware she'd had an abortion but didn't know who'd performed it.'

'Was it the same woman?'

'I expect so,' said Ingiborg. 'Though I never heard any more about it.'

23

The army jeep made easy work of the rough track leading up to the concrete farmhouse among the small hills east of the Ellidaár. Flóvent noticed that their jolting progress up the slope was being observed from a window by two inquisitive faces which vanished the moment the men stepped out of the car.

On the way there he had recounted the details of his visit to Vigga. Thorson was astonished to hear that there was another girl, in a distant part of the country, who might also have been raped and, like Rósamunda, had mentioned the hidden people.

'Is that even possible?' was Thorson's first response.

'Looks like it.'

'There are two cases? Related cases in two different parts of the country?'

'It's conceivable,' said Flóvent. 'It's hard to avoid the conclusion that the same man could have attacked them both.'

'The link being the reference to the elves?'

'Yes. Rósamunda learnt from Vigga that she wasn't necessarily the man's only victim. Clearly, their attacker wanted them both to give the same explanation.'

'And one is taken in by it and confides in her sister, while the other thinks it's totally crazy?'

'But it has the same upshot,' Flóvent pointed out. 'Neither one of them reported him. Neither would say who her rapist was. Either they were protecting him or they were afraid to expose him.'

'Why?'

'For various reasons the girl up north was more receptive to the lie. She believed in the *huldufólk*. Had heard tales of people's dealings with them. No doubt she was familiar with the folk tales in books and genuinely believed some of them. Maybe even swallowed the lot.'

'Still, we can't rule out coincidence,' said Thorson.

'No, of course we can't rule anything out,' conceded Flóvent, 'though I find it highly unlikely. And we do know one thing we didn't know before.'

'What's that?'

'We're looking for an Icelander. I can't imagine the foreign soldiers here know the first thing about the elves.'

The woman opened the door before they had a chance to knock and looked them both up and down.

'And who are you fine gentlemen?'

'We're from the police,' said Flóvent.

'The police? That's all we need. What do you want with me?'

'We'd like to ask you a few questions about a girl who came to you for help,' said Flóvent. He added tactfully, mindful of the two

147

children he'd seen in the window: 'We gather you provide certain services behind closed doors.'

'Services? What are you on about? I sell eggs sometimes. That's no crime.'

'That's not what we're talking about,' said Flóvent. 'I believe you know what I mean. As it happens, we're not here about that. Though you can expect a visit from our colleagues shortly. What we're interested in is a young woman who came to see you recently, seeking your help.'

'A young woman? That's not much to go on.'

'You talked about the *huldufólk*,' said Thorson.

'Remember her?' asked Flóvent.

The woman stared at him. 'Did she come crying to you, telling tales?'

'I'm afraid I'm not with you,' said Flóvent.

'That other one. She chickened out. It was her who reported me, wasn't it? Snooty little madam. Brittle as a china doll. Was it her?' The woman stepped out over the threshold, pulling the door carefully shut behind her. 'I'm not a bit ashamed of what I do,' she went on. 'You bloody men don't have to worry about a thing. You leave all that to the women. So what if I help those poor girls? I haven't hurt anybody, let me tell you. I've –'

'As my colleague said, we're not concerned with that side of things,' Thorson interrupted, noticing the fingers curled, clawlike, into her palms as Ingiborg had described. 'You'll have to explain to someone else what kind of charity it is you run here. What can you tell us about the first girl? Did she give you her name?'

'No.'

'Or tell you what she did for a living?'

'She said she worked as a seamstress, not that I asked.'

'Is this her?' asked Flóvent, showing her the photograph of Rósamunda.

The woman examined the picture. 'Yes, that's her.'

'Did you know she was found murdered behind the National Theatre a few days ago?'

'Murdered? No. I hadn't heard. Well, I knew a young woman had been found . . . Was that her?'

'Did she tell you who the father was?' asked Thorson.

'No.'

'Did you get any feeling about who it might have been?'

'How do you mean "feeling"? I don't know what that's supposed to mean.'

'Well, whether it could have been a soldier, for example,' said Thorson.

'No, I don't know. Was it a soldier who killed her?'

'We're aware that soldiers have referred women to you,' said Flóvent, ignoring this.

'I don't know anything about that.'

'You said she'd babbled on about the hidden people,' said Thorson. 'What did she mean?'

'The poor girl, she was desperate when she came here. Could hardly get a word of sense out of her. All she wanted was to get rid of . . . for me to help her with her problem. She wouldn't hear of anything else. Couldn't bear the thought of having the child. Couldn't bear it.'

'Why not?' asked Flóvent.

'She claimed it wasn't her fault . . .'

'How do you mean?'

'I took it that she'd been raped rather than done it willingly . . .'

'But she never said who the man was?'

'No, but it sounded like he wanted her to blame it on the *huldufólk* or something. She couldn't stop crying and saying sorry, swearing it wasn't her fault, that she wasn't responsible and couldn't stand the thought of having the baby. My heart went out to the poor girl. Someone had attacked her all right, but it was a man who did it. Forget any talk about elves. You can bet your life he was all too human.'

The US Navy had made major improvements to the road between Reykjavík and Hvalfjördur when they began to store fuel oil on the northern shore of the fjord. As the war went on, more and more warships and cargo vessels docked there, and the naval base now sprawled across the neighbouring ports of Midsandur and Litlisandur. Huts for the workers and huge fuel tanks had sprung up, along with depots providing supplies for naval repairs. A horde of Icelanders worked in the area, including two of Rósamunda's brothers.

Flóvent and Thorson headed straight up to Hvalfjördur after their visit to the farmhouse on the hill. It was a beautiful, cloudless February day, but cold, and they drove carefully because the road was icy in patches and difficult to negotiate. Thorson had brought chains in case they got stuck in one of the snowdrifts that often blocked the road.

As they travelled along the shores of the fjord, Flóvent pointed out places of interest and three times they stopped for Thorson to hop out and examine the bridges they encountered, all of which were only wide enough for one vehicle and consisted of concrete supports with a wooden roadway. The young man clambered around in the snow in his uniform, tapping concrete piles, bouncing on timber decks and jotting down observations in a small notebook. Although Flóvent was becoming frustrated by their slow progress, he held his tongue.

'Just above here is Glymur, the highest waterfall in the country,' he commented as they stood by the bridge over the River Botnsá at the head of the fjord. 'You ought to walk up there sometime. It's a pleasant hike – easy, not too far.'

'How come some Icelanders don't want to break with Denmark?' asked Thorson suddenly, as he leant over the rail. 'Isn't it about time?'

'I think everyone wants independence really,' said Flóvent. 'But some feel the timing's not right. The Danes are vulnerable because they've got their hands full with Hitler, so there are those who think we should postpone our declaration. They don't want to offend the King.'

'Does his opinion still matter to people here?'

'Not to me,' said Flóvent.

Thorson was aware that the inauguration of the republic that summer would mark the end of almost six hundred years of Danish rule. The struggle for independence in the last century and the start of this one had reduced Denmark's influence in Iceland, but the two nations had to be formally separated before the process could be completed. The Republic of Iceland was to be established at the ancient assembly site of Thingvellir on 17 June, the anniversary of the independence hero Jón Sigurdsson's birth.

'What's worse,' said Flóvent, once they were seated in the jeep again, 'is the talk of the American army staying on once the war's over.'

'Wouldn't that be a good thing?' asked Thorson. 'Don't you need military protection? It's not like you have an army of your own.'

'What we need is neutrality,' said Flóvent, as they set off again. 'We've no business having an army.'

'Is neutrality really feasible? I mean, would you want to be neutral in this war?'

'Others have managed it.'

'Are you saying you're just swapping the Danes for the Americans?'

'Honestly, I don't know. These are strange times.'

They were stopped at a checkpoint when they reached the military zone, but were waved through after Thorson flashed his police badge. Rósamunda's brothers both worked at the depots and Thorson had phoned ahead to request the assistance of the officer in charge, one Colonel Stone. The colonel had spoken in turn to the man in charge of the Icelandic contractors who had passed on the message to his men. When Flóvent and Thorson arrived, the brothers were waiting for them in the overseer's office. British and American destroyers lay at anchor in the fjord and a large oil tanker was taking on fuel to supply the fleet out at sea. Dense ranks of Quonset huts, with their curved green roofs and pairs of windows at each end, ran up the slopes from the shore, housing dormitories, offices and stores, while the giant oil tanks loomed over them all.

The brothers were both in their early twenties, one dark, the other red-haired, both lean, though one was appreciably stockier. His name was Jakob, he was the more self-assured of the two and did the talking. Egill was a bit younger and had little to say for himself, seeming shy and withdrawn in his brother's presence. Both were dressed in khaki trousers, black military boots and hand-knitted *lopapeysur* instead of jackets. All they had been told was that the police wanted to talk to them about their sister.

'Are we under arrest?' asked Jakob.

'No,' said Flóvent. 'Of course not. Is that what you were told?'

'That's what everyone will assume,' said Jakob.

'We just wanted some information from you. That's all.'

'Should we talk to them individually?' Thorson asked Flóvent.

'Why?' asked Jakob immediately.

'We can start with you,' said Flóvent. 'If you'd wait outside, Egill, thank you.'

Egill looked at his brother, who gave him a sign to do as he was told. Once he had left the room, they sat down and Jakob pulled out a packet of American cigarettes and offered them round. They declined. He lit up with a new American Zippo lighter, flipping back the lid with a loud snap.

'Did your family up north have a good relationship with Rósamunda?' asked Flóvent. 'Did you stay in touch with her while you were growing up?'

'Not really,' said Jakob, expelling smoke.

'Why not?' asked Thorson.

'She was given up for adoption. We didn't talk about her much. Me and Egill were sent away for several years too. Life was tough at home.'

'But she was your sister.'

'So? It's not like we knew her at all. I don't remember her. Nor does Egill. So there's no point asking us about her.'

'What do you think happened to Rósamunda?' asked Flóvent.

Jakob shook his head. 'Dunno. There's plenty of stuff going on in Reykjavík with all those soldiers around.' He looked pointedly at Thorson.

'Do you think she could have been mixing with the soldiers?'

'Haven't a clue. I didn't know her.'

153

'When did you last see your sister?'

'I already told you: I don't remember her. Neither does Egill.'

'We gather she was corresponding with her father – your father. Were you aware of that?'

'She wrote to the old man,' said Jakob. 'Said she was planning to visit us. But nothing came of it.'

'Do you know why she got in touch?' asked Thorson.

'No.'

'Maybe she wanted to get to know her family?'

'Maybe.'

'Didn't you have any interest in meeting her?'

Jakob thought, then shook his head.

'Do you know if she was happy with her adoptive parents?'

'No. Haven't a clue.'

'Whether she wanted to leave them? Move home to be with your father? Was that why she wrote to him?'

'Dad didn't mention anything like that. There was only the one letter. He told her she'd be welcome up north.'

They persevered with their questions, but Jakob seemed remarkably indifferent to his sister's fate. His callousness didn't escape them.

'Doesn't she matter to you at all?' asked Thorson.

'I didn't know her.'

'She was your sister,' said Flóvent.

'She probably had a much easier life than us. I can't think why she wanted to get in touch.'

'To get to know you? Her family?'

'Yeah, well, nothing came of it.'

'It seems likely that she was raped.'

Jakob's expression didn't change.

154

Flóvent asked if he had been in Reykjavík the evening Rósamunda's body was found, but he said no. He and his brother had been here in Hvalfjördur as usual. They'd worked all day, then played poker with some Yanks in a hut that served as a bar.

Jakob's younger brother Egill was not as offhand with them. He took the chair facing them, sniffed loudly and wiped his nose on the sleeve of his jumper. They asked him many of the same questions as they had put to his brother, and he backed up Jakob's statement that they had been in Hvalfjördur when Rósamunda died.

'When did you last see your sister?' asked Flóvent.

'I don't remember,' said Egill. 'I was so young when she was adopted.'

'Was there no contact at all between your family and Rósamunda in Reykjavík?'

'No.'

'Never?'

Egill shook his head. 'Well, she wrote to Dad.'

'Did you see the letter?'

'No, he told us.'

'What was her letter about?'

'She wanted to meet us or something.'

'Was your father in contact at all with the couple who adopted Rósamunda?'

'No. Never. We were . . .'

'What?'

'We were told it was best for everyone if there was no contact. She was theirs and that was that. We always knew we had a sister in Reykjavík. We knew what had happened – she had to be given away. Dad couldn't look after all of us when Mum died. Me and Jakob were sent to other farms. The family was split up. That's nothing new.'

'So you didn't do anything to her?'

Egill sniffed again and rubbed his nose on his sleeve. 'No. We didn't know her. Not at all.'

24

Following his visit to Ingiborg, Konrád went for a meal at a decent steakhouse on Skeifan. It was still early; there were few other diners, and he took a corner table. While he was eating, his thoughts wandered back to Vigga in the nursing home. To the other girl she had mentioned, who had gone missing and never been found, and that obscure reference to the *huldufólk*. This couldn't have been Rósamunda. Her body had definitely been found behind the theatre. Thorson had been investigating her case during the war, if Ingiborg was to be believed. But something had prompted him to start asking questions again, all these years later. At least, he had spoken to Vigga, and possibly to others as well. What had sparked his interest? And why had he gone to talk to Vigga? How had she been mixed up in it all? Vigga had been under the impression that she was talking to Thorson when Konrád visited her. As if they had once known each other. Had the other girl suffered the same fate as Rósamunda? Was their story similar? Had Thorson unearthed some new piece of evidence in his old age?

Konrád was startled out of his thoughts by a crash. He looked up to see one of the customers standing in momentary bewilderment among the shards of a glass he had dropped. A waiter came to his aid, and Konrád decided to make a move.

There was a line of inquiry he wanted to pursue. He'd been putting it off, but decided that now was as good a time as any to get in touch with the person who had originally sold Thorson his flat. He might just know something. Konrád had made a note of the name when he came across the sales contract among the old man's papers.

Konrád enquired after the man in question at an attractive townhouse in the east end and was directed to a garage where he worked as a mechanic. The man got the shock of his life when he saw Konrád, as he assumed he must be from the tax office, and that someone had shopped him for working cash in hand, an offence of which he was all too guilty. When his fears turned out to be unfounded, he relaxed and became very pally. Yes, he could remember selling the flat to Stefán Thórdarson, and had indeed heard how the old man had met his end. He hadn't been acquainted with Stefán at all, but recalled that he had been a cash buyer. Remembered thinking that he must have managed to put quite a bit aside. It turned out that the man had a clearer memory of his old neighbour Birgitta, and the conversation soon veered towards a subject that had been strangely close to her heart.

'Me and Birgitta used to argue about it,' said the mechanic. He had a broad face and strong hands marked by many years of tinkering with engines. 'She could never convince me. But she was totally in favour.'

'Of what?'

'You know she was a nurse?' The man removed the battery from the car he was working on.

'Yes,' lied Konrád. In fact, he'd made no effort to research her background.

'Naturally she was speaking from experience. Said she'd seen it all in her job.'

'Speaking from experience? About what? I'm not with you.'

'Assisted suicide,' said the man, putting down the battery. 'She wanted it legalised in this country.'

'Assisted suicide?' Konrád had difficulty hiding his surprise.

'She wanted them to allow assisted suicide in specific, difficult cases. She used to be pretty hard line about it in the old days. Actually, I had half a mind to ring you about the old man. When I heard his death wasn't violent – if you know what I mean – I immediately thought of her.'

'That she might have suffocated him?'

'I'm not saying that's what happened. That's not what I'm saying at all. I just happened to think of her when I heard about the old man. Remembered her views. The way he died sounded like that – like an act of kindness.'

Konrád talked to the mechanic for a while longer without learning anything else of interest. After saying goodbye, he set off home and rang Marta on the way.

'Have you given any thought to assisted suicide?' he asked without preamble. Judging by the sucking and smacking noises at the other end, Marta had just finished eating.

'Assisted suicide? What are you on about?'

'Have you given it any thought?'

'Not particularly,' said Marta. 'Do you mean would I choose that way out myself?'

'No, not you,' said Konráð. 'Were you eating?'

'Some crap I picked up at a burger joint. What's all this about assisted suicide?'

'Has it crossed your mind in relation to Thorson? There he is, lying in his bed, no sign of a struggle. No resistance on his part. It's like he lay down and went to sleep, only someone put a pillow over his face.'

'So?'

'Two points. There's a suggestion that Birgitta and Stefán, or Thorson, were more than just neighbours – according to another occupant of the building. And I've just heard that Birgitta was a great believer in assisted suicide – was passionate about it, in fact. She used to be a nurse. Did she tell you that?'

'No. Where did you hear that?'

'From the man who originally sold Thorson his flat. He remembered Birgitta because of her views.'

'Assisted suicide? It's not like Thorson was ill. The post-mortem didn't reveal anything wrong. What sort of relationship *did* they have? Maybe you ought to check it out.'

'Want me to have a word with her?'

'Please,' said Marta. 'We're unusually short-staffed at the moment. See what you can winkle out of the woman and let me know how it goes.'

25

It was late evening. Candles were burning here and there on various tables, and thick curtains were drawn over the windows. The medium was waiting for them in the sitting room. He was about forty, on the small side, with a friendly manner, soft, smooth hands, and a warm smile. He wore a threadbare dark suit and looked a little peaky, as if he was suffering from a hangover. The couple, sensing a whiff of mysticism about him, were surprised to find how down-to-earth and approachable he was when he spoke to them. Konrád's father had pulled out two chairs for them, which they now took. There were three other people attending the seance: a father and son and a very deaf old man, all of them poor, judging by their clothes. The son had lost his mother after a gruelling illness, and he and his father wanted reassurance that she was better off in the next world. The deaf old man wasn't seeking contact with anyone in particular and seemed preoccupied with the issue of which language the spirits would use. The medium had no need of a chair. He alternately stood in front of them or paced the floor, trying to pick up the currents flowing through the ether – as he was only the conduit, he explained to his audience.

'All I do is relay messages to you.'

'Don't you fall into a trance then?' the woman wanted to know. Although she and her husband were no strangers to seances, they hadn't encountered this psychic before.

'No,' the medium replied, 'that's not how it works. It's more that the currents flow through me.'

The old man cupped a hand to his ear. 'What's that you say?'

'I'm explaining how it works.'

'They will be speaking Icelandic, won't they?' the old man bellowed.

The medium reassured him on this point and he began the seance by asking the sitters a series of questions. Names floated around the room, which they either did or didn't recognise. If a name didn't sound familiar to anyone, the medium was quick to move on to the next one. But if he received a positive answer from his audience, he would continue to question the spirit and describe any distinguishing features until a consensus was reached about who it could be. Once this was established, he would convey the message that all was well on the other side, and sometimes pass on thanks to somebody in the room. Some spirits, according to him, were accompanied by a sweet smell, others were associated with pieces of furniture, paintings or articles of clothing. The father and son recognised some of these, the old man others. Once the medium had taken his time in attending to them, he turned to Rósamunda's parents.

'I . . . it's cold and dark here,' he said, standing in front of them with half-closed eyes, his head tilted to one side. 'Cold and dark and there's a man standing . . . he's standing in the cold and I . . . I think he's got mittens on, it's as if he's got mittens on and he's cold. Mittens knitted from two-ply yarn. Does that sound familiar at all?'

The couple didn't immediately answer.

'He's . . . could he be wet from the sea?' asked the psychic. 'Could he be drenched with seawater?'

'Yes,' said the woman hesitantly. 'If it's him. Did you say two-ply yarn?'

'The mittens,' her husband added in explanation.

'He says you were always good to him and he wants to thank you for all the coffee,' said the medium, not letting himself get distracted. 'I have the feeling his name might be Vilmundur or Vilhjálmur, something like that.'

'Could it be Mundi?' the woman said, her eyes on her husband.

'I get the feeling he drowned,' continued the medium. 'That he's dead. Am I right?'

'He was lost in Faxaflói Bay,' said the husband. 'Off Akranes. There were three of them.'

'I knitted those mittens for him,' said the woman. 'The poor, dear chap.'

'I can see . . . it's like a painting or maybe a view from a sunny house and there's this strong smell of coffee. A beautiful house. And *kleinur*. Such a strong smell of coffee and something else too – cinnamon, from the doughnuts, something like that.'

'Mundi often used to say how good my *kleinur* were,' said the woman, nodding as if to confirm this to the father and son who were sitting quietly listening.

'I sense that he's in church and I think . . . I can hear music. Could that be right? Was there a lot of music around him?'

'That could well be right; he used to play the organ,' said Rósamunda's father.

'Thank you,' said the medium. 'He's telling you not to worry about . . .'

He broke off and appeared to be listening intently for messages from the spirit world. A long time passed in absolute silence, as if the messages couldn't get through. Then all of a sudden the medium took a step backwards and froze, as if riveted to the spot, his eyes still half-closed.

'He says she's with him. She . . . that you'll know who she is.'

The woman gasped: 'Our little girl!'

'Can you see her?' asked her husband eagerly.

'He doesn't want . . . says you'll know what he means and that you're not to worry.'

'Our darling little girl,' said the woman and began to cry. Her husband tried to comfort her.

The medium fell silent again and they didn't dare interrupt, convinced that he was straining for messages from the depths of eternity, until finally Rósamunda's father could hold back no longer.

'Does she want to tell us who it was?' he whispered.

The medium stood in the middle of the room, perfectly still, for what felt like an age. The sitters didn't move a muscle. The eyes of father and son were fixed on him and the deaf old man was trying not to miss a thing. Rósamunda's parents held hands.

'Does she want to tell us who it was?' the husband asked again.

The medium didn't answer but remained silent and motionless, until he began shaking his head and pacing around the room, saying the connection had broken and he didn't have the strength to continue.

The seance was over. The psychic sank into a chair as if exhausted and Konrád's father brought him a drink of water. Rósamunda's parents sat there dazed, as though they could hardly believe what had happened. It took a while for everyone to get their bearings again. They were all convinced that something important, something extraordinary, had occurred.

Konrád's father pulled back the thick curtains to admit the light spring night, then went out to the kitchen and came back with coffee for the sitters and offered round some boiled sweets. The deaf old man poured the coffee into his saucer and drained it with loud slurps.

'Odd about those mittens,' remarked Rósamunda's father. 'That he should bring them up.'

'I was telling the host only yesterday how fond Mundi was of my *kleinur*,' said his wife. 'And about the mittens. The two-ply ones.'

The father and son looked at them.

'Did you tell him that?' the widower asked, his eyes on Konrád's father.

'What was that? What did she tell him?' shouted the old man.

'I'm sure I did,' said the woman. 'I told him about Mundi and how he drowned.'

'Did that seem wise to you?'

'Wise? I don't understand.'

Konrád sat at the kitchen table, watching the sun go down and recalling his father's account of the incident. He remembered it vividly. He was eighteen when his father told him about the seance with the couple who had lost their daughter, and how he used to go about swindling a few krónur out of gullible types, many of whom were mourning the loss of a loved one. He had never spoken of it before, though he had often talked of the other dubious activities he had been mixed up in. But on this occasion he had been drunker than usual and mawkish with it, willing to open up to his son about some of the murkier episodes in his past.

'It was laughably easy,' he had said in his hoarse voice, smoking non-stop as he talked. 'People were ready to swallow anything, and the more they paid, the more they'd lap it up. Damn it, the whole thing was a piece of cake.'

Konrád couldn't detect any remorse in his father's manner. He never made excuses for what he was or what he had done to others, but Konrád couldn't stop himself from asking how he could stomach profiting from people's misery like that.

'If they want to be taken in, that's not my problem,' was all the answer Konrád got. 'Mind you, he did have powers of some kind, the bloke who played the medium for the girl's parents. We held a lot of seances together, him and me, and we weren't found out because he did have a certain gift, I reckon, though he was a bloody amateur. I didn't get everything from the woman – not the organ, for example – but maybe that was just luck. You needed a bit of luck to do it well. I'd tipped him off about the other stuff, like the mittens and how the bloke drowned, before they arrived. But when the father and son got wind of the fact that the woman had talked to me beforehand, they went mad and called the police, and that was that. A phoney medium exposed. And I was described as his accomplice.' Konrád's father burst out laughing. 'Like I was his sidekick!'

'Was that how you usually did it?' asked Konrád. 'Chatted to people beforehand, then passed it on to the medium?'

'There was no set way of doing it,' said his father. 'This particular psychic held a whole load of meetings at our place, and I was in charge of finding out a little bit about the sitters. The same people often came back again and again, so he got to know them himself. Like the father and son. They'd been twice before. But sometimes he didn't know them at all and said he preferred to have some facts up his sleeve before he started – helped him warm up, he said.'

Konrád's father paused. 'He should never have described those mittens like that,' he continued eventually. 'But the strange part was that the silly sod did actually sense a presence. He told me, when the fuss about that bloody seance was at its height, that he was sure he'd sensed the presence of their daughter, and another girl too, who was with her. He had the feeling she'd come to a bad end as well.'

'There was another girl with her?'

'That's what he claimed.'

'What happened to her? What sort of bad end?'

'He didn't say. Didn't like to discuss it, any more than he did the other stuff that happened at that seance. After we'd been found out no one would listen to him any more.'

'Didn't he tell you anything about her?'

'No. Except the bit about the cold. He said she'd been accompanied by this powerful feeling of cold. But listen, Konrád, he was a bloody amateur, this bloke, and most of what he came out with was stuff I'd fed him.'

The story of the seance had remained etched in Konrád's memory because it was the last conversation of the kind that he'd had with his father. One evening in mid February, Konrád had come home near midnight to see a police car parked in front of their basement flat and two officers hanging about outside. He wasn't particularly surprised, as his father was certainly known to the police and whenever there was a burglary, or a bootlegger was busted, or a major smuggling ring was exposed, they would come round to question him, even haul him off to the station on Pósthússtræti. It was 1963. Konrád had recently dropped out of technical college where he had been training to be a printer and started drinking heavily. His father had never interfered much in his life, and he seldom heard from his mother who had moved with Beta to Seydisfjördur in the East Fjords. Konrád's drinking companions were generally other layabouts on a fast track to the gutter, or else his father. Konrád took cash-in-hand jobs on building sites, shoplifted, broke into cars, and ran errands for his father for a minor share in the profits of whatever shady activity he was involved in at the time. In spite of this, Konrád had never been caught or had any kind of brush with the law.

One of the officers approached him and asked if he lived in the building and knew the tenant in the basement. Konrád, who had learnt to be wary of the police, opened his mouth to trot out a lie but nothing came to mind. So he admitted that his father lived in the basement – they lived there together – and asked if it was him they were after.

'No, we're not looking for him,' said the policeman. 'Were you with him this evening?'

'No,' said Konrád. 'Why are you asking?'

'Are you sure?'

'Yes, I'm sure.'

'Any idea who he was going to meet?'

'Why do you want to know?' asked Konrád.

'Had he fallen out with anyone recently? Was there anyone after him?'

'After him? What are you on about?'

'Your father's dead, mate,' said the other policeman. 'Do you know if he was planning to break into the abattoir down on Skúlagata?'

Konrád wasn't sure he'd heard right. 'What do you mean?' he said. 'What did you say?'

'He was found lying in the alley by the abattoir,' said the policeman. 'Stabbed. Do you know what he was doing there?'

'What are you talking about? Stabbed! Was he stabbed?'

'Yes, stabbed to death.'

Konrád gaped at the policemen. They had been sent to inform the dead man's next of kin, but they knew his father well and saw no reason to be compassionate towards drunks and petty crooks. Just then a car drew up and yet another policeman climbed out. But this one wasn't in uniform, and it soon became apparent that he was a detective.

'What are you talking about?' Konrád shouted furiously, shoving at one of the officers. He would gladly have punched him but the man's partner immediately grabbed Konrád, knocked him down in the road and got him in a stranglehold. Konrád flailed wildly and it took both officers to overpower him. When they had managed to subdue him, they raised him to his feet again.

'Let him go,' ordered the detective wearily. 'Leave him be.'

The two officers grumbled but eventually relinquished their grip on Konrád.

'They've told you what happened?'

'Yes.'

'Are you his son?' asked the detective.

'Yes. They said he was stabbed. What happened? Why . . . ? Is he dead?'

'Are you sure you don't know what happened?'

'Yes, I . . . I can't believe it.'

'You don't know who attacked him?'

'Attacked him? Me? No, I was in town. What the hell happened? Is . . . is he really dead?'

The detective nodded. Speaking in a level tone and, unlike the other officers, without a trace of superiority, he explained that a passer-by had found Konrád's father lying in a pool of blood near the gates of the abattoir on Skúlagata. He had been stabbed twice and left lying in the road. There were no witnesses and they didn't know the identity of his killer. Konrád couldn't tell them anything about his father's movements. He didn't know what business his old man could have had at the abattoir or down on Skúlagata, and hadn't a clue who he'd gone to meet or who he could have run into there. His father had fallen out with countless people over the course of his life and had always kept questionable company. Konrád quickly realised that his death was bound to be viewed in that light.

'My condolences, son,' said the detective. 'I'm sorry you had to find out like this. If there's anything I can do for you, anything that bothers you, anything you want to know, whatever it is, please get in touch.'

His father's killer was never found. A comprehensive murder investigation was launched but eventually shelved due to lack of evidence. However, his father's death did have a profound effect on Konrád: he eventually turned his back on his dead-end life-style, re-enrolled in technical college and finished his training as a printer. And, as fate would have it, some years later he joined the police and ended up a detective himself. From time to time his fellow officers would whisper about his father and once or twice even asked him outright about the case, but Konrád would bite their heads off. He never forgot, though, the kindness and consideration the detective had shown him in his hour of need.

26

The day after their trip to Hvalfjördur, Thorson and Flóvent met up again at the offices on Fríkirkjuvegur at noon. This time they were going to speak to the foreman of the road crew in Öxarfjördur. Flóvent had learnt his name from Vigga and after a few phone calls discovered that he had quit his job with the National Road Administration and started working instead for the Americans at Patterson Field in Sudurnes on the Reykjanes Peninsula.

They headed south-west along the Sudurnes road. The day was overcast but the sun broke through the thick layer of cloud here and there to strike a glittering light from the surface of the sea. As they drove, Flóvent took the opportunity to educate Thorson about the wealth of folk beliefs that had survived for centuries among ordinary Icelanders, passed down from generation to generation during the long, dark winter nights, when every sound carried on the wind might herald a terrifying revenant with gaping wounds; when every knoll or outcrop of rock might house the *huldufólk*. When the landscape was populated with ogresses and trolls who turned to stone at sunrise, or creatures like the *nykur*, a horse with hooves facing backwards, which left a trail that vanished into cold lakes, or the *tilberi*, a fetch-like creature that suckled from teats on women's thighs. Fantastical tales like these had grown out of man's relationship with nature, out of the Icelanders' arduous struggle for survival in a harsh environment, out of their fear of the winter darkness. All of which, when combined with a love of storytelling and a fertile imagination, gave rise to magical worlds that could seem as real to people as their own.

'But that all belongs in the past, surely?' said Thorson as they entered the airfield. 'It sounds like something out of the grey mists of time.'

'Yes, I expect the modern world's sweeping it all away,' said Flóvent. 'Though a surprising number of people still believe in the *huldufólk*.'

He parked behind a large hangar and turned his head to study Thorson. The Canadian had been quiet for most of the journey, his thoughts clearly miles away.

'And it's not just the *huldufólk*,' Flóvent added, on reflection. 'Many ordinary Icelanders still believe in all kinds of creatures and folk tales. The old beliefs run deep.'

They were told where they could find the Icelandic foreman, Brandur, who was in charge of a small airstrip-maintenance crew. Patterson Field had been constructed two years earlier on the Njardvíkurfitjar wetlands in an area formerly known as Svidningar. Named after a young pilot who had died while serving in Iceland, Patterson Field was home to US fighter planes defending the south-western corner of the country. It was one of two airfields in the area. The other, Meeks Field, which catered for bombers and transport aircraft, was named after another young pilot who had lost his life off the Icelandic coast.

When Flóvent and Thorson arrived, the crew were busy putting in new markers along the runway. Flóvent did the talking and asked to speak to the foreman.

'What do you want with him?' asked a man with a big paunch, a dirty flat cap and a cigarette clamped between stubby fingers. He was leaning against a green army truck, watching the men work. His manner was so brusque that Flóvent dropped any attempt to be polite.

'Are you Brandur?'

'What's it to you?' The man took off his cap and scratched his bald head.

'We'd like a word with you about your time in charge of a road crew in Öxarfjördur a few years ago. I'd like to talk somewhere we won't be overheard.'

The man looked them both up and down, taking in the civilian dress of the older man and the uniform and military police arm-band of the younger. The workers stopped what they were doing to stare at the new arrivals.

'Öxarfjördur? What's that about?'

'Would you accompany us into the hangar?' asked Flóvent. 'Then we can explain in a more private setting.'

Brandur hesitated, uncertain what was going on but now thoroughly intrigued. Eventually, after barking at his men to quit slacking and get back to work, he offered Flóvent and Thorson a lift in his truck. They clambered into the front seat and Brandur drove them the short stretch to the hangar. Once they were inside, Thorson positioned himself by the door to ensure they were left undisturbed in the small office. Brandur plonked himself down in the only chair. Flóvent, left standing, didn't beat about the bush.

'Do you remember the disappearance of a young girl from a farm in the Öxarfjördur area when you were working there with the road crew?'

'You mean the one who threw herself into the waterfall?'

'Did she?'

'That's what some people thought.'

'So you're familiar with the case?'

'I remember it well. A very sad business. It really shook people, as you can imagine.' He fished a cigarette out of a packet of Camels with thick, yellow, smoker's fingers. 'But what's it got to do with me?'

'Were you acquainted with her?'

'No.'

'Was anyone from your crew acquainted with her?'

'Not to my knowledge. Are you suggesting one of my crew bumped her off?'

'Where did you get that idea?'

'There were a lot of rumours doing the rounds.'

'Such as?'

'That she threw herself into Dettifoss because of a broken heart. That was one. Nobody knew what had become of her, so they had to fill in the gaps.'

'I'm not suggesting anyone killed her,' said Flóvent. 'Did any of your men talk about her in your hearing? Before or after her disappearance?'

'Well, they were shocked and sad about it, as you'd expect, and I remember we joined the search party, but if you're suggesting any of my men harmed her, I wouldn't believe it. Not for a minute.'

'So you didn't hear any comments about her that struck you as strange or inappropriate? A bit off colour?'

'I don't know what you're driving at, mate,' said Brandur, taking a drag on his Camel. 'Have you found her? The girl?'

Flóvent shook his head. 'Do you remember hearing any talk about local superstitions?' he continued. 'About the *huldufólk*, for example?'

'No,' said the foreman, with an expression that showed he no longer understood where on earth Flóvent was going with this.

'These men you've got working for you here on Patterson Field, were any of them up north with you?'

'No, they're all Sudurnes men. The crew up north were mostly locals.'

'We've heard there were British troops in the area,' chipped in Thorson.

'Yes, they had a base at Kópasker,' said Brandur. 'Fine lads. Still wet behind the ears most of them – still reeling from finding themselves up there at the arse-end of nowhere.'

'Were they involved with the local girls?'

'I daresay. But I didn't take any notice.'

'Do you know if the girl in question was mixed up with them?'

'No, you should talk to her family. Why are you asking me?'

'Are you acquainted with her family?'

'No. All I know is . . .'

'What?'

'They were the salt of the earth,' said Brandur. 'Decent folk. It was terrible to see how badly they were hit by that business.'

'Do you remember any visitors who happened to be passing through the area at the time?' asked Flóvent. 'There must have been plenty of summer guests on the farms.'

'Yes, there was quite a bit of coming and going. We couldn't help noticing because we were working on the roads.'

'Anything that struck you as unusual?'

'No . . . Unusual . . . ?'

Flóvent gave Thorson a glance as if to say they were wasting their time with Brandur.

'I'm not sure what you mean by unusual,' the foreman went on. 'Of course there were a bunch of big shots hanging around there all summer, as always. War profiteers from Reykjavík, there for the salmon fishing. Another lot from Akureyri; the director of the Co-op, that lot who spend their time sucking the lifeblood out of the farmers – Co-op capitalists. Oh, yes. My mate Stalin would send those gentlemen packing in no time. And they had two or three MPs in their pockets.'

'Co-op capitalists?'

'Yeah, you know the type.'

'And local MPs?'

'I wouldn't know where they came from, though I'm assuming it was from the north. You heard stories about them in the district – about all the drinking that went on in the fishing lodges. The kind of debauchery that the working man never gets to enjoy. No, we're just expected to foot the bill.'

'You didn't harm the girl yourself?' interrupted Thorson.

'God, no!'

'Are you interested in Icelandic folklore?' asked Flóvent.

'You what?'

'*Huldufólk*? Elves? Are you interested in that kind of thing?'

'Me? No. Not in the slightest. I've no time for bullshit like that.'

'All right,' said Flóvent, catching Thorson's eye. 'I think that about wraps it up. We don't want to keep you all day. Thank you for your time.'

Brandur got up and they walked out with him. All the aircraft were out on reconnaissance and the place was quiet. Mechanics sat around, smoking and playing poker, and ignored them. A Glenn Miller number was playing on the radio.

'Mind you, there was a lad in my crew who was crazy about that sort of stuff,' said Brandur as he hauled himself into the truck.

'What?' asked Thorson.

'Elves and so on. Pupil at Akureyri College he was – bookish type. A loner and a bit of an oddball. They used to tease him, the boys, called him the professor and so on, all pretty harmless. He was a hard worker, though. Couldn't fault him on that.'

'And he was interested in the *huldufólk*?'

'Yes, in folk tales and all that. Reckoned he knew the where-abouts of some elf dwellings by the road. Bit peculiar like that, if you know what I mean, but totally harmless.'

'Know where we can get hold of him?' asked Flóvent.

'If I remember right, he was heading south to study at the uni-versity,' said Brandur. He started the engine with a load roar, shoved the truck into reverse, then slammed the driver's door and leaned out of the open window. 'But I've no idea what became of him.'

27

Stefán's neighbour Birgitta gave Konrád a friendly welcome, apparently unsurprised to see him again. He took a seat on her sofa, and she asked how the investigation was going, whether the police were any closer to finding out what had happened to Stefán. He said he couldn't really answer for the police as he was mainly looking into the case on his own account, given that it touched him personally, though only in a very remote way. She was immediately intrigued, so Konrád gave her a brief account of the Rósamunda affair, leaving out his father's involvement and saying only that he was acquainted with Rósamunda's parents. It appeared that the case had never been solved as there was no record of it in the police archives, though it was possible the US military might be sitting on some papers if the matter had been handled by them. Konrád knew Marta was planning to send a request for information to the American authorities.

'Did you ever hear Stefán talk about the Rósamunda case?' he asked.

'No, never. Why should . . . Were they acquainted?'

'Do you know what Stefán did during the war?'

'Not really. Only that he was stationed in Reykjavík.'

'Apparently he was in the US Military Police,' said Konrád. 'Rósamunda's death was one of the cases he investigated. He never told you?'

Birgitta had been completely unaware of Stefán's stint in the police. He'd never referred to it; in fact he'd spoken very little about the war years. 'I had no idea,' she said. Do the police think . . . Do you think there might be a connection between the case and the way he died?'

'Naturally, I can't talk about the investigation, except to say that the police are exploring all avenues, considering various factors. Including, for example, the way he was found.'

'In bed?'

'Lying flat on his back like that, looking almost peaceful.'

'Wasn't he smothered?' asked Birgitta.

'All the evidence certainly points that way,' said Konrád. 'One of the possibilities we're considering – one of the factors I mentioned – is his state of mind immediately prior to his death. Another is his great age. Then there's the question of what he was up to shortly before he died. And his views on death. Were you familiar with them, by any chance? Did he ever talk about how he'd like to make his exit?'

'I'm not with you.'

'Well, for example, do you know if he wanted to be cremated or buried?'

'He never spoke about it,' said Birgitta. 'At least not to me.'

'We can't find a will in his flat. Do you know if he made one?'

'No, I've no idea.'

'Did you two ever discuss issues like assisted suicide?'

Birgitta didn't answer straight away. 'Why do you ask?' she said at last.

'Did you?'

'Do you have any reason to think so?'

'No, none. But we know you're not opposed to the idea in principle,' said Konrád. 'We heard that you are, or were, in favour of assisted suicide. As a nurse you must have encountered terminally ill patients who were suffering terribly. You wanted them to have the option of a dignified exit.'

'I support the legalisation of assisted suicide, you're right about that,' said Birgitta. 'Like in the Netherlands and a number of other countries. There's nothing sinister about it.'

'And you –'

'I haven't helped anyone take their own life,' said Birgitta, 'if that's what you're insinuating. There's a big difference.'

'I'm not suggesting you did.'

'Then why are you asking me about assisted suicide?'

'How close were you and Stefán?'

'Close?'

'When he died. What was the nature of your relationship? Or when your husband Eyjólfur was alive, for that matter?'

Birgitta got up from her chair. 'I think you'd better leave.'

'Why?'

'Because I've nothing more to say to you.'

Konrád sat tight. He had been prepared for a reaction like this. 'Forgive me, I really didn't mean to upset you. It's just one of the angles the police are exploring and I wanted you to know.'

'You can't just walk in here and accuse me of something like that,' said Birgitta. 'Assisted suicide! I didn't do anything to Stefán. Perish the thought. He wasn't even ill.'

'Was he in favour of the idea?'

'In favour?'

'Of assisted suicide.'

'I don't think he was opposed to it. But it never came up.'

'You lost your husband –'

'Why are you dragging him into this?'

'I –'

'You're not implying I killed him too?'

'No. Honestly, I didn't mean to upset you.'

He recalled that the first time he met Birgitta she had mentioned that her husband Eyjólfur had been on friendly terms with Stefán, and that after her husband died she and Stefán had seen quite a bit of each other. But she hadn't gone into any details about the nature of their relationship. They had lived opposite each other for years and there had been quite a bit of coming and going between their flats. One of the police officers who found the body had quoted her as saying that Stefán must be glad to be at peace.

'Were you and Stefán more than just neighbours?'

Birgitta nodded. 'He was very private. It wasn't until after my Eyjólfur died that . . . I mean, he very rarely talked to us about himself. After I was widowed, I got to know him a bit better. He began coming round more often and somehow we ended up . . .' She glanced at Konrád. 'You're not under the impression . . . ?'

'I'm simply trying to get my head round your relationship.'

'It wasn't like you think.'

'What sort of relationship did you have after your husband died?'

181

'We were friends.'

'No more than that?'

'No.'

'Sure?'

'What do you mean? Of course I'm sure. Stefán wasn't that way inclined.'

'That way inclined?'

Birgitta glared at him. 'You asked me about his friends,' she said after a moment. 'I expect you saw the photo he kept in the drawer by his bed.'

'Yes.'

'That was his friend.'

Konrád pictured the elegant man in the photo. 'And?'

'His very dear friend.'

'You mean Stefán was . . . ?'

'Yes.'

'Let me get this straight. You're telling me that's his lover in the photo?'

'Yes. So I hope you understand that there could never have been anything other than friendship between me and Stefán.'

'What happened to the man? To his friend?'

'He died of heart failure after they'd known each other a few years. Of course they kept their relationship completely secret, as people did in those days. Shortly after his friend died, Stefán upped sticks and moved to Hveragerdi. From then on he lived alone and kept a low profile, isolating himself from people, making few friends.'

'That figures. He kept the photo in a drawer rather than on display.'

'Yes. I expect that was an old habit from when you had to keep that kind of thing secret.'

'Your relationship must have been very close for him to have confided in you.'

'We . . . we became very fond of each other in the last few years and I miss him a lot, but I never had an affair while Eyjólfur was alive, let alone with Stefán, if that's what you're implying. And the idea that I played some part in Stefán's death is utterly absurd. Preposterous.'

'Did he have any relatives – the man in the photo, I mean? Anyone I could meet? Anyone Stefán stayed in touch with?'

'Apparently he had a brother. But he's dead. I don't know of anyone else.'

'So Stefán never told you he'd been a policeman here in Reykjavík during the war?.'

'He never mentioned it, no. He didn't like talking about those days.'

'Any idea why?'

'No, I just sensed that he didn't like dwelling on the war years. And I never heard him mention any Rósamunda.'

'What was he up to in the weeks and months before he died? Did he mention how he passed his time?' asked Konráð.

'Haven't we been over that already?' asked Birgitta wearily. Konráð's visit was proving to be a strain, and he could tell she was keen to get shot of him and all his questions, his prying into her private life.

Deciding to call it a day, Konráð stood up. But it seemed Birgitta hadn't finished.

'You were asking about visits or people he met,' she said. 'When I thought about it afterwards I remembered him saying to me shortly before he died that he'd met a woman who had told him something, and he didn't know what to do about it. He said it was all so long ago now . . . I don't know if it could have any bearing on the case you mentioned.'

'Who was the woman?'

'She gave him some information about an old dressmaking shop.'

'A dressmaking shop?'

'That's right. He said it didn't exist any longer. The shop, I mean. Its heyday was during the war.'

'Any idea what the information was?'

'He didn't explain, just said it was probably too late.'

'Do you know who the woman was?'

'No, I don't. Though, come to think of it, I believe there were two of them, and one was called Geirlaug or some unusual name like that.'

'How long ago was this?'

'Oh, about three weeks, I should think.'

'And you have no idea what it was about?'

'No, I'm afraid not.'

Konrád spent the evening searching for information about old dressmaking companies. There had been several shops offering mending services and tailoring in Reykjavík during the war and for a number of years afterwards, from what he could discover. At the time seamstresses had been part of everyday life since there weren't that many off-the-peg clothes available in the shops. People used to buy material and have it made up into dresses and coats or bedclothes and curtains The larger stores ran their own tailoring and dressmaking services, using material offered on their shop floor, an arrangement which had long since gone out of fashion.

As Konrád knocked back the Dead Arm, he felt his mood mellowing and let his thoughts stray back to his father and the spirit world, to human remains that were reinterred at the behest of psychics and to bones that were never found.

Finishing the bottle, he reflected on Birgitta's revelation about Thorson and his lover, remembered the small stains on the photograph of the young man in the drawer. He had assumed something had spilled on it, but now he felt sure the marks were from Thorson's tears.

28

Since Geirlaug wasn't that common a name, Konrád decided his best bet was to ring all the Geirlaugs listed in the online telephone directory and ask whether by any chance they had a connection to an old dressmaker's in Reykjavík, had heard of a man called Thorson and, if so, had met him shortly before he died. He couldn't find any Geirlaug listed with 'seamstress' as an occupation, and assumed that the term had gone out of use long ago anyway. If the woman he was looking for turned out to be ex-directory, he would simply have to track her down by other, more circuitous means.

He started systematically working through the list of Geirlaugs at lunchtime the next day. Unusually, he had overslept. He had gone to bed late, been unable to get to sleep in spite of all the wine, and lain awake for hours, brooding over the fate of the elderly Thorson. He thought about Thorson's lover and how, ever since losing him, the engineer appeared to have lived alone, withdrawn from the world. From there his mind turned to Thorson's relationship with Birgitta, and he asked himself whether there was any chance, despite her categorical denial, that she could have helped him on his way as an act of mercy.

Having woken in the grip of a hangover, he drank several cups of coffee, gulping down water in between, but found he had little appetite. He sat staring into space until finally he summoned up the energy to start phoning Geirlaugs. There were landlines and mobiles listed for most of them, so if they didn't answer at home, he tried their mobiles. He posed as an acquaintance of Stefán's – avoiding any mention of 'Thorson' – and explained that he needed to get in touch with a woman called Geirlaug who had been in contact with him recently. Most of the women answered his call. One, who hadn't been able to take it at the time, rang him back and asked if he had been trying to reach her. None of them knew Stefán Thórdarson, though two had a vague recollection of hearing the name in the news. The conversations were brief and the women generally showed little interest in who Konrád was. 'You must have got the wrong number,' was the most common response. Only one or two of the older-sounding women were curious to know more about him, but he didn't waste time explaining. When they turned out not to know Stefán, he quickly brought the call to a close.

The task took him most of the afternoon. In between calls he listened to the radio or flipped through the papers, or wasted time surfing the Internet. Late in the afternoon his phone rang.

'Yes, hello,' he answered.

'Was someone from this number trying to get hold of me?' asked an elderly sounding female voice.

'It's possible,' said Konrád. 'Is your name Geirlaug?'

'Yes, who is this, please?'

187

'My name's Konrád. Sorry to bother you like this but I knew Stefán Thórdarson. He died recently.'

'Oh?'

'You may have seen it on the news. He appears to have been murdered in his own home. I gather you spoke to him not long before he died.'

'Yes, I did, I did speak to him,' said the woman. 'He rang me. Just like you.'

'Did he?'

'Yes, I've no idea how he dug up my name. He didn't explain, just said he'd heard I knew a woman he was trying to get hold of.'

'So you two didn't meet?'

'Oh no, we only talked on the phone.'

'What exactly did he ask you?'

'Who did you say you were again?'

'My name's Konrád and I knew Stefán. I'm helping the police with the inquiry into his death.'

'Have you found out what happened?'

'No, not yet. Could you tell me why he wanted to speak to you?'

'He was trying to trace an old friend of mine,' said Geirlaug. 'It took me ages to work out what it was he actually wanted but we got to the bottom of it in the end. He'd heard I might be able to put him in touch with her. He didn't even know her name.'

'And what is her name?'

'My friend? She's called Petra. It was about her mother, Petra told me afterwards. He was asking questions about her.' Geirlaug lapsed into silence, as if she had finished what she had to say.

'What about her mother?' prompted Konrád.

'Petra's mother?'

'Yes.'

'She ran a mending and dressmaking business during the war and Stefán was very interested in it for some reason.'

'In the dressmaking business?'

'Yes, specifically in a girl who used to work there, called Rósa-something, I think Petra said. She rang me after they'd talked. Knew I'd passed on her name to him.'

'Could the name have been Rósamunda?'

'Yes, Rósamunda, that sounds right.'

'What about her?'

'She was found murdered behind the National Theatre during the war. Does that sound familiar?'

'Yes, it does, actually,' said Konrád. 'Why was Stefán so interested in her?'

'I don't know, but he asked lots of questions about her. Maybe you should talk to Petra yourself. Would you like her number? I've got it here somewhere. Just a minute . . .'

29

Petra clearly hadn't followed in her mother's footsteps: she was neither a dressmaker nor did she run her own business. In fact, judging by her outfit, she was completely indifferent to fashion. And, looking around her home, Konrád couldn't see any needlework, or any hint of enthusiasm for handicrafts. It was almost as if, despite being well past middle age, she was still rebelling against everything her mother had stood for. It turned out that she was a few years older than he was and had got herself an education, as they used to call it when people stayed on at college to take their matriculation exams, though she hadn't continued on to university. Instead she had taken the boat to Europe and gone travelling, before coming home and taking an admin job at the National Hospital, where she had worked for most of her career up until the banking collapse. At that point she had been made redundant as a result of cuts in the health service. She was, in addition, a divorcee with four children and what she described as heaps of adorable grandchildren.

As Konrád soon discovered, she never wearied of talking about herself, but he was reluctant to interrupt the flow. She lived in a block of flats in the east end, where she had wound up following her divorce, having been forced to part with the large detached family home in the smart suburb of Garðabær. Apparently she and her husband had quickly grown bored of each other once their children had flown the nest.

When Konrád finally managed to get a word in edgeways, Petra proved extremely interested in Stefán's death and asked a lot of questions. He did his best to field them without giving away any details that might compromise the inquiry, saying only that the circumstances of Stefán's death had been highly unusual and the police investigation was making good progress. He himself wasn't directly involved, but he had been asked to look into one aspect of the case. Petra proved no less inquisitive about Konrád himself and bombarded him with questions. He tried to reply to them as best he could, feeling that it was only fair for him to be a little forthcoming, given that he had come here to extract information from her.

At long last he managed to steer the conversation round to Stefán's visit. He had come to see her, Petra reckoned, about two weeks before she read of his death in the papers. She had recognised him immediately when his picture was splashed all over the media, but it hadn't even crossed her mind that she might be able to help the police with their enquiries.

Her mother had run a dressmaking business until the mid sixties when she sold it. By then cheap imported clothing was fairly common; there were many more shops, and large firms offering mending and tailoring were closing down right, left and centre. Petra's mother had died in 1980, her father sometime later.

Petra and Geirlaug had been friends since college. From what Stefán had told her, he'd been chatting to an old engineering acquaintance who knew Geirlaug well, and somehow it had emerged that she used to know Petra's mother, who ran a dress-making business during the war. Stefán had seemed familiar with the company in question and became very attentive, saying he felt sure he had once met the owner.

'Do you know where Stefán encountered this engineer?' asked Konrád.

'At a funeral, he told me. He'd read the obituary of a woman who used to work for my mother. For some reason he went along to her funeral and that was where he bumped into the engineer.'

'So the woman had worked for your mother during the war?'

'Yes, during the war and for a number of years afterwards, I believe. It was all described in the obituary.'

'And . . . ?'

'She'd been a friend of that girl Rósamunda who was murdered, and Stefán had interviewed her at the time in connection with the police investigation, or that's what he led me to believe. He'd come across the reference to the dressmaking company in the obituary, and I suppose he felt the urge to find out more about her. Perhaps because he remembered her from the old days. Anyway, he decided to attend the funeral and that's where he ran into an engineer he was acquainted with – I don't know how – and started telling him how he'd met the dead woman, and about the link to my mother's sewing business. The engineer happened to mention Geirlaug and that we were friends . . . And one thing led to another. Or that's what he told me. I don't know if there's any truth in it.'

'I very much doubt he was lying,' said Konrád. 'Stefán seems to have been a man of strict integrity.'

'Yes, that's how he struck me too,' said Petra. 'He said he'd interviewed my mother at the time, together with another man, a policeman whose name I forget, as part of the murder investigation.'

'Did he come to see you about anything specific?' asked Konrád. 'Anything directly related to the inquiry?'

'No, I don't think so, not to begin with, at any rate. He said he used to think about Rósamunda from time to time and would be grateful for a chance to meet me. He was terribly polite, and you'd never have guessed how old he was from looking at him. He didn't seem at all arthritic or doddery. But then he said he'd always led a healthy life.'

'Yes, he seems to have been very fit for a man his age.'

'Yes, so . . . I regretted giving him such a turn.'

'A turn?'

'I didn't think it was at all important, but it evidently struck him very differently and he suddenly got all worked up. Started saying he couldn't understand my mother. How she could have done a thing like that – failed to let them know.'

'What? What did she do? Failed to let them know what?'

'About a little thing that my mother told me about long afterwards, many years later. In fact I was grown up by the time she told me. It never occurred to me that it was important.'

'What did she tell you that got Stefán so worked up?' asked Konrád, struggling to conceal his impatience.

'You really need to understand my mother. I tried to make him see that,' said Petra. 'She was a funny woman in some ways. You'd have to have known her well to appreciate the way her mind worked. Especially in the old days, as regards her clients. She was – I admit it – a snob. A raging snob. People were in those days. They looked down on other people a lot more, called them common and so on. She still used to talk down to shop assistants, for example, right up until she died. She was stuck in her ways. And she was unbearable when it came to her social superiors, always name-dropping, boasting about how so-and-so used to be her client and always treated her like an equal – you know the kind of thing. "She always used to patronise my shop," she'd say whenever some toffee-nosed old bag came up in conversation.'

Not entirely sure how this was relevant, Konrád felt it best to keep his mouth shut. Now at least he understood the complete absence of needlework from her home, though. He was detecting a distinct chill in Petra's attitude to her mother.

'For example, she used to give some of her clients preferential treatment. She felt that confidentiality was the cornerstone of her business, and she honoured this principle right up to her death. That's the way she operated. She never gossiped about her customers, felt she was almost part of their private lives, felt they trusted her and came to her with their requirements precisely because of this discretion.'

'But how did that affect Stefán? Why should that have upset him?'

'Oh, no, it wasn't because of that – not because of what she was like, but because of what she failed to tell them.'

'Which was?'

'It was about Rósamunda. I don't really know why I started telling him about it – Stefán, I mean. I don't know why it should have mattered so much.'

'*What* did you tell him?' Konrád asked, his patience really wearing thin.

'That my mother said she once came across Rósamunda in the yard behind the shop – in tears and dishevelled, in Mother's words. Rósamunda refused to say what was wrong but Mother sent her home anyway because the poor girl was in such a state. All Mother knew was that earlier that day Rósamunda had gone to deliver a dress to a house in town and had just come back from there when Mother saw her in the yard. The girl never referred to the incident again but flatly refused to take any further deliveries to that particular address. My mother never discussed it with anyone because she didn't know the full story. I told Stefán this was typical – my mother would never have cast suspicion on those people. Never in a million years.'

'Why suspicion?'

'Because of what happened later. To the girl.'

Konrád stared at Petra as the significance of her story gradually dawned on him, its relevance to the investigation and to Thorson. How had he felt on learning this detail so long after the event? According to Petra it had given him a bit of a turn. That was probably an understatement.

'Did your mother believe there was a connection between the incident and Rósamunda's death?' he asked at last.

'My mother suspected she might have had a nasty experience at the house. At least, the possibility bothered her in her later years.'

'Was this shortly before Rósamunda was murdered?'

'Yes, a few months before,' said Petra. 'Mother hadn't meant to tell me. She blurted it out accidentally. Though I got the feeling she'd been brooding on it. But she obviously felt uncomfortable talking about it, so I let it drop.'

'Why was Rósamunda crying? And why wouldn't she go near the place afterwards?'

'Mother didn't know. Rósamunda clammed up and wouldn't say another word about it. Mother knew the people concerned – they were important customers, and she didn't want to believe they could have mistreated the girl. She was desperate not to draw any attention to the incident in light of that, if you follow me. You'd have to understand what Mother was like. Her clients were sacrosanct in her eyes.'

'Was your mother the only person who knew?'

'Yes, I'm pretty sure.'

'So Rósamunda was hiding in the yard, in tears, all dishevelled?'

'My mother guessed that she'd been assaulted, but when she tried to help her, Rósamunda wasn't having it, so Mother left it at that. I think she regretted it later – that she hadn't done more for the girl.'

'And she'd just come back from taking a delivery to these clients?'

'Yes. But Mother would never have suspected them. That's just the way she was.'

'Yet it was still preying on her mind?'

'Yes, it seems so. She was still thinking about it right before she died.'

30

The young man known to the road crew up north as the Professor was out when Flóvent and Thorson drove up to his digs, a poky basement flat on Öldugata. They'd raced back to Reykjavík after their meeting with Brandur at Patterson Field, with the young man's name as a new lead. Working on the foreman's hazy recollection that the boy had come south to study, they had headed straight over to the new university building in the west of town, where they discovered that he was in the second year of a degree in Icelandic and history. They were permitted to see his timetable and concluded that he had probably left for the day. The university office made no objections to supplying his address.

Flóvent and Thorson sat in the car, a stone's throw from the basement, watching the odd passer-by hurry along the street as dusk fell. They were still waiting for the student. They had spoken to the other tenants but they didn't have much to report. The student had moved into the basement last Christmas and never made any noise or caused any trouble, quite the reverse in fact. He was considered a quiet, polite young man, inoffensive in every way. No, they didn't get the impression he was much of a womaniser, or indeed met any girls at all. Naturally, being a student, he wouldn't have time for that sort of thing. He always had his nose in a book, though he did have at least one interest outside his studies, and that was birdwatching. They used to see him from time to time with a fine pair of binoculars on a leather cord and knew he was off on one of his birdwatching expeditions to the nearby Seltjarnarnes Peninsula or further afield.

Flóvent was all for hanging on to see if the young man came home, before trying to track him down by other means. But the car's heater didn't work properly and the temperature dropped as evening came on, so they sat there frozen and hungry, waiting. Since most people would be sitting down to dinner at this hour, there was hardly anyone around. Flóvent's thoughts went to his father, who always waited for him to come home before eating, though Flóvent had repeatedly told him to go ahead without him. He pictured the old man napping on the couch in the kitchen, worn out after a long day's drudgery on the docks.

'If he turns out to be our man, there's no need for you to be involved any longer,' Flóvent remarked after a long silence. 'It'll have nothing to do with the military.'

'Why don't we wait and see?' said Thorson.

'Yes, of course, but it looks to me as if the focus of the investigation's shifting away from your charges – from the troops, I mean.'

'It certainly looks that way,' admitted Thorson. 'But if you wouldn't mind, I'd kind of like to see this case through, all the same. So long as you don't mind.'

'I wouldn't object,' said Flóvent. 'All help gratefully received.'

'Good.'

'I thought maybe you had other fish to fry. You've been unusually quiet all day.'

'Yes, sorry, I've had a lot on my mind.'

'Of course, you must have plenty of cases of your own to be getting on with,' said Flóvent. 'I daresay they're no picnic either.'

'You can say that again.'

Flóvent was right: he'd been distracted all day. With tens of thousands of troops crowded into a confined area, new incidents were inevitably brought to the attention of the military police every day. Minor brawls were common – you always got the odd troublemaker – but some cases were sadder, as you might expect when morale was low, the world was at war and the young men being sent across oceans and continents to fight the enemy were not all equally suited to the task. Sure, there were the daredevils who actively looked forward to combat, eager for a chance to take a shot at the enemy. But others lived in dread of what the future would bring, far from their loved ones, far from normality, far from the life they knew. The evening Rósamunda's body turned up, Thorson had been over at Nauthólsvík Cove, on the other side of Öskjuhlíð, at the cluster of prefab huts that comprised the naval air station. Driving there, Thorson was reminded of the time he'd glimpsed Winston Churchill when he stopped over in Iceland in August of '41, on his way back from a mid-Atlantic meeting with President Roosevelt. On the present occasion, though, Thorson had been called to a shoe-repair workshop housed in one of the huts, where a young serviceman had chosen to take his own life rather than face the enemy guns. The boy, who had only just turned twenty, came from a small town in Kentucky and was described by his friends as cheerful and friendly, but fearful, like many others, of being sent to the front. Rumours had been rife about the imminent transfer of troops from Iceland to Britain in preparation for the Allied invasion of France. No one could think of another explanation for his desperate act. He hadn't left a suicide note, and none of his buddies had any idea what he was going to do; though, in retrospect, he had seemed kind of down in recent weeks and apprehensive about the future. They didn't think it was a broken heart. There was no sweetheart back home, and he hadn't been involved with any Icelandic girls. His wallet was found to contain a few dollars and a photograph of his mother and two sisters.

'Those cases are always tough,' said Flóvent when Thorson had explained about the young man.

'They certainly are,' said Thorson. 'A lot of the boys are scared.'

'What about you? Do you give it much thought?'

'Not really. I've got enough to think about.'

'Did you know the soldier from the Nauthólsvík camp?'

'Not, not at all. I only learnt yesterday that he'd been having a terrible time since he got here.'

'Oh?'

'Yes, he was badly bullied.'

'Why?'

'A man in his squadron told me it was because he wasn't one for the ladies. Quite the opposite –'

'Is that him?' Flóvent interrupted, nudging him.

Glancing up, Thorson saw a young man approaching along Öldugata. He was tall and fair-haired; he wore a thick down jacket and sturdy boots and was carrying a pair of binoculars in one hand. He strode along the road, head down, deep in thought, then turned down the narrow path that led to the basement door.

Flóvent and Thorson stepped out of the car and followed a little way behind. The young man had gone inside but hadn't yet closed the door when they appeared at the entrance. He nearly jumped out of his skin when they loomed out of the darkness; he clearly hadn't been expecting visitors.

'Wha . . . ?' he said, gaping at the two men.

'Good evening, sir. Are you Jónatan, by any chance?' asked Flóvent.

'Me? Yes.'

'We're from the police. We'd like to talk to you about a case we're investigating. Mind if we come in, sir?'

'The police?' he echoed, startled. 'What case?'

'Might we come in for a minute?'

The young man looked searchingly from Flóvent to Thorson, clearly perplexed.

'What case?' he asked again.

'It concerns a young woman by the name of Rósamunda,' said Thorson.

'And a second young woman from Öxarfjördur, whose name was Hrund.'

The student was halfway through taking off his jacket, still with the binoculars in his hand. He put them down, then hung his jacket on a peg. Flóvent and Thorson waited.

'Yes, I'm sorry, do come in,' said the young man. 'I don't see what . . . how I can help you. Did you say you were policemen?'

'Were you birdwatching, sir?' asked Flóvent, nodding at the binoculars.

'I was watching the cormorants on Seltjarnarnes. Look, there's no need to call me "sir".'

'Are you interested in birds?'

'Yes, I am rather.'

'Tell me, were you part of a road crew working in or around Öxarfjördur about three years ago?' asked Flóvent, closing the door behind them. The young man showed his unexpected visitors into a small bedsit. There was a camp bed in one corner, made up with a quilt and blankets, a desk below a window set high in the wall, bookshelves on two walls. The cramped basement also contained a tiny kitchen and an even smaller washroom.

'I was working on the roads there, yes.'

'We gather you come from the north,' said Thorson. 'You were at school there?'

'Yes, that's right. At Akureyri College.'

Flóvent looked round the small room, taking in the books on the shelves and desk, the files, the materials related to Jónatan's studies, an old typewriter containing a sheet of paper with a few lines he had written before giving into the lure of the cormorants on Seltjarnarnes. Next to the typewriter was an ashtray containing several cigarette butts, and, on the other side of it, a packet of Lucky Strikes and a box of matches.

Flóvent eyed the packet, then shot a look at Thorson, who had spotted it too.

'What are you working on?' Flóvent asked, gesturing at the typewriter.

'I'm writing a thesis. For my degree in Icelandic and history at the university. What exactly is it you want with me? What . . . why are you here?'

'Were you acquainted with a girl called Rósamunda?' asked Thorson.

'No.'

'Are you sure about that?'

'Yes, I ought to know. I'm not acquainted with anyone of that name.'

'What about Hrund?'

The young man watched as Flóvent rooted around among the files on his desk, then stepped over to the bookcase and squinted at the spines.

'Did you meet a girl called Hrund when you were working on the roads in Öxarfjördur?' Thorson tried again.

The student's gaze remained fixed on Flóvent. 'What are you looking for?' he asked, as if he hadn't heard Thorson's question.

'These books . . . ?'

'What of them?'

'What are you writing about?' Flóvent asked, turning to him.

'I'm writing a thesis,' repeated Jónatan. 'It's about . . . well, all sorts of things.'

'Are you collecting them?'

'No, I'm not a collector. Lots of them come from libraries. I need them for my research.'

Turning back to the shelves, Flóvent took out a book and opened it.

'Your foreman certainly wasn't lying.'

'Who?'

'Your foreman from the road crew. He said you were fascinated by folklore.'

'What are all those books about?' asked Thorson.

'Most of them are about Icelandic folk tales and legends,' answered Flóvent, giving him a meaningful look. 'Ghost stories. Elf rocks. Forbidden ground. *Huldufólk*,' he added, reading from the contents page of the volume he was holding.

'I use the books for my research,' said the student. 'My thesis is concerned with Icelandic folk beliefs, from the settlement right up to the present day.'

'Did you know Hrund, the girl I mentioned?' asked Thorson, returning to his earlier theme.

Jónatan's gaze swung back and forth between the two men. 'I knew who she was,' he admitted at last. 'You mean the girl who's supposed to have thrown herself into Dettifoss?'

Flóvent nodded.

'I was aware of who she was. But I didn't know her at all.'

'Can you tell us if she was interested in folk tales?'

'If *she* was?'

'Yes.'

'Why . . . I didn't do anything to harm her if that's what you're asking. Never touched her. Is that why you're here?'

'Now why would you think someone harmed her?' asked Flóvent. 'We haven't said anything to give you that idea.'

Jónatan's gaze flickered from one of them to the other in that poky little bedsit, as if the walls were closing in on him.

'I know nothing about her,' he protested. 'I swear.'

31

Moving almost imperceptibly, Thorson stationed himself by the door to the hall. Flóvent studied the young man. He was looking decidedly rattled now that he had worked out the reason for the policemen's visit. His eyes darted back and forth between Flóvent and Thorson, and he hunched his lanky frame defensively. His sudden vehement denial had taken them both by surprise and roused their suspicions. Anyone would have thought he'd been expecting to be questioned sooner or later about his relationship to Hrund.

Flóvent asked if he would mind accompanying them down to Fríkirkjuvegur for a more leisurely chat about his interest in folklore and his acquaintance with Hrund. He refused politely, saying he had other business to attend to and that her case had absolutely nothing to do with him. Flóvent and Thorson insisted, finally informing him that if he didn't accompany them voluntarily, they would be obliged to use force.

Eventually they succeeded in persuading him to come with them and, pulling on his jacket again, Jónatan accompanied them out to the car. They drove in silence to Fríkirkjuvegur where they took a seat in Flóvent's office. He closed the door carefully behind them.

'Are you going to throw me in jail?' asked Jónatan, when Thorson enquired if there was anything he wanted, like coffee or a drink of water.

'Is there any reason why we should?' asked Thorson.

'No, this is . . . this is all a misunderstanding.'

'Do you have family here in Reykjavík?' asked Thorson.

'No.'

'Any friends then? Anyone you'd like to inform that you're sitting in here with us?'

'No, I'd just like to go home again as soon as possible, if you don't mind. I don't need anything except to get this over with. No one else need know, surely?'

'Need know what?'

'That you've brought me in for questioning?'

'No,' said Flóvent. 'Not necessarily. Does the thought make you nervous?'

'I'd rather people at the university didn't know I was being questioned by the police. That's all. I still don't understand why you wanted me to accompany you here. I haven't done anything wrong.'

'Well, that's good, that's excellent,' said Flóvent. 'Can you tell us how you knew Hrund?'

'I ran into her a few times. There was a petrol station with a restaurant not far from our camp and sometimes when I walked over in the evening she'd be there – a friend of hers served in the shop – and we got chatting. She said there wasn't much going on in the countryside and asked about life in Akureyri. About the soldiers and so on. I think she wanted to move there. Or maybe even south to Reykjavík.'

'Did you tell her about your fascination with the *huldufólk*?'

'She was very interested to hear I was going to university. I told her I wanted to read Icelandic and history; perhaps do research into folk beliefs and . . . that sort of thing.'

'Are you familiar with stories about the *huldufólk* attacking humans?' asked Thorson.

'There are examples of that, yes.'

'Did you tell her any stories like that?'

'I don't remember if . . . We may well have talked about it. I forget.'

'Did she believe in supernatural beings? In the hidden people?'

'I think . . . She kept an open mind,' said Jónatan. 'She struck me as being a bit naive and unworldly, a child of nature.'

'Meaning what exactly?'

'Well, she was deeply rooted in the countryside, had grown up very close to nature and knew everything about the plants and birds, and had such – I don't know how to put it – she . . . I can't explain it better than by describing her as a child of nature. People like her probably find it easier to believe in supernatural phenomena, spend more time than the rest of us thinking about elves and demons and trolls.'

'Do you believe in those kinds of phenomena yourself?'

'No, I don't,' said Jónatan firmly. 'Except as a mirror of human society. I believe folk tales provide us with an insight into the mindset of the common man. They can reveal a great deal about people's attitudes over the centuries, whether it's their fear of the unknown or their desire for a better life or dreams of a better world. They can tell us so much both directly and indirectly about life in the past. That's how I look at them. Not as true stories or representations of reality.'

'Did Hrund view them like that?'

'I can't give you a simple answer to that.'

'But she was a child of nature?'

'Yes, that was my impression.'

'Had Hrund ever been molested by – what shall we call them – supernatural beings?' asked Flóvent.

'Molested? No, I don't believe that for a minute. But please be clear that I didn't know her very well. Hardly at all, in fact. We only met a few times and chatted a little. I can't say I really got to know her, so I may be reading too much into what she said. Look, I don't know what it is you want from me. I don't understand these questions. What have folk tales got to do with anything?'

'Did any of the other members of the road crew share your interest in folklore?' asked Flóvent.

'No. None of them.'

'Were any of them involved with this girl?'

'Not as far as I know.'

Jónatan had grabbed his packet of Lucky Strikes as he was leaving his digs and now extracted a cigarette and lit it, sucking in a lungful of smoke and blowing it out again. Flóvent pushed over an ashtray.

'Good cigarettes?'

'Yes, great. I get them from a friend of mine at the university – his sister's seeing a Yank.'

'Are you absolutely sure you didn't know a girl here in Reykjavík called Rósamunda?' asked Thorson.

208

'Yes, I'm sure.'

'She worked as a seamstress.'

'No, I don't know anyone by that name . . . Isn't it, wasn't that the name of the woman found behind the theatre?'

'That's right.'

'Why are you asking me about her?'

'Rósamunda had no interest in the *huldufólk* or folk tales, yet she and Hrund both shared a bizarre experience related to them, and we wondered if you might be able to shed some light on it for us.'

'What was that? What kind of experience?'

'Before she disappeared, Hrund let it be understood that she had been assaulted by one of the *huldufólk*,' said Flóvent, leaning closer over the desk. 'And Rósamunda said that a man who raped her had told her to blame it on the *huldufólk*. Their stories are so alike that you'd think they'd both fallen victim to the same perpetrator. The alleged attacks took place three years apart. One up in Öxarfjördur where you happened to be working on a road construction team. The other here in Reykjavík where you happen to be studying at the university. We've established that you knew one of the girls and now I'm asking you again: did you know Rósamunda?'

As Jónatan listened to Flóvent it gradually dawned on him what the police were really after when they came round to his digs and why he had been brought to their offices.

'Am I under arrest?' he asked, aghast.

'Is there any reason why you think you should be?' asked Thorson.

'Are you . . . Do you actually believe I harmed them, both of them? That I . . . that I . . . killed them?'

'Did you?' asked Flóvent.

His astonishment was unmistakable but something about his manner struck a false note.

'No,' Jónatan burst out, the spittle frothing from his mouth. 'Are you mad?'

'Did you persuade Hrund to lie about being attacked by one of the hidden people, to cover up what you did to her?'

'Lie about the hidden people?'

'Did you repeat the game with Rósamunda when you moved down here to Reykjavík?'

'No!'

'Did you force yourself on both girls?'

'Force myself? No! You've got it all wrong. It's . . . I can't believe you're serious. I don't believe it. This is . . . This is crazy,' said Jónatan, rising from his chair. 'I have to go home. I need to get on with my thesis and I . . . I've got a lot to do. I'm far too busy for this.'

He rushed towards the door but Thorson blocked his way, seized his arm and led him back to the chair where he pushed him down again. Jónatan offered no resistance.

'I'm afraid you can't go home yet,' said Thorson calmly. 'Not until we've had a chance to talk some more.'

32

Frank Ruddy listened to the approaching footsteps. Two men, he thought, in a hurry by the sound of it. They halted outside his cell and he heard the jingling of keys. He was lying on a mattress, smoking and reading a pornographic comic. Propping himself up on his elbow, he listened to the jingling. He was expecting to be released any minute; he'd wasted enough time in the slammer. Last time he checked, there was no law against assuming a false name and lying to Icelandic girls. He shouldn't have to spend days locked up for that kind of crap. The police said they were checking his criminal record in the States. Well, good luck to them. They wouldn't find a thing. They said he was still a suspect in the killing of the girl he and Ingiborg had found. A lame excuse. They had nothing on him.

He was on his feet by the time the door opened and the prison guard appeared – with Thorson.

'You?' Frank exclaimed.

'We'd like to ask you to do us a favour.'

'Favour? How about you do me a favour and let me out of here? How long am I going to be stuck in this hole?'

'Come take a ride with me,' said Thorson. 'And we'll see.'

Frank stared at him for a beat without answering. The last thing he wanted was to do that son of a bitch Thorson any favours, but on the other hand the monotony was driving him nuts. He wouldn't mind going for a ride in a car, even though he had no idea what it was about.

'I've run out of smokes,' he said, eyeing the guard.

'We can pick some up on the way,' said Thorson.

'What kind of a drive?'

'There's something I want you to do for me.'

Frank's curiosity was roused. 'I didn't touch that girl. I only found her. That's no crime.'

'No, you're right,' said Thorson. 'That's no crime.'

'So, what do you want me to do?'

'Come on, it really won't take any time at all.'

Frank followed him out along the passage. The guard closed the cell door and turned to watch them leave.

'Is it about that girl I was with?' asked Frank as Thorson opened the passenger door for him. 'About Ingiborg?'

'No.'

They drove off towards the centre of town.

'She's claiming I got her pregnant,' Frank added after a lengthy pause.

Thorson swung the jeep into Hverfisgata and headed for the National Theatre. 'And did you?' he asked.

'No, there's no way she's pinning it on me,' said Frank. 'How do I know how many other guys she's been screwing?'

'I don't believe she's been seeing any other men,' said Thorson. 'She strikes me as a very honest young woman who thought she'd found an equally honourable man. Looks to me like she got that wrong.'

'Have you talked to her?'

'Briefly. The worst part for her is the lies. The shabby way you treated her. I don't suppose she was expecting much when she told you about the baby. She just felt you ought to know, and I think she wanted your advice – in spite of everything.'

'I gave her advice all right.'

Thorson parked a short way from the barricade of sandbags in front of the theatre. He didn't anticipate any trouble from Frank but needed to keep him in a cooperative mood, so, curbing his anger, he left off the handcuffs and did his best to keep him sweet. There were no other police in sight.

'What are we doing here?' asked Frank.

'Come on,' said Thorson. 'We're going round the back.'

Frank baulked. 'Why?'

'Relax, I'm not planning any surprises. I'm not trying to pin anything on you. I just want you to do me a small favour.'

'What favour?'

'Come with me.'

Mystified, Frank followed him round the back of the building to the doorway where he and Ingiborg had found the dead girl. Thorson asked him to position himself where he had been standing that evening. Frank did as he was told. Thorson had brought along a torch which he now flashed several times in the direction of Skuggasund. After a short delay, a figure appeared on the corner of Lindargata and Skuggasund, tall, round-shouldered, smoking a cigarette. His outline was clearly discernible in the darkness, silhouetted against the faint glow of a street light further down Skuggasund. There was another lamp post on

Lindargata, a few yards from the corner, but it was still broken, as it had been on the evening the girl's body turned up.

'Is that the man you saw across the street?' asked Thorson.

Frank looked over at the figure for a while. 'If I say it's him, will you let me out of jail?'

'What do you mean?'

'If I play along?'

'Don't say what you think I want to hear,' said Thorson angrily. 'This isn't about playing along with me. Tell me what you think you remember.'

Frank shook his head.

'I'm not bargaining with you,' said Thorson. 'Tell me if you think it's the same man you saw standing on the corner that night. I'm not cutting you a deal here. Was that where he was standing when you saw him?'

Frank looked across the road. 'Yeah, he was standing there.'

'And?'

'The light's poor,' said Frank, 'and I was in a hurry of course, but I reckon it's the same guy.'

'Are you sure?'

'Yeah, I guess so.'

'Take a good look and try to remember what you saw.'

Frank did as Thorson ordered and studied the figure on the corner for a minute or two. 'I can't be a hundred per cent sure it's the guy I saw,' he said eventually. 'I can't swear to it. But it's possible.'

'OK,' said Thorson. 'I'm going to ask you to look away, just for a second.'

Frank did as he was told. Thorson flashed the torch again three times and the figure disappeared from the corner, to be replaced by another. Thorson ordered Frank to turn round again.

'Or was that the guy you saw?'

This time the man standing on the corner was shorter, with more of a stoop, and definitely looked older.

Frank studied him for several seconds. 'What do you want me to say?'

'I want you to tell the truth.'

'No,' said Frank at last. 'The other guy. He was much more like the man I saw.'

Flóvent saw Thorson's torch flash for the third time. It was over. Frank had given his statement and, judging by the signal, he had identified Jónatan. Seeing Thorson lead Frank away, he gave his father, who was still standing on the corner holding a cigarette, a sign that they were done.

'We're finished,' he called. 'You can come back now.'

Jónatan was standing at Flóvent's side. He had come with them of his own free will, protesting his innocence all the way, and had obligingly taken up position on the corner opposite the theatre where Frank claimed to have seen a man standing the evening he and Ingiborg made their grim discovery. He had lit a cigarette as requested and smoked it unhurriedly. Flóvent had picked up his father on the way and asked if he could help out. Naturally he was willing, and once Jónatan had stood on the corner for a while, the old man had taken his place, holding a cigarette in one hand, though he had never smoked in his life. Flóvent had felt it would be better for Frank to have a point of comparison.

'What happened?' asked Jónatan. 'What did you find out?'

'Come along, son,' said Flóvent, leading Jónatan back to the car. He dreaded having to break the news to him: all Jónatan had to look forward to now was a prison cell on Skólavördustígur.

33

It was the second time in a matter of weeks that a total stranger had come round to Petra's house to ask questions about her mother. Both men had listened to what she had to say and looked utterly stunned. The first time it was the polite old man who had knocked on her door and chatted to her about everything under the sun before finally getting to the point and asking about her mother and Rósamunda. He was badly shaken when she told him about the girl. Now the other man – Konrád he said his name was – was sitting in the same chair, and she had managed to knock him sideways as well.

Petra couldn't understand what was so significant about the story she had told them, but then she didn't know much about the case. She explained to both men that her mother had hardly ever spoken about Rósamunda, either to her or to anyone else, as far as she knew, so she couldn't really answer their questions. She'd never bothered to familiarise herself with the details of the case.

216

In fact, all she knew was that her mother had been one of the people questioned by the police about a murder that had been committed during the war. She didn't even know if it had ever been solved.

She suspected that the old woman had her reasons for not wanting to discuss it. On the rare occasions when Petra had asked her about Rósamunda's death, if she was reading about a murder in the papers for instance, she had sensed her mother's reluctance to dredge it up. But it had never entered Petra's head that her mother might be sitting on information that could shed new light on the case.

She looked at Konrád curiously. She had conscientiously related everything she knew as accurately as possible, just as she had done previously for the old man, Stefán. They had both seemed so extraordinarily interested in her mother and Rósamunda, and she'd been eager to help.

'Was it common for the women working for your mother to react like that? To refuse to take deliveries?' asked Konrád.

'I wouldn't know.'

'Your mother found it very unusual, didn't she?'

'Well, yes, she gave that impression. Though I think mainly because it was so rare for one of her staff to disobey her. Especially when it came to a simple task like that.'

'And Rósamunda wouldn't explain?'

'No, but as I said Mother reckoned she'd had a nasty experience at that house the day she found her in tears.'

'Do you know if Thorson – Stefán – was intending to act on this information?'

'No, but he seemed very upset when I told him about it, though he didn't explain why. As I said, I know very little about the case. He left shortly afterwards and I never heard from him again.'

'Which house was it that Rósamunda refused to visit?' asked Konrád. 'Who lived there?'

'My mother said she knew the woman very well and wasn't aware that she had ever been rude to Rósamunda. Not that Mother ever raised the matter with her of course. She never told a soul, so the family in question wouldn't have had a clue that there was a problem. The woman's husband was a politician, an MP, according to my mother. That's why she didn't want to make a fuss.'

'An MP?'

'Yes, he died years ago. Mother said he was a person of considerable standing at the time and his wife sat on all kinds of committees, was involved in the Women's Institute and so on. They were both Oddfellows, or whatever it's called. She was pretty sure he was a Freemason too. Their son later became a cabinet minister.'

'And Rósamunda refused to deliver a dress to the wife?'

'Yes. Not just a dress but bedclothes as well. All terribly smart, according to Mother, with the couple's monograms embroidered on the quilt and pillowcases – she remembered it vividly. Mother was always very proud of the quality of her seamstresses' work.'

'And when you told this to Stefán, he was startled?'

'To be honest he seemed stunned,' said Petra. 'He kept asking me questions, like you're doing now, kept repeating the same questions over and over again, as if he wanted to be sure he'd understood correctly.'

'But you don't know what action, if any, he intended to take?'

'No. I haven't the foggiest.'

'And you didn't hear from him again?'

'No.'

'But you gave him the names of the family involved?'

'Yes, I did.'

'Was he going to look them up?'

'I don't know.' Petra paused, then added: 'I got the feeling . . .'

'Yes?'

'I got the feeling he wasn't satisfied with how the case was handled at the time. He wouldn't have come round otherwise.'

'Can you be more specific?'

'I think that was why he came to see me. I sensed that he felt the case wasn't closed. That he was unhappy about how he'd left it. Even before I told him about Rósamunda I could tell something was still nagging at him after all these years. It was like he was searching for reassurance that he'd done the right thing.'

'Did he actually come out and say that?' asked Konrád.

'No, and I didn't ask him,' replied Petra. 'It was just a hunch. But I could have been mistaken.'

'As if he had a bad conscience about some aspect of the case?'

'That was my instinct. That he wasn't happy about it, and was even less happy after what I told him. When he left he was muttering something about a student.'

'Oh?'

'I didn't quite catch it, but I heard him say "the student".'

'The student?'

'Yes.

'What student?'

'I don't know. I've no idea what was troubling him but the poor man seemed genuinely distressed.'

34

Jónatan offered no resistance when they led him through the doors of the prison on Skólavördustígur. On the way there he had protested against his detention, saying he needed to go home. There was so much to do and he had lectures first thing in the morning. Eager though he was to help the police, he didn't have the time right now. He was polite, never descending into rudeness, but imploring, as if they'd be doing him a great favour if they let him go. Flóvent told him it was probably too late to continue the interview that night but they would resume their chat in the morning. Until then he would have to stay in the police cells.

'But I've got lectures in the morning,' pleaded Jónatan.

'Perhaps you'd better take tomorrow off,' said Flóvent.

'But I haven't got time to take a day off.'

The prison guards signed him in and escorted him to a cell, Flóvent following just behind. Jónatan kept up a constant stream of protests. When Flóvent asked if there was anyone he wanted to inform of his circumstances, Jónatan merely shook his head as if he still couldn't fully grasp that they were going to lock him up.

'I don't want anyone to know,' he said. 'This is ridiculous. Surely you'll have to let me go in the morning?'

He grabbed Flóvent's arm as the door to the cell opened. 'Don't shut me in there, I beg you.'

'We'll have another chat tomorrow morning, son,' said Flóvent. 'It's late. I'm afraid we have to do it this way. It can't be helped.'

'But I can't bear it,' said Jónatan, in a choked voice. 'There's been some terrible mistake. I don't understand why you're treating me like this. I didn't . . . I haven't done anything.'

'Then we'll straighten it all out tomorrow,' said Flóvent reassuringly. 'Don't worry. If you've done nothing wrong, you'll soon be able to go home again. You have nothing to be afraid of – if that's the case.'

'Don't do this to me. Please, I beg you.'

The door closed on Jónatan.

'Don't shut me in here!' He raised his voice for the first time and it carried through the cell door. Flóvent lingered outside for a moment or two, then headed back down the corridor, the sound of sobbing echoing behind him.

He and Thorson had felt they had no alternative but to detain Jónatan. The evidence was stacking up against him. He had known Hrund and had dealings with her when he was labouring on the roads up north. He was an enthusiast, practically an expert, in Icelandic folklore. Frank Ruddy had thought it possible he was the man he'd spied standing on the corner of Skuggasund the evening Rósamunda's body was found. Jónatan smoked Lucky Strikes, just like the cigarette butts they had found in the street.

221

Admittedly they were very popular, but all things considered it was another mark against Jónatan that he smoked them.

'I guess Frank's not the most reliable witness in the world,' commented Thorson as they re-emerged onto Skólavördustígur.

'Have you let him go?'

'I told him he could rejoin his regiment. There's no reason to hold him any longer. At any rate, he doesn't seem to have attacked Rósamunda. We've found nothing to support that theory. And there's been no news yet from the States about a criminal record.'

'But he reckoned it could have been Jónatan standing on the corner?'

'Yes. Rather than your father, anyway.'

'During my training in Edinburgh they told me that criminals are sometimes drawn back to the scene of a crime. Particularly in cases of murder or other serious incidents.'

'So you think Jónatan may have been drawn back to the theatre?'

'Hard to say. Criminals go back for a variety of reasons. Guilt is one. It gnaws away at them until they're on the brink of giving themselves up – and some actually do turn themselves in. Another is fear of being found out. They're scared they've left something incriminating at the scene and want to double check.'

'So you think the man on the corner was Rósamunda's killer? Whether or not it was Jónatan?'

Flóvent shrugged. 'Did you tell Frank to steer clear of Icelandic women from now on?'

'What good would that do?'

'His testimony isn't everything,' said Flóvent. 'Jónatan's strongest link to the two girls is the folk tales. That's where we should apply the pressure when we question him.'

222

'We've got the link to Hrund,' said Thorson. 'All we really need is to connect him to Rósamunda. Any reason to put off searching his apartment?'

Flóvent glanced at his watch. 'It's pretty late,' he said, thinking of his father. 'Maybe we should leave it till tomorrow morning, before we talk to the boy.'

Thorson nodded. It had been a long day, and he was tired. They drove down to the centre of town where they parted company. Flóvent said he wanted to walk home; he had a lot to think about. Thorson headed into Hótel Borg, hoping to grab a bite of supper before bed. He was staying there for a few nights while the barracks were undergoing some modifications. It didn't bother him in the least, except when the drinking got out of hand at the weekends.

The restaurant was packed but he found an out-of-the-way table and decided to order the roast lamb. A waiter came over and started to apologise in broken English that the kitchen was closed. Thorson replied in Icelandic and asked if the man could fix him a snack instead since he was a guest at the hotel. The waiter promised to see what he could do.

Sitting back and surveying the crowded room, Thorson spotted the proprietor, a strapping, broad-shouldered man, standing by the door to the kitchen in conversation with a waiter. The proprietor was a champion in the ancient art of Icelandic wrestling known as *glíma*, and had toured the world in his younger years, taking on all challengers. His fame had spread all the way to Manitoba. He had done so well out of these tours that when he returned home he was able to build the hotel out of the proceeds, and ran it now with great panache.

That evening the restaurant was largely filled with American

223

servicemen, officers mostly, accompanied by several Icelandic women whose shrieks of laughter frequently punctuated the roar of male voices. Thorson was only too familiar with the so-called Situation. Numerous cases involving relations between soldiers and Icelandic women had landed on his desk at military police headquarters. In a rather draconian effort to tackle the problem, the Icelandic authorities had set up a juvenile court to process cases involving minors, but the initiative had proved short-lived since there were few solutions available short of exiling the younger girls to the countryside to remove them from temptation. It was against regulations to bring women back to barracks and the age limit for admission to dance halls was sixteen, but neither rule was observed in practice. Every now and then fights broke out between locals and servicemen, and there were instances of women seeking to press charges because of the way they had been treated. Cases where soldiers turned out to be married back home were common and invariably a source of distress.

His mother had asked in her letters how he liked his ancestral home. He knew his parents missed Iceland at times; they always spoke well of their homeland and fellow Icelanders. They had emigrated while still young, at the turn of the century, in search of a better life in the new world, and had the good fortune to be allotted a decent piece of land when they arrived in Canada. Thorson's mother had relatives in Manitoba who had fled a life of poverty in Iceland several decades earlier, and they gave the young immigrants a warm welcome. His parents were hard workers and had been quick to establish themselves and put down roots in their new country. Although they often thought of home and missed family and friends, they never regretted their decision to leave. Thorson had written that most Icelanders were still dirt poor but their situation had greatly improved with the outbreak of war, since now there was plenty of well-paid work to go round. As a result, people were flocking from the countryside to Reykjavík in search of a better life – new homes, opportunities that had never been open to them before, a brighter future. He omitted to mention the Situation, preferring not to cast a shadow on his parents' rosy image of the old country, but said the occupation was proving such a watershed in the history of the nation that it was bound to change it for ever. The traditional farming society that his parents had known was fast disappearing.

Having finished his snack, Thorson returned to his room and went to bed. He could hear a muffled echo of the carousing from the restaurant and thought of his home in Canada, as he often did in his lonely state. His parents had told him so many tales of their old homeland, their memories tinged with nostalgia. But the society that awaited him bore little relation to their stories. From the moment he arrived, he'd had the inescapable feeling that he was in a completely different country from the one his parents had left.

Early next morning Flóvent and Thorson drove round to Jónatan's bedsit to search for conclusive evidence that he had known Rósamunda. They had no idea what precisely they were looking for and wouldn't know until they found it. Jónatan had handed over the keys himself the evening before, saying they were welcome to search his room. His only concern was that they would muddle up the papers on his desk: the notes, source references and other carefully ordered material. He offered to go with them and prove that he had nothing to hide, but they declined his offer. 'Maybe later,' Flóvent had said.

The tiny bedsit was exactly the kind of place you would expect a university student, a bookworm too engrossed in his research to take care of himself and his surroundings, to live. In addition to the volumes of Icelandic folk tales and legends, they found a range of other scholarly works related to his studies in the Icelandic Department, as well as books and papers devoted to his other interest: birds. When they'd visited him the previous evening he claimed he'd been out watching cormorants, and Flóvent unearthed a brief composition Jónatan had written about the bird, stating that it was large, black, almost prehistoric in appearance, with a broad wingspan and talons, that it was impressive in flight and a good diver.

In the bookcase they discovered a file of sketches Jónatan had made of the cormorant and other seabirds, which revealed an above-average skill in draughtsmanship – even artistic flair. Some were painted in clear watercolours, with every detail accentuated.

'Nice work,' remarked Thorson.

'The boy's an artist,' agreed Flóvent, holding up one of the drawings and inspecting it closely.

'A sensitive soul, perhaps.'

Flóvent replaced the picture and surveyed the room. He was aware of a flutter of excitement in the pit of his stomach, a feeling that had been present when he woke up that morning and had now returned. 'There's nothing here to suggest that he attacks and harms women.'

'No,' said Thorson. 'He's an innocent student. A birdwatcher and bookworm who happens to be interested in Icelandic folklore.'

'They used to say –'

'Don't tell me – in the Edinburgh police?' finished Thorson.

Flóvent smiled. 'They used to say that you should disregard

everything but hard evidence. Any gut feelings we may have about the boy or his digs or his skill at drawing or the fact he's an innocent bookworm are beside the point. Irrelevant.'

'Isn't that just Scottish cynicism?'

'They knew a thing or two,' said Flóvent.

He began to examine the source material Jónatan had amassed for his thesis, leafing through the papers until his gaze alighted on an account relating to the *huldufólk* that appeared to derive from old court records. The handwriting was almost illegible, however, and after peering at it for a while, Flóvent abandoned the attempt to decipher it on the spot and decided to take the pages away to peruse them at leisure.

Thorson was out in the hallway investigating a small wardrobe. He opened it to find two shirts, a folded jumper and some rolled-up socks. Picking up a pair of smart trousers that had been lying in a crumpled heap at the bottom, he searched the pockets and turned them inside out, noticing, as he did so, a rip in the crotch that had been mended so skilfully as to be almost invisible.

Ten minutes later they located the invoice for the mending service, buried in a kitchen drawer.

35

Jónatan hadn't slept a wink during his night in the cells. The guards heard him muttering to himself and sobbing quietly. When breakfast was delivered to his cell, he asked after the two policemen who had brought him there. He wanted to get a message to them that he mustn't miss his classes; he should already have been in a lecture by now and was hoping he would be released as soon as possible. The gravity of his situation still seemed to elude him. He had little appetite and hardly touched his breakfast of porridge served with two slices of liver sausage and a glass of milk.

When Flóvent and Thorson arrived at the prison towards midday, he had finally fallen asleep but started awake when the key was turned in the lock and his cell door opened. Sitting up on the bed, he stared blearily at the two policemen in the doorway.

'I must have dropped off.'

'Would you come with us?' said Flóvent. 'There's a room where we can talk.'

'Are you going to let me go?' asked Jónatan, standing up.

'We're going to have a little chat,' said Flóvent. 'We need to ask you a few questions concerning the two girls. After that we'll see.'

'I explained to these men that I haven't got time for this; I've already missed some of my lectures.'

Nevertheless, he accompanied them down the corridor and into a small room next to the guards' coffee room. It contained a table and three chairs, and they all sat down. Flóvent asked if they could have some coffee but Jónatan declined his. He seemed calm and composed; brief as it had been, his rest had done him good. Flóvent reached into his pocket for the composition about the cormorant that he had found in Jónatan's room and handed it to him.

'Informative stuff,' he said. 'Have you always been interested in birds?'

'Yes, actually. Ornithology's a hobby of mine. I've always been fascinated by nature, birds especially.'

'By the cormorant in particular?'

'No, by seabirds generally. The cormorant is . . . I like watching it in flight, its elongated neck, the way it plummets into the sea. It's a wonderful bird.'

'Did Hrund share your interest in ornithology?'

'Hrund?' said Jónatan. 'I wouldn't know. I don't think so.'

'Tell us again how you knew Hrund,' said Flóvent.

'I didn't touch her,' said Jónatan. 'I hope you don't think I harmed her. Because I didn't.'

'Did you talk about birds? You told us yesterday she knew a lot about nature, about birds and plants and so on.'

'Well, maybe we did. But I can't really remember.'

Flóvent nodded understandingly. Thorson sat silently at his side. Facing them across the table, Jónatan embarked again on the tale of how he had met the young girl who often used to hang around the petrol station. His account was largely consistent with the one he had provided the day before: they would chat from time to time; she had asked a lot of questions about Akureyri and wanted to move south to Reykjavík, and she was open to the idea that the hidden people really existed.

'And the subject came up because she knew of your interest in such things?' said Flóvent, once Jónatan had finished.

'Yes. She knew I was going to university. I told her I wanted to read Icelandic and history.'

'Did you regard her as a subject for your research?' asked Thorson.

'A subject for my research? No.'

'Well, she told you her ideas about the *huldufólk*, didn't she?'

'Yes, I suppose so.'

'Which were?'

'All the usual stuff about enchanted mounds and elf rocks. She knew lots of stories too. Nothing out of the ordinary, though.'

'Had she had any encounters with supernatural beings herself?'

'She didn't say.'

'She didn't discuss it with you?'

'She never mentioned it, no.'

'She'd never been molested in any way by a supernatural being?' asked Flóvent.

'You asked me that before. I've no idea.'

'She didn't tell you?'

'No.'

'Are you sure about that?'

'Yes. Anyway, I don't believe in that sort of thing. If she had, it would have been a figment of her imagination.'

'Oh, that's right, you don't believe in the existence of such creatures. They belong purely to the world of fairy stories.'

'Yes. Of course. Not that I'm familiar with the type of malevolence you're referring to in tales of the *huldufólk*. After all, they're mostly told by women, passed down from mother to daughter. That's essentially how they've survived. And because they've been kept alive by women, they reflect a female view of the world, feature concerns close to their hearts. They tend to be stories about faithless lovers, childbearing, the exposure of infants.'

'Exposure of infants?' queried Flóvent.

'Some things don't change much.'

'What do you mean?' asked Thorson.

Jónatan looked from one of them to the other, seeking to make himself understood. 'The stories often describe the harsh lot of women. Such as giving birth to a child out of wedlock and being forced to dispose of it. Exposure of infants was the abortion of its day. Naturally it would have been a harrowing experience and the *huldufólk* stories were a way of glossing over the harsh reality and easing the mental anguish. They offered an alternative world in which women have children with handsome, gentle men of the hidden race, who are the antithesis of their brutish human counterparts. The infants are left out in the open for their fathers to find, and grow up, cherished, among their father's people, and may even return one day to the human world. In other words, the stories serve to alleviate a distressing experience.'

'Handsome, gentle men?' repeated Thorson.

'Like the Yanks,' said Jónatan.

'Are they the new *huldufólk*?'

'In a manner of speaking.'

'How do you feel about that?' asked Thorson.

'Me? I don't have an opinion.'

'Are you involved with any women yourself?'

'What's that got to do with anything? Why are you asking me that?'

'Maybe everything we're asking is relevant; maybe none of it is,' said Flóvent. 'We'd appreciate it if you simply gave a straight answer to the question.'

'I've never had a girlfriend,' said Jónatan.

'What about Hrund?'

'What about her?'

'Did you have a crush on her?'

'No,' said Jónatan. 'I hardly knew her.'

'Did she go running after the soldiers up north?'

'Not that I could see.'

'Did you assault Hrund?'

'No, I didn't.'

'Did she turn you down?'

'Turn me down?'

'We mentioned Rósamunda yesterday,' said Thorson.

'Yes.'

'You claim you didn't know her.'

'I didn't.'

'And you had no idea where she worked?'

'No.'

'Tell me, what do you do if your clothes need mending?'

Jónatan was confused by the question. 'I . . . what do I do?'

'If you tore a hole in your trousers, for example. Or needed to get the elbows of your jumpers patched. Are you good with a needle and thread yourself?'

Jónatan looked wonderingly from Flóvent to Thorson and back. 'Why . . . why are you asking me that?'

'You're not much cop at sewing, are you?' said Flóvent.

'No.'

'Rósamunda worked for a dressmaker's in Reykjavík. The shop also offers a mending service. It's called The Stitch. Does that jog your memory?'

'I took my trousers to be mended once,' Jónatan faltered.

'Did you take them to that company, to The Stitch?'

'It's possible.'

'Possible?'

'Yes.'

'Perhaps this will refresh your memory.'

Flóvent took out the invoice they had found in Jónatan's digs and placed it on the table in front of him. It bore the stamp of The Stitch and listed a fee for repairs made to one pair of trousers. Jónatan reached for the invoice, but Thorson was quicker off the mark and, snatching the piece of paper, held it up to him.

'Yes, that's right.'

'Were you aware that Rósamunda worked for this company?'

'I don't know any Rósamunda. I don't understand why you're holding me here. I've done nothing wrong. All I want is for this to be over.'

'It might be advisable for you to get yourself a lawyer at this stage,' said Flóvent.

'I don't want a lawyer. I don't know any lawyers. I want to go home. I haven't got time for this. You have to understand – I'm innocent. I haven't done anything. You've got to believe me.'

233

Jónatan stood up. 'You can't keep me here. You've no right to hold me. I'm leaving.'

By now Flóvent and Thorson were also on their feet. Jónatan walked to the door, which was unlocked. He opened it and was about to step out into the corridor when Thorson grabbed his arm.

'Let me go.'

'I'm afraid you can't leave yet,' said Flóvent.

For an instant it looked as if Jónatan was going to try to make a break for it. Then, conscious that he was outnumbered, he seemed to wilt.

'Don't do this to me,' he begged. 'Let me go.'

'I'm sorry, son,' said Flóvent. 'I'm arresting you on suspicion of murdering Rósamunda. We have no alternative. I advise you to cooperate and also strongly recommend that you get yourself a lawyer.'

An hour later Flóvent was back in his office on Fríkirkjuvegur, poring over the notes he had found in Jónatan's room. They consisted of an account the student had scribbled down over five sides of paper. The handwriting was barely legible yet Flóvent thought he could make out the gist. Pulling over the desk lamp, he shone it on the pages. They were unnumbered, so it took him a while to figure out what order to read them in. The style was familiar from the old court records he had occasionally consulted, and before long he had worked out that the pages described a nineteenth-century rape case. The more Flóvent was able to decipher, the more convinced he became that he had the right man in custody.

36

Konrád pushed one drawer of the filing cabinet shut and opened the next. He hadn't entirely given up hope of finding a police report on Rósamunda's death. The fragment of the witness statement, from which he'd learnt Ingiborg's name, had turned up in an otherwise empty folder, marked only with a case number and filed under 1944. After sifting through everything he could find in the archives for that year without success, he tried widening his search to include files from the years immediately preceding and following 1944, in case any documents had been misplaced. The police must have written reports about such a major crime; he was convinced of it. It was simply a matter of finding them.

His thoughts kept returning to Petra's description of the elderly Thorson's agitation on learning that Rósamunda had been afraid of entering a certain house in Reykjavík. According to Petra's mother, it had been the home of a prominent family: a member of parliament and his wife, pillars of society, important customers, in whose patronage the dressmaker had taken a snobbish pride. Oddfellows, and he might have been a Freemason, Petra had said. Since she had also passed on their names to Thorson, it was a fairly safe assumption that he must have attempted to approach the family, seventy years after the event.

'I'm glad you came,' Petra had told Konrád as he was leaving. 'I hope I've been able to help. To be honest, my mother was terribly bothered about all this before she died. Plagued with guilt about withholding information.'

'Surely there was no need for that,' Konrád replied, not knowing what else to say.

'She was afraid she'd unwittingly caused trouble for someone,' said Petra, 'but felt it was far too late to make amends. She was desperate to relieve her conscience. Do you think this Stefán – Thorson – could have been killed because of what she knew?'

'Oh no, that's very unlikely,' Konrád said reassuringly, though privately he was beginning to wonder.

'Or someone else could have suffered because she kept quiet? Though Mother didn't think anyone had been arrested or tried for the murder.'

'No, I can't find any evidence of that either.'

'Perhaps she should have told the whole truth.'

'Presumably she was reluctant to report unfounded suspicions, as you said. She must have been in a real quandary.'

'Do you think you'll ever find out what happened?'

'Who knows? It's probably too late now.'

Konrád pulled out one file after another. As he flicked through their contents he kept an eye out for references to Rósamunda, Thorson or a student connected to the case. Every now and then he came across the name of the detective, Flóvent, who had been conducting the inquiry with Thorson, but never in connection with Rósamunda. Flóvent had investigated all kinds of routine offences: burglaries, smuggling, car thefts and cases of assault, as well as the odd serious incident, until his name disappeared from the records shortly after the war.

While Konráð was leafing through paperwork from the time of the occupation, he reflected on what he knew about the Situation. He had recently read a newspaper article about the prejudice that Icelandic women who had fraternised with soldiers had faced for many years after the war and the stigma attached to the children of such unions, though attitudes had gradually changed and softened with the passing of time and the influence of the feminist movement. According to the article, the war had effectively emancipated Icelandic women from the patriarchy of the old farming society. The unprecedented degree of independence they enjoyed was one reason why resentment about the Situation had been so fierce. After all, a woman who washed laundry for the army was an independent businesswoman with an income many times greater than that of her unskilled sisters. No longer subject to the traditional authority of the male householder, and spared the need to find herself a husband straight out of a turf hovel, she found herself free to indulge her desire for adventure, to sail to far-off lands with a man from another world on her arm. Besides, as the women themselves pointed out, the foreign soldiers – polite, personable and clean – seemed like fairy-tale princes compared to the Icelandic men on offer.

Smiling to himself at the thought of his boorish countrymen, Konráð kept going back in time, looking for information about a girl who might have paid a heavy price for that new-found freedom. He had got back as far as 1941 when he discovered two loose handwritten sheets. They weren't in a file and lacked both date and author; presumably they had ended up in the wrong place when someone was clearing out old files or in the midst of a move. Perhaps someone had just forgotten to throw them out. The handwriting was neat and legible, and the pages appeared to sum up an interview with a man who was not identified by name. It wasn't an official report, more like a policeman's notes to himself, stating that the man had been brought in for questioning and held in the cells on Skólavördustígur under strong protest. During questioning it had emerged that he knew 'the girl up north' – as it was phrased – and had taken some mending to a shop called The Stitch, where Rósamunda used to work. He was a student of Icelandic and history at the University of Iceland, it continued, with a special interest in folklore and legends, on which he was writing a thesis. Added at the bottom in different ink but in the same hand was a sentence which seemed strangely at odds with the dry tone of the preceding account, like a heartfelt outburst by the author: *What happened was a tragedy.*

That was all that the pages told him. Konrád tracked down some typewritten reports signed by Flóvent, and, comparing them to the notes, concluded that the handwriting on the loose sheets of paper could well be his. He continued rummaging through the filing cabinets, pulling out drawers and leafing through reports, but turned up nothing else of interest. Although the reference to the girl up north was puzzling, it appeared that the student in question had been suspected of Rósamunda's murder. Evidently, the case had not been solved by his arrest, though, since it never went to court and nobody was ever found guilty. It was as if the inquiry had been abruptly terminated. Was there any chance that the suspect could have been linked to the influential family Petra had mentioned? A member of parliament was involved, after all. Could the investigation have been dropped as a result of political pressure?

A student of Icelandic and history.

A student.

Was this unnamed suspect the student Thorson had muttered about as he was leaving Petra's home?

Two hours later, when it was clear that he was getting nowhere, Konrád abandoned his ferreting and went to see Marta. She told him glumly that they were making next to no progress with the inquiry. On her desk was a pile of recordings from CCTV cameras near Thorson's home, labelled with the names of a shop, a bank and a school.

'We're starting to slog through this lot,' said Marta, gesturing to the pile as she pulled on her coat. 'In case we spot any of the usual suspects. Apart from that we haven't a clue what we're looking for.'

'Have fun,' said Konrád.

'Have you got anything for us?'

'Nothing concrete.'

'We're starting to think that the old guy took his own life,' said Marta.

'Smothered himself? Is that possible?' asked Konrád incredulously.

'Think about it, Konrád,' said Marta. 'He was old and knackered.' She was late for a meeting, and clearly had no time to talk. 'We've hit a brick wall. We can find no one who had any reason to harm him. There was no forced entry. Nothing was stolen. Motive? Absolutely no idea. He had no family here, no circle of friends as far as we know. Nothing to look forward to except spending the rest of his days mouldering away in a nursing home. See what I mean?'

'Wrong,' said Konrád. 'Totally wrong. That's a million miles from what was going on in his head. On the contrary, he had every reason to live. He was actively engaged in looking into that cold case involving the girl behind the theatre, a case he himself investigated back when he was a military policeman during the war. And I have reason to believe he was making progress with his enquiries. That's where you'll find the reason for his death. There's your motive.'

'All right,' said Marta. 'Could you send us a short report? We'll take a look at it.'

The phone on her desk was ringing and the instant she picked it up, her mobile chimed in.

'My report-writing days are over,' said Konrád curtly. 'You know where to find me.'

He left.

Afterwards, wondering if he could glean any more information from Vigga, he paid another visit to her nursing home. The corridors were alive with residents on the move, many of them inching along on Zimmer frames; they were overtaken by members of staff dashing to and fro with trays and bowls. The air was filled with music from a radio. Vigga was lying in her usual spot, oblivious to it all. Reluctant to disturb her, Konrád took a seat beside her bed. The carer he consulted had told him she never received any visits, so people had been surprised when an elderly gentleman had come to sit with her a couple of weeks ago, and now Konrád had turned up twice.

He had been sitting there for twenty minutes or so, flipping through an unbelievably tedious lifestyle magazine, when he heard the old woman stirring. He put down the magazine. Vigga opened her eyes and looked at him.

'Vigga?' said Konrád.

'Who are you?' she asked weakly.

'My name's Konrád. I came to see you the other day.'

'Oh?'

'Do you remember?'

Vigga shook her head. 'Who are you?' she asked again.

'My name's Konrád. Naturally you won't remember me, but I used to live near you in the old days.'

Vigga showed no sign of recognising him, either from the past or from his recent visit.

'I came to see you the other day to ask about a visitor you had, a man called Stefán. He was stationed here during the war and went by the name of Thorson; he was in the military police. Do you remember his visit at all? Do you recall talking to him?'

'Do I know you, Mr –?' asked Vigga, suddenly turning formal.

'No, I doubt you'd remember me – it was too long ago. This Thorson wanted to know if you could help him with a case he was investigating during the war – a young woman found strangled behind the National Theatre. When I came to see you recently, you mentioned another –'

'Are you from the management?'

'No, I'm just visiting,' said Konrád. 'I don't know if you talked to Thorson at all, but you told me about another girl, a girl who'd vanished. They never found her bones, you said, and you mentioned the *huldufólk*.'

'She was attacked by one of the *huldufólk*.' With difficulty,

241

Vigga raised herself up from her pillow, her eyes resting on Konrád's face.

'Who?'

'The girl up north. Hrund, her name was. They never found her. She threw herself into the waterfall. Was your father a medium?'

'No,' said Konrád, disconcerted.

'Yes, he was.'

'No, he –'

'The fake medium!'

'No, he wasn't. He was a member of the Society for Psychical . . .'

'He was a crook,' hissed Vigga, lying back on her pillows. 'He was a dirty, no-good piece of scum.'

'Vigga?'

She didn't answer. Her eyelids drooped again.

'Vigga?'

Three quarters of an hour later Konrád stood up and left. Vigga was out for the count. He had sat by her side, waiting for her to wake up so he could ask her more about the girl, Hrund. Everything she'd said was a mystery to him. The *huldufólk* had attacked Hrund and she'd thrown herself into a waterfall. He had no idea what she was talking about. Was Hrund the same girl she had referred to last time, the one who had vanished and never been found?

He was sitting in his car, about to start the engine, when he suddenly remembered the two pages of notes he had found in the police archives, which appeared to be in Flóvent's hand. They had mentioned that the suspect knew 'the girl up north'.

Could that have been this Hrund?

He recalled his father's account of the seance with Rósamunda's parents. Because of the subsequent furore, no one else had learned that the disgraced medium had sensed the presence of another girl who had also suffered a cruel fate, and Konrád, who was not the credulous type, wondered all the same if he could have meant the girl Vigga had referred to as Hrund.

37

The woman was a little younger than Konrád. She had held a number of office jobs over the years, most recently with the social security department. She suggested they meet up at a cafe in the centre of town. Though their fathers had worked together, conspiring to defraud the innocent, Konrád had never spoken to her before. Her name was Eygló and she was the only child of the medium who had held the seance for Rósamunda's parents.

He explained over the phone that he'd found her father's obituary online and got her name from it. Eygló told him her father had been reluctant to talk about his time as a medium, but she turned out to be familiar with the Rósamunda affair and said she'd sometimes wondered how it ended. Konrád informed her that the inquiry appeared to have been abandoned and the case was never solved.

'So you're his son,' was her opening gambit as they greeted one another in the cafe. She held on to his hand when he made to withdraw it, scrutinising him for a moment before suddenly releasing it. 'I have to admit I was a little curious after we talked on the phone.'

'Curious?' said Konrád as they sat down.

'Your father nearly destroyed my dad,' she said. 'I wanted to see what you look like.'

'I hope you're not too disappointed.'

'We'll see. Those kinds of character flaws tend to run in families.'

'Character flaws? What do you mean?'

'Dad never used to speak ill of anyone, but that's what he said about your father – that he was a bad character. Were you brought up by him?'

'I don't see what . . . what that has to do with anything.'

'You want to bombard me with questions – why shouldn't I return the favour?'

'This isn't about me.'

'Are you sure?'

'Yes, I am.'

'Then why are we here? Isn't it because of your father? That seance? Isn't that why you rang me?'

Eygló studied him intently as she waited for his reply. She was petite, dark-haired, dressed almost entirely in black, and looked much younger than her years. Her eyes were bright and searching below her high forehead, her movements brisk and decisive; she had a quick mind and got straight to the point. Over the phone she had informed Konrád that she had followed in her father's footsteps and worked as a psychic for a while. Konrád toyed with the idea of asking if she'd inherited her talent from her father but hesitated. She added that she wasn't well known and kept very quiet about what she called her 'gift'.

'I rang about Rósamunda,' said Konrád. 'I wanted to know if your father had ever said anything about her. If he'd researched any of the details of her case before he held the seance. If he had any prior knowledge, let's say.'

'Wasn't that your father's job? To collect information?'

'So I gather,' said Konrád. 'He told me how they used to go about rigging the sessions, and about that particular seance, but he didn't tell me anything about Rósamunda. I was wondering if your father had . . .'

'You don't believe in any of it, do you?' said Eygló. 'Psychics. Seances.'

'No.'

'Not even in life after death?'

'No.'

'Are you sure?'

Konrád smiled. 'Yes.'

'You can't be as sceptical as you say or you wouldn't have dragged me down here. Are you sure you don't have a touch of the second sight yourself?'

'Did your father ever talk about Rósamunda?' asked Konrád, quickly changing the subject.

'No, not that I recall. Though he did tell me about that seance. He said your father coerced him into working with him. Did you know that?'

'No.'

'He had something on Dad – I don't know what – and forced him to take part in the deception. Dad had the gift, but that wasn't enough for your father. He wanted dramatic results, so people would pay more. They met through the Society for Psychical Research. Dad was weak, I admit, and longed for recognition. He had a drink problem too. Used to go on benders. He'd vanish for weeks at a time and sometimes had blackouts lasting days. But he was a good man. Deep down. He didn't mean to hurt anyone. And he had certain qualities as a medium. A degree of sensitivity not granted to everyone. A sympathetic understanding of people's search for answers.'

'Do you know why he told my dad he'd sensed the presence of another girl during that seance for Rósamunda?' asked Konrád. 'Where that detail came from? Or who she was? My dad hadn't fed him any information about a second girl. She was supposedly there with Rósamunda and was accompanied by an intense feeling of cold. Did your father ever talk about that? Did he know any more than he let on?'

'He knew what he sensed,' said Eygló, 'but you don't believe in any of that, do you? You've already decided that everything he said was a lie, so I can't imagine why you're asking me.'

'Well, I don't know what to make of it,' said Konrád, 'but the strange thing is there may actually have been a second girl connected to the Rósamunda case. A girl who was never found. I wanted to check if your father had any prior knowledge of this.'

Startled, Eygló put down her coffee cup. 'I had no idea she was connected to Rósamunda,' she said. 'Do you know how?'

'That's what I'm trying to find out. I thought maybe our fathers might have had some inside information, like when they pretended to sense the mittens or the shipwreck.'

'Pretended? My father had psychic powers, and if he said he sensed the presence of another girl with Rósamunda, he wasn't making it up. He wasn't a pathological liar, unlike . . .'

'My dad?'

'Yes.'

'So he sensed a presence, you say? Who was she? Did he ever discuss it with you? It's possible her name was Hrund.'

'He didn't know her name, but she visited him powerfully during that seance. He had no idea who she was or what had happened to her. All he knew was that she was unhappy and cold. He spoke about the chill you mentioned. The intense cold.'

'So he didn't know any more than that?'

'No.'

'Nor how she died?'

'No.'

'Have you heard of a man called Stefán Thórdarson, or Thorson, as he used to be known in the old days?'

'Thorson? No.'

'He didn't get in touch with you?'

'No.'

'And your father died years ago, of course.'

'Yes,' said Eygló. 'He . . . It was suicide. He'd been in a bad way for a long while. Couldn't find any peace in his soul, as my mother used to say. Actually, it happened not long after he heard the news about your father.'

'My father?'

'Wasn't he stabbed to death by the abattoir?'

'Yes. But what's that got to do with your father?'

'Mum said he was knocked sideways by the news. Only a few months passed between that and his . . . his death.'

'But they weren't in contact at all, were they?'

'Not that I'm aware, but then I don't know everything. I didn't really know my dad that well. I was so young. But my mother told me he'd been affected by the news of your father's stabbing. She assumed it was because they'd once worked together but . . .'

'But what?'

'Maybe there was more to it.'

'What do you mean?'

'I don't know,' said Eygló. 'I'm completely in the dark, I'm afraid. All I know is that my father wasn't well, obviously. No one in their right mind would resort to an act like that.'

She sat there for a while, lost in the sad memories Konrád had stirred up, then abruptly pushed back her chair and rose to her feet, saying she had to get going.

'Sorry I couldn't help you at all,' she added.

'Thanks for meeting me anyway,' said Konrád, rising to his feet as well and shaking her hand again. This time the contact was fleeting and she avoided his gaze.

'I hope I haven't made you uncomfortable,' he said. 'It really wasn't the intention.'

'No, it . . . no, not at all,' said Eygló.

He could tell that she had noticed his withered arm during their conversation and was trying not to stare at it. 'I've got to be somewhere else,' she added, and hurried out of the cafe.

Konrád sat down again, stroking his arm absently and turning over her words in his mind, thinking about the way she'd talked about his father. It didn't surprise him. He'd heard similar sentiments before and knew from experience – from his own childhood memories – how unreasonable and violent his old man could be. Konrád's mother had tried repeatedly to bring her ex-husband to his senses and persuade him to allow their son to come and live with her, but it was no good. On one occasion he had refused to let her in to speak to Konrád and left her standing in the basement doorway. Usually when she came to town from her new home in the east she would stop by and spend some time with Konrád.

Sometimes she would start crying and begging his father not to drive them any further apart. But on this occasion his father had had enough.

'At least let me say goodbye to him,' she had pleaded, trying to catch a glimpse of her son.

'Oh, shut the fuck up,' his father had said and slammed the door in her face.

38

A little online sleuthing soon revealed when the member of parliament and his wife had died, and the fact that they had been survived by several children and grandchildren. No wonder their names had sounded familiar. When Konrád looked them up he remembered that one of the sons had been an influential politician, a cabinet minister, and a leading light in Icelandic society. Of the MP's four sons and one daughter, only two of the sons were still alive. One had died in his early sixties. Checking the obituaries, Konrád saw that he had passed away suddenly at home. A weak heart was mentioned. The other brother and the sister, however, had lived to a ripe old age. Their descendants were scattered all over the country and as far afield as Britain and Australia.

Konrád decided his first move should be to visit the younger surviving brother, who lived in sheltered accommodation in the little town of Borgarnes on the west coast. He was in the mood for a trip out of town, so the day after his visit to Vigga he got in his car and headed north. The drive took him almost two hours, as he decided to give the tunnel a miss and take the longer, more scenic route around Hvalfjördur. It was a beautiful day, and because most people now used the tunnel he had the road largely to himself. There wasn't a breath of wind and the fjord lay smooth as a mirror. On a whim, Konrád turned off by the old wartime barracks that still stood above the Thyrill Service Station, which was a shadow of its former self now that traffic around the fjord had dwindled to a trickle.

The old barracks had been painted red and lovingly restored; Konrád had read recently that some were used as summer holiday homes by employees of the nearby whaling station. He drove slowly through the little colony, trying to picture how the area would have looked during the war when there were far more huts and the whole place was alive with activity, iron-grey warships lying at anchor in the fjord. Now silence reigned, broken only by the occasional roar of a passing car. A lone gull was floating on the wind above the old whaling station, as if hunting for the long-lost days of prosperity.

He reached Borgarnes just after midday, quickly located the retirement flats, continued on down the hill and parked outside. The man's name was on the entryphone in the lobby. Konrád had given no advance warning of his visit, so he had no idea if the man would be home. After waiting for a decent interval, he pressed the bell again but no one answered. Then he rang the bell of what he assumed was the flat next door and a woman picked up. She said she hadn't seen her neighbour that morning but he often went swimming at lunchtime. Konrád thanked her, returned to his car and drove over to the pool.

He had always liked Borgarnes, a friendly little town with a pretty church, perched on a strip of land surrounded by the sea and set against a dramatic backdrop of mountains. It was of historic interest too, as the area featured heavily in the medieval sagas. The only thing that spoiled it for him was the constant stream of tourists pouring into the snack bars and cafes, since Borgarnes was one of the main rest stops on the routes heading north and west.

None of the swimmers leaving the pool looked the right age to be the man he was after, so he cruised back down the main street. There his hopes were raised when he spotted an elderly man emerging from the local shopping centre with a plastic bag from the state off-licence in one hand and a small sports bag in the other. But they were dashed again when the man climbed straight into a car with a woman at the wheel and they drove away, heading out of town.

Konráð swung by the retirement flats again, tried the bell in the lobby and this time heard a sharp crackling over the entryphone.

'Yes?' blared a voice.

'Is that Magnús's flat?'

'Yes, this is Magnús.'

'Ah, my name's Konráð and I'd like a brief word if that's OK. It's about your parents.'

'My parents?'

There was a long pause, then the door to the lift area buzzed. When Konráð reached the second floor, Magnús was waiting for him outside his flat. They shook hands and Magnús invited him in, explaining that he had just come home from a swim. Konráð pretended this was the first he had heard of it.

'How did you know my parents?' the man asked, closing the

door behind them and showing Konrád into the sitting room. 'Are you one of those genealogists?'

The flat was compact, with an open-plan kitchen and sitting room, a small bedroom, and a fine panorama over the fjord and Mount Hafnarfjall. Its owner, Magnús, appeared to be in good physical shape for his age. He was of average height, straightbacked and sprightly, his head completely bald and his face round. No doubt the swimming kept him fit.

'No, actually,' Konrád said, 'I'm not into genealogy. But I do have an interest in old criminal cases and –'

'Criminal cases?' interrupted Magnús.

'That's right. One of the cases I've been looking into recently dates back to the Second World War.'

'Really? And that's why you're here?'

'Yes.'

'Which case?'

'A young woman who worked as a seamstress was found strangled behind the National Theatre in 1944. Her name was Rósamunda. I should think plenty of older people from Reykjavík would remember the incident.'

'It does sound vaguely familiar,' said the man, frowning slightly.

'May I ask if you've received another visitor recently – he'd have come from Reykjavík like me – a man called Stefán?'

'Stefán? No.'

'He used to go by the name of Thorson; he was from the Icelandic settlement in Canada.'

'No, that doesn't ring any bells.'

'So he didn't come here to talk to you about the case?'

'No. I'm not acquainted with any Stefán or Thorson. I don't get many visitors out here. My daughters both live in Australia. They

254

moved there during the recession in the late sixties and can't be bothered to fly up to the frozen north that often. What . . . Why would this man have wanted to talk to me?'

'He came over here during the war – he was in the military police and investigated the death of the girl I mentioned.'

'So? I'm not with you. Where do I come in?'

'He was still making enquiries about the case right up until his death a couple of weeks ago. You may have heard about it on the news. A pensioner was found dead in his home under suspicious circumstances. That was Thorson.'

'I'm afraid I don't follow the news very closely, and I still don't understand what all this has to do with me.'

'No, of course, I'm sorry; I'll try and explain. The girl found by the theatre worked for a dressmaker's in Reykjavík, quite a large enterprise called The Stitch, which had a wide range of customers – from all walks of life, as you might say. Thorson recently stumbled across a new piece of information – namely that the girl had refused to take any deliveries to a certain house in Reykjavík, whose owners were regular customers of the company.'

'Thorson?' repeated the man, distractedly.

'Is it coming back to you now?'

'He was in the military police, you say?'

'Yes, that's right. I assume he would have worn a uniform at the time. He was in the Canadian Army, but as far as I can work out he was seconded to the American forces stationed in Reykjavík and served in the military police.'

Magnús hadn't offered Konrád a seat, and they were still stand-ing, face to face, by the door.

'Maybe you'd like to sit down?' suggested Konrád.

'Yes, I must admit I'm a bit tired after my swim,' said the man, crossing the room to sink into an armchair. 'What were you saying about the girl? Which house was it she didn't want to visit?'

'Your parents' house, as a matter of fact. It seems likely that she had a bad experience when she delivered something there, and after that she refused to go anywhere near the place.'

The man didn't seem to grasp the implication. 'What are you driving at?' he asked.

'I imagine that to Thorson, all these years later, it must have suggested that she had reason to be afraid of a member of your household.'

'Afraid?'

'Yes. That might explain why she refused to go round there.'

'But why? What would she have been frightened of?'

'I was hoping you'd be able to answer that,' said Konrád.

'Me? I don't know what you're implying. I can't imagine what she would have had to fear at our house.'

39

Towards evening on the day of his formal arrest, Jónatan was escorted back to the same small room, where Flóvent and Thorson were waiting. He had refused to eat, refused to contact any of his friends or relatives or provide Flóvent with their details. He still seemed to be labouring under the illusion that he would be released at any moment. Although Jónatan had declined the services of a lawyer, Flóvent had gone ahead and made arrangements for a legal representative to meet him later that evening. Flóvent started off by trying to put the young man at his ease, before returning to a tougher line of questioning.

'Where do you go birdwatching?' Flóvent asked once they were seated.

'The Seltjarnarnes Peninsula usually, that's the most rewarding spot. Or to Skarfaklettur on Videy Sound. Or Nauthólsvík Cove.'

'Do you always take your binoculars along?'

'Yes.'

'Do you see anything other than birds on these trips?'

'Like what?'

'People, for example?'

'Yes, of course. Sometimes.'

'Soldiers?'

'Yes. They're quite active along the coast.'

'Do you ever come across any women on these trips?'

'I don't watch them deliberately, if that's what you're implying. I don't spy on people. I don't use my binoculars for that.'

'You said you didn't have any views on the Situation, on Icelandic women fraternising with soldiers – walking out with them, marrying them, you know. What are your feelings about that kind of behaviour?'

'I don't have any feelings, really – I don't give it much thought.'

'So it doesn't make you angry?'

'No. It has nothing to do with me. I can't understand why you're bringing it up. Of course . . . of course it's an odd state of affairs and I know lots of people are unhappy about it, but I don't give it a moment's thought. It really doesn't interest me. So, as I said, I really don't understand the point of the question.'

'Did you meet Rósamunda on one of your birdwatching trips?'

'I've told you over and over again – I never met her.'

'Not long before she died, she told someone that she'd been attacked and raped,' said Thorson. 'Her attacker told her to blame it on the *huldufólk*. Can you imagine why he would have ordered her to give such an outlandish explanation?'

'No.'

'You've gone out of your way to study tales of the hidden people. Why on earth do you suppose this man would have brought them up?'

'I haven't a clue. I didn't know the girl. I don't know what you're talking about.'

'You didn't know her?'

'No.'

'Did you rape her?'

'No. I . . . you . . .'

'Did you put pressure on her to get rid of the baby?'

Jónatan was speechless.

'Did you assault her, then order her to invent some tale about being attacked by the elves or she'd be sorry?'

'No!'

'You used the same method three years ago on Hrund, didn't you?'

'No.'

'You forced yourself on her, then told her to blame it on the *huldufólk.*'

'That's not true.'

'Can you tell us where Hrund is?' asked Flóvent.

'Where she is?'

'Yes.'

'How am I supposed to know that? I never touched her.'

'Did you have any contact with her after she claimed she'd been attacked?'

'No. I've told you, I barely knew her. I only ran into her a few times at the petrol station.'

'You knew Rósamunda from the dressmaker's, of course.'

'No, I didn't.'

'You took your trousers there to be mended.'

'Yes, but I didn't know anyone there. Lots of people take their trousers to be mended there. I'm not the only one.'

'You could have struck up an acquaintance with her like you

259

did with Hrund, without anyone else knowing. You trusted the girls to keep quiet.'

'The only one I met was Hrund – we'd chat from time to time, as I've told you repeatedly. But I wasn't acquainted with this Rósamunda at all. Why can't you get that into your heads? This is all a serious misunderstanding, and while you're sorting it out, I'd be grateful if you'd let me go home.'

'It would be a great comfort to her family if you could tell us where you think Hrund's body is,' said Flóvent.

'Haven't you been listening to a word I've said? I never touched her. Ever. Look, I've got to get out of here. I'm not feeling well. You can't keep me here. I'm finding this whole business terribly upsetting and utterly incomprehensible. It's incomprehensible that you would even think I'd be capable of harming another person. Killing someone. It's . . . I just don't understand how such an idea could enter your head.'

'Perhaps you should wait for the lawyer,' said Flóvent. 'A lawyer would help you understand what will happen next.'

'I don't want a lawyer. I just want you to stop this. I want to go home. I'm missing my lectures. This is absurd. It's complete madness.'

Flóvent now took out the pages he had found in Jónatan's room and placed them on the table in front of him. Thorson was already familiar with their contents. Jónatan stared at the pages, his face suddenly blank.

'Are these yours?' asked Flóvent.

Jónatan didn't answer.

'Is this your handwriting?'

'Yes,' said Jónatan. 'It's my handwriting. Where did you get them?'

'From your room,' said Flóvent. 'Then you know what these pages contain?'

'Of course I do,' said Jónatan. 'I'm collecting material for my thesis. You mean you actually took these from my room?'

'This account is taken from old court records, isn't it?' said Flóvent.

'Yes.'

'I looked up the case. You've copied it down almost word for word.'

'Of course I have. It's a source.'

'Would you care to tell us what the trial was about?'

'You ought to know if you've read it,' said Jónatan.

'It's a rape case,' said Flóvent.

'Yes.'

'Involving a young girl and a farm labourer.'

'Yes.'

'The circumstances of the case were highly unusual, to say the least. And strangely relevant to our present investigation.'

'I wouldn't know.'

'Would you like me to refresh your memory?' asked Flóvent.

'Do what you like. What you do is your affair. I want you to let me go. I've done nothing wrong. I'm innocent.'

Flóvent studied Jónatan in silence for a moment, then began to summarise the student's notes. The court case dated from the early nineteenth century and involved a young woman, a servant on a farm in the south-west of Iceland, who had grown up with stories of the elves; she had even learnt to identify the local rocks and knolls reputed to be their dwelling places. Once she was dispatched on an errand to another farm some distance away, and as she was coming home towards evening she met a labourer from a neighbouring farm. Their paths crossed near a mound where the hidden people were said to dwell. She was already acquainted with the labourer, who had tried to court her in the past, so when he began to make advances, trying to fondle her and saying he wanted to lie with her, she steadfastly rejected him. When she tried to continue on her way, however, the man seized hold of her, intending to have her in spite of her refusal. A violent struggle ensued. She received several wounds to her face and body and her clothes were torn off before eventually he succeeded in forcing himself on her. The labourer then threatened that she'd be sorry if she reported him – saying he could easily kill her – and when she asked how she was to explain the state she was in, he glanced up at the mound and said that she could blame it on the *huldufólk*. Afterwards the girl went home and did as the man told her. Some believed her while others did not, among them her own mother, who eventually got the truth out of her. In the end the young woman pressed charges against the labourer, who confessed to the crime and duly received his punishment.

'Have I got the story right?' asked Flóvent when he had finished.

'That's just one aspect of my research,' said Jónatan. 'The various forms folk beliefs can take. It's the record of a case I found particularly intriguing.'

'So it didn't give you any ideas?'

'Good God, no. I don't understand . . . I don't know what I'm supposed to say. This is ludicrous.'

'So you didn't tell Hrund to blame it on the *huldufólk* like the assailant in the historical case?'

'No,' said Jónatan. 'I did nothing of the sort.'

'And you didn't repeat the whole thing with Rósamunda?'

'No, this is utter nonsense.'

'Are you telling me that the idea didn't come from this case?' asked Flóvent, waving the pages at him.

'I don't know what you're talking about,' said Jónatan. 'You're confusing me. I just want to go home.'

'This is exactly the same kind of incident as the ones we're investigating,' said Flóvent, 'and we find an account of it in your room. Coincidence? Is that what you're claiming?'

'I don't know what I'm claiming,' said Jónatan. 'I don't know what's going on. Nothing you say makes any sense.'

'We'd like to contact your parents,' said Thorson. 'Why won't you tell us how to get in touch with them?'

'Because this has nothing to do with them.'

'They're bound to be wondering how you are. They might be worrying about you already. Do you write to them regularly?'

'No. I . . . I don't want anyone to know I'm in prison.'

'What about your brothers and sisters? Are you in touch with them?'

'I don't have any brothers or sisters.'

'Are you their only son, then?'

'Their only son, exactly,' said Jónatan, grinning at some private irony. 'Will you let me go? Will you stop making these crazy accusations?'

'Why don't you tell us a bit about yourself?' said Thorson. 'Help us understand you better so we can get this over with sooner.'

'What can I possibly say? You turn everything against me. Everything. If I take my trousers to be mended that makes me a dangerous criminal and I'm locked up in prison. What on earth am I supposed to tell you? You both twist everything I say.'

'All right,' said Flóvent amiably. 'Have it your way. We'll track down your parents and get word to them whether you like it or not – before the evening's over, with any luck. I was hoping you could help speed things up, but have it your own way.'

Flóvent stood up and summoned the prison guard who came and escorted Jónatan back to his cell at the end of the corridor. They heard the heavy door clang shut just as they were stepping out onto Skólavördustígur. They stood beneath the glass lantern that shone over the prison entrance, discussing their next move. A faint mist of snow was settling on the streets and houses, making the paving stones slippery underfoot.

'He's going to be a tough nut to crack,' remarked Thorson.

'Perhaps because he knows he's in a tight spot,' said Flóvent, watching three army jeeps drive past.

He had noticed the ships massing in the harbour mouth, the increased activity among the armed forces. It was all part of the build-up to the long-awaited invasion. If the Allies managed to get a foothold on the Continent and the German retreat continued on the Eastern Front, the end of the hostilities couldn't be far off. The war might be over in a year or so. The day couldn't come soon enough as far as Flóvent was concerned: not only would it ease the appalling suffering in Europe and around the world, but there was a chance that Icelandic society might possibly revert to its familiar, pre-war state. But that was wishful thinking. The longer the war dragged on, the more convinced he became that nothing would ever be the same again.

Thorson seemed to read Flóvent's mind as he watched the jeeps receding from view.

'The troop movements have begun,' he said.

'The beginning of the end?'

'Hopefully.'

'Will you be going?'

'Yes.'

'Do you know when?'

'In a couple of days. I received my orders this morning.'

'Will you take part in the fighting?'

'I expect so.'

'Not a very pleasant thought.'

'No, it isn't.'

'The Germans will put up a hell of a fight.'

'Yes. Though they don't know where we'll be landing. Nobody knows. So we . . .'

'You'll have the advantage of surprise.'

'That's the idea.'

'Any plans for what you'll do after the war?'

'No.'

'I suppose talking about it feels like tempting fate?'

Thorson shrugged with apparent indifference.

'That's understandable,' said Flóvent. 'I imagine it's . . . going to be tough.'

'They're expecting heavy casualties over the first few days, at the very least. While we're establishing a bridgehead.'

'Is there any way you can avoid going?'

'Avoid it?' said Thorson, gazing up into the haze of tiny snowflakes. 'I asked to be sent.'

40

They heard the door of the prison opening behind them.

'Ah, I thought you were still here,' said the guard who had escorted Jónatan to his cell. 'He wants to talk to you. Shall I bring him back to the interview room?'

Flóvent and Thorson exchanged glances.

'What does he want?' asked Flóvent.

'I don't know,' said the guard. 'He's got something he wants to say to you. He asked if you'd left already.'

'All right, go and get him then,' said Flóvent.

They waited in the interview room without sitting down or removing their coats. Soon Jónatan was brought in and took a seat at the table.

'I can't cope with being locked up,' he began in a strained voice, and they sensed his mounting desperation. He looked imploringly from one to the other.

'I'm afraid there's not a lot we can do about that,' said Flóvent.

'You can speak to a chaplain – I expect they've already offered you the opportunity.'

'I've nothing to say to a chaplain. You're in charge. You're the ones deciding my fate.'

'You haven't exactly been cooperative,' Flóvent pointed out.

'What am I supposed to do when you don't believe a word I say?'

'Was that it?' asked Flóvent.

'I . . .' Jónatan broke off.

'Why did you call us back?' asked Thorson.

The student didn't answer.

'We'll continue our conversation tomorrow, Jónatan,' said Flóvent. 'I haven't got time for this now.'

He opened the door and called the guard.

'Don't go!' cried Jónatan.

They didn't answer. The guard took him by the arm, raised him from the chair and led him out into the corridor and back towards the cells. His keys jingled as he opened the cell door. But when he tried to steer Jónatan inside, the prisoner dug in his heels.

'I can't spend another night here,' he whispered, so quietly it was almost inaudible.

'What was that?'

'I'll show them,' Jónatan whispered.

The guard hesitated. 'What did you say? I didn't catch that.'

'I'll take them there.'

The guard turned and shouted after Flóvent and Thorson, who were just passing through the door at the end of the corridor. They paused when they saw him waving.

'What now?' called Thorson.

'He's got something to tell you,' the guard called back.

Jónatan took a deep breath. 'I'll show you where I met her in . . . in the Shadow District.'

'What did you say?' asked Flóvent, retracing his steps with Thorson on his heels.

'I'll show you the place,' said Jónatan more loudly.

'In the Shadow District?' said Flóvent. 'Is that where you met Rósamunda?'

Jónatan nodded. 'I'll show you where.'

'Now?' said Thorson.

'Yes, right now. I'll take you there and show you where we met.'

'All right,' said Flóvent. 'If that's the way you want it, we can go now. Does that mean you're prepared to tell us what happened?'

'First I'll go with you to the Shadow District, then I'll talk to you. I'll need my jacket, though. Isn't it cold out?'

'What made you change your mind?' asked Thorson.

'Do you want me to do this or not?' retorted Jónatan angrily. There was no sign of hesitation now.

'Of course we do,' said Flóvent.

'You can ask me all the questions you like afterwards.'

'All right. Are you going to confess to having killed Rósamunda?'

'Do you want me to take you there or not?' Jónatan asked, glaring stubbornly at Flóvent.

'Fetch his coat,' Flóvent said to the guard. 'We'll wait here.'

The guard hurried away down the corridor. The door to the cell was still wide open and Jónatan looked inside with a shudder.

'I can't bear being shut in,' he murmured in a voice barely above a whisper.

They stood in silence while they waited for the guard to return with the jacket. Flóvent felt sorry for the young man. He wondered if he ought to cuff him, but the handcuffs were in the car, so he decided it could wait until they were seated in the vehicle. He didn't anticipate any trouble now that Jónatan seemed ready to give in and work with them. Flóvent was keen to meet him half-way. If Jónatan wanted to take them to the scene this late in the day as a means of postponing the evil hour when he was locked up again, that was his affair. He seemed to have undergone a change of heart and decided to cooperate, and that was all that mattered.

Once the guard had finally returned with Jónatan's coat, they left with the prisoner between them, Thorson holding his arm. The car was parked only a few yards from the jail. Thorson opened the rear door for Jónatan and was about to usher him inside when, quick as a flash, the young man tore himself loose and broke into a run.

'Damn!' exclaimed Thorson, taking off after him. Flóvent, who was halfway behind the wheel, sprang out of the car after them.

Jónatan fled round the corner of the prison and followed the wall down Vegamótastígur towards Laugavegur, with Thorson pounding along a few yards behind him. Flóvent was further back still, slowed down by his shoes. The streets were treacherous and, with no grips on his soles, he was in serious danger of falling flat on his face. Thorson gained on Jónatan as the student sprinted down the narrow side street and, without looking, shot out into Laugavegur, where an army jeep, hurtling down the street at breakneck speed, hit him head on.

Thorson watched as Jónatan was thrown in the air then slammed down onto the bonnet of the jeep. He bounced off, land-ing head first on the icy paving stones. The driver lost control of the vehicle, swerved up onto the pavement and crashed into a wall, narrowly missing a pedestrian, who just managed to dodge out of the way. Both the soldiers in the jeep were flung against the windscreen, which shattered, cutting their faces. One crawled groggily out of the wreckage and collapsed in the street. The other, trapped inside, screamed in agony. He had cracked his ribs when he hit the steering wheel and his shin had snapped clean in two; the bone was protruding through his trouser leg.

Thorson raced over to Jónatan and crouched down beside him. Blood was welling out of his head, forming a large pool beneath him. His eyes were staring emptily at the sky. Thorson imagined he must have died the instant he hit the ground.

Flóvent knelt down beside them. A light mist of snow was still falling and the tiny flakes settled on Jónatan's eyes, melting into them like tears.

41

Konrád drove back to Reykjavík deep in thought. Night was falling but he hardly noticed. Even the violent gusts of wind that caused the car to swerve in the notorious black spot at the foot of Mount Hafnarfjall failed to rouse him from his reverie. Nor did he realise that he had shot past a speed camera in the Melasveit area. His mind was entirely preoccupied with his visit to Magnús in Borgarnes. They had discussed Rósamunda's murder exhaustively, but Magnús either didn't know anything about it or was pretending not to.

'The fact that the girl refused to make a delivery to our house doesn't prove anything,' Magnús had argued. 'Doesn't prove anything at all.'

'No, maybe not,' Konrád conceded. 'Nevertheless, it may be relevant to the bigger picture.'

'The bigger picture,' echoed Magnús. 'You sound like a politician.' He said it as if he had little time for the breed.

'Am I right in thinking that your father was a member of parliament?'

'Yes, he was involved in politics.'

'And you were one of five children – your parents had four sons and one daughter?'

'I'm not sure I appreciate all these questions about my family,' said Magnús. 'Just what are you insinuating?'

'Did you have any domestic staff? Did anyone else live in the house?'

'What are you driving at?' asked Magnús.

'I'm wondering who the girl was so keen to avoid. I suppose it could have been your mother or sister. Do you think that might have been the case?'

Magnús looked at Konrád for a moment. 'My mother had quite a temper,' he replied at last. 'But my sister was sweetness personified. Is that what you wanted to hear?'

'What about you and your brothers?'

'What about us?'

'Did any of you know Rósamunda?'

'No,' said Magnús. 'I don't recall any of us associating with a seamstress.'

'But you remember Rósamunda's murder?' persisted Konrád, ignoring the contempt implicit in Magnús's reply.

'Vaguely, as I said before.'

'Do you remember talking about it at home? And, if so, how your family felt about it?'

'No, though obviously we'd have regarded it as a shocking crime. Just as any other family would. We were no different from other people. Are you trying to implicate us somehow in the girl's death? Isn't that absurdly far-fetched, more than half a century later?'

'I'm not trying to implicate anyone in her death, I'm simply attempting to discover why she refused to set foot in your house shortly before she was found murdered. I hope you don't find that unreasonable?'

Magnús had no reply to this.

'Is it conceivable that your father could have applied political pressure to ensure that the investigation went no further?'

'Political pressure?'

'I don't know how else to put it,' said Konrád. 'I can understand if this has come as a bit of a shock to you, but I can't find any record of the case. Of course, those were unsettled times and the paperwork may have gone astray or never been completed, but the fact remains that I can hardly find a single sheet of paper relating to the Rósamunda inquiry. No police reports. Hardly anything in the newspapers beyond reports of her body being found. Nothing in the court records. It's as if the whole affair was swept under the carpet. So, not unnaturally, it occurred to me that your father, as an influential figure at the time, might have had a hand in suppressing the matter.'

Magnús listened, his face giving nothing away. 'I don't understand what you're implying,' he said when Konrád had finished. 'As far as I'm aware, my father never abused his position in that way. Naturally, he fought for his constituency and did people favours here and there, but that sort of behaviour was taken for granted in those days. He may not even have known about the case.'

'One of your brothers is still alive,' said Konrád.

Magnús nodded.

'Do you know if he received a visit from Thorson? The man I asked you about?'

'I haven't spoken to my brother or his family for many years.'

'Oh?'

'Yes, and I have no intention of discussing the matter with a stranger. Look, I've had enough of this. It's time you were leaving.'

'All right,' said Konrád. 'Thanks again for agreeing to have a chat. Just one final question: do you, or rather did you, know a girl, or young woman, during the war, whose name was Hrund?'

Magnús shook his head.

'It's possible she and Rósamunda had similar experiences, but the facts are a bit hazy.'

'During the war?'

'Yes.'

'No. Not unless . . .'

'What?'

'I once heard about a girl who was supposed to have thrown herself into Dettifoss. She was from the Öxarfjördur area. Now you come to mention it, I'm pretty sure her name was Hrund.'

'Where did you hear about her?'

'From my father originally, I expect. He was travelling up there when it happened.'

'Your father was in the area?'

'Yes. The name stuck in my memory. Whenever I visited the waterfall I would think of her sad end. We've got relatives up there, and my father used to visit them. In the summers mainly.'

'Do you know what happened?'

'It was such a long time ago that I've forgotten the details,' said Magnús. 'But some people said she wasn't right in the head. Or maybe it was a broken heart. Apparently she used to see things. She believed in the supernatural and supposedly had some kind of encounter with the *huldufólk* before she died.'

'You couldn't elaborate?'

'No, sorry, the story was very muddled. But then delusions like that usually are.'

'And she was never found?'

'Not to my knowledge. Her body never turned up.'

Magnús rose to his feet, eager to end the visit. 'I need to go for my rest now,' he said. 'Would you excuse me?'

'Yes, of course. I didn't mean to tire you.' Konrád stood up as well.

'We fell out over the will,' Magnús volunteered suddenly, as they made their way to the front door. 'My brother and I. I felt Hólmbert grabbed the lot in his typical domineering manner. Things never got really acrimonious – I didn't take him to court – but the upshot is that we haven't spoken for years. So it's perfectly possible that this man, this Thorson, went to see him. But if so, I wouldn't have heard about it.'

'Right, I see,' said Konrád.

'Not that there would have been much point.'

'For Thorson? Why not?'

'It would be a waste of time asking my brother if he'd received a visit.'

'What makes you say that?'

'And it's too late for me to try and bring about a reconciliation.' Magnús fell silent. Then he added: 'I gather the illness is in its final stages.'

'He's ill?'

'Hólmbert has Alzheimer's and, from what I've heard, he's gone downhill very rapidly,' said Magnús. 'Apparently he's in a world of his own these days.'

'I'm sorry to hear that.'

'Yes, it's a grim fate,' said Magnús, opening the front door.

'Apart from that I believe he's always been healthy. Never known a day's illness in his life. But that makes no difference when you're dealing with a degenerative disease like Alzheimer's.'

'No, I suppose not,' said Konrád. 'So there's no point my going to talk to him?'

'No, you can forget about that,' said Magnús, giving him a firm handshake.

Konrád was forced to slow down when he ran into congestion near the suburb of Grafarvogur. All the way back his mind had been grappling with the implications of what he'd learnt from Magnús, about Hrund and the waterfall, Rósamunda and the theatre. He racked his brain, trying to think of anything that might connect the two girls. Thorson had gone to see Vigga in his search for answers about Rósamunda. Did she tell him about another girl called Hrund? Or had he already been familiar with Hrund's story from his time in the police? Konrád considered the newest piece of the puzzle: that the MP, Magnús's father, had been visiting the Öxarfjördur area when talk of Hrund's disappearance would have been on everyone's lips. Later, Rósamunda had refused to enter his house. Was that the connection? Did Magnús know more than he was prepared to let on?

Konrád sat in the traffic jam thinking about the former MP and his connections to both cases, however tenuous. He reflected on the fact that the two girls had mentioned the *huldufólk* and remembered what he had been taught about coincidences when he was just starting out as a detective.

Never, under any circumstances, believe in them.

42

It was very late before Flóvent and Thorson were able to return to the Fríkirkjuvegur offices. By then, Jónatan's body had been taken to the mortuary, the soldiers injured in the crash were being tended to in hospital, and their jeep had been towed away to the base in Skerjafjördur. Flóvent and Thorson had given the Reykjavík police a preliminary account. A more detailed report would have to wait until the following morning.

They still didn't know who they should inform of Jónatan's death. Their investigation into his background had only just got under way; they hadn't yet identified his next of kin, and Jónatan himself had stubbornly refused to reveal any information about his personal life.

They sat in silence. The only illumination came from Flóvent's desk lamp. Outside the snow had thickened and was now coming down heavily over the town. Their guilt felt as oppressive as the enshrouding darkness. Both men were haunted by the same thought: a young man in their care had lost his life. For as long as he was in their custody, they were responsible for him, and they had failed him. His death was their fault, though they had only meant to be kind. Their momentary lapse of concentration had cost him his life.

'Do you think he was really going to take us there?' asked Thorson, finally breaking the silence. 'Or was that just a ploy?'

Flóvent didn't seem to hear. Recalling Jónatan's extreme distress at being locked up, he wondered if they should have foreseen what might happen; if they had ignored the danger signs. He should have been handcuffed to one of them when they left the prison. They should have read the situation better, guarded him more closely.

'Flóvent?'

'What was that?'

'Was he using the Shadow District as a ploy? Did he really plan on taking us there?'

'You mean in order to escape?'

'Yes.'

'I'm not sure,' said Flóvent. 'Impossible to say. I don't suppose we'll ever know the answer to that. For God's sake, why didn't we handcuff him? We were so careless.'

'I didn't see it coming,' said Thorson. 'Neither did you. We didn't forget. It was a gesture of goodwill. We were trying to create an atmosphere of trust. That was important. Then he gets hit by a car. We would have caught him. I was only a few yards behind when he ran in front of that jeep. It was a crazy attempt. And look how it ended.'

Flóvent nodded distractedly.

'There's no way we could have predicted that he would make a run for it,' continued Thorson. 'He was being cooperative . . . OK, he was upset at being in jail – we knew that. But wasn't that because he'd been caught? Because he didn't want to confess his guilt?'

'Perhaps,' said Flóvent. 'But it's also possible that we had the wrong man. He didn't say anything to you?'

'No. I believe he died instantly. I don't think he even knew what hit him.'

The soldiers had been driving well over the speed limit, from what Thorson could remember, and he assumed there would be consequences. He had spoken to the man who had been sitting on the pavement, covered in blood, beside the wrecked vehicle. 'There was nothing we could do,' the soldier had said, distraught. 'We didn't even see him till he landed on the hood.' He had been informed that Jónatan was dead.

Flóvent was finding it hard to master his despair. 'The poor boy,' he whispered, his voice cracking.

'It was his decision,' said Thorson. 'He didn't have to do it.'

Flóvent said nothing. He knew Thorson was trying to comfort him, and perhaps one could take the view that the student had been responsible for his own fate, but Flóvent was painfully aware that they had badly misjudged the situation.

'We didn't handle it right,' he said. 'We didn't handle it right. We should have traced his family. Got him a lawyer straight away . . .'

'We were going to,' Thorson reminded him. 'You told him we were going to fix that this evening. Maybe that's what upset him. Maybe that's why he was willing to try something that desperate. Maybe he wanted to speak to his family before we did. Who knows what was going through his mind? He wouldn't open up to us.'

'No, he was obstinate,' admitted Flóvent. He grimaced, clutching at his stomach. 'He was bloody obstinate.'

'Are you OK?' asked Thorson.

'Yes, it's nothing. I keep getting these twinges. I expect it's this case. It . . . It's all been rather a strain.'

Early the next morning Flóvent went to speak to Jónatan's tutor at the university in the hope that he might be able to provide some information about the student. Thorson didn't go along. They had agreed that there was no call for the military police to have any further involvement in the case. In fact, this had been apparent for some time, but Thorson had wanted to help out. Now that he had received his embarkation orders, he had only forty-eight hours to prepare for his transfer.

The news of Jónatan's death came as a heavy blow to his tutor. The young man had been reserved, he told Flóvent, but a good student. The tutor had twice invited him round to discuss his studies and discovered that they had a shared passion for birdwatching. As a result they had struck up a friendship, in the course of which the tutor had learnt that Jónatan was adopted and had never known his real parents. He was brought up as one of the family on a farm not far from Húsavík, on the north coast, showed promise at school and was sent first to college in Akureyri, then south to Reykjavík to attend the university under the guardianship of some relatives of his adoptive mother: her sister, Sigfrídur, and Sigfrídur's husband, who was a member of parliament.

'Did he have any contact with the opposite sex, that you're aware of?' asked Flóvent.

'No,' said the tutor. 'Not that he mentioned. At least not to me.

I don't think he had many friends, to be honest – he was a bit of a loner.'

Next, Flóvent paid a visit to Jónatan's relatives. They lived on Laufásvegur, not far from Flóvent's offices, in a large, detached house, set in a sizeable garden, which contained a small pond. As Flóvent passed it he noticed that the pond was frozen solid. A maid answered the door and showed him into the drawing room. When she enquired after his business, he said he would prefer to explain in person. The girl went to alert her employers and before long a woman of about fifty appeared at the drawing room door and greeted him formally.

'Good day. Were you hoping to see my husband?'

'Yes, ma'am, I should probably speak to him too. Are you by any chance Sigfrídur, ma'am?'

'Yes, I am,' said the woman. 'And you are . . . ?'

'Flóvent, ma'am. I'm from the police and I'm here about a student called Jónatan.'

'Oh, what about him?'

'I'm very sorry to have to inform you that he's passed away. He was hit by an army jeep on Laugavegur yesterday evening and died instantly.'

The woman stared at him blankly. 'Jónatan?'

'Yes, I'm afraid so, ma'am. It was an accident. He was –'

'What are you saying? Is he dead?'

At this point a slightly older man entered the room. Flóvent recognised him immediately as the member of parliament.

'This . . . man has come here with some absurd story about Jónatan being dead,' the woman said, turning to her husband.

'Jónatan?' he repeated. 'What . . . how is that possible?'

'According to him he was hit by a car.'

The husband turned to Flóvent. 'Is this true?'

'I'm afraid so, sir. I'm a detective from the Criminal Investigation Department. He was hit by a car on Laugavegur late yesterday evening. And there's another matter . . .'

He had the couple's undivided attention now.

'Another matter?' said the member of parliament.

'I'm sorry to have to break it to you but Jónatan was in police custody at the time of the accident,' said Flóvent. 'He didn't want anyone to know, so he refused to supply us with the names of any relatives or friends, and turned down the services of a lawyer. He was being detained in connection with the murder of a girl called Rósamunda, who was recently found strangled behind the National Theatre. I'm afraid to say he broke free of us outside the prison and fled down to Laugavegur, straight into the path of an oncoming jeep.'

The couple seemed stunned by this. He gave them a moment to assimilate the news. They exchanged glances, then turned their attention back to him, their faces registering utter disbelief.

Flóvent had already been called to a meeting with his superiors, and he had provided a blow-by-blow account of all that had occurred between the discovery of Rósamunda's body and the moment Jónatan ran in front of the jeep. He had received a stern dressing-down for allowing Jónatan to slip out of his grasp, but in spite of this they had proved broadly sympathetic and agreed that he could remain in charge of the inquiry for the time being.

'I don't believe it,' groaned the woman, groping for a chair. Flóvent quickly helped her to sit down.

'Murder?' exclaimed the MP.

Flóvent nodded. 'I'm afraid so.'

'Surely there must be some mistake? How could you have arrived at such a conclusion?'

'The evidence is fairly overwhelming, sir,' said Flóvent. 'He was about to show us the place in the Shadow District where he met her . . . or rather, where he subjected her to an assault. We were on our way there when he eluded our grasp and ran in front of the jeep. We were powerless to stop him. He tore himself free and fled.'

'Shouldn't you have been guarding him more closely?' asked the MP.

'Yes, of course, sir,' Flóvent admitted. 'But he was being cooperative, so we were keen to demonstrate a degree of trust in him. That's why we didn't use handcuffs. We simply couldn't have foreseen that he would resort to such a desperate act. It was an accident. Deeply regrettable, it goes without saying, but an accident nonetheless.'

'What then? Was he taken to hospital or . . . ?'

'No, sir. He was killed instantly, and his body is now in the National Hospital mortuary. You can –'

At that moment the door opened and a young man entered the room.

'There you are,' he said, then immediately sensed from the tension in the air that something serious was afoot. 'What's – ?'

'Hólmbert, dear,' said the woman, rising and going over to him. 'This policeman says Jónatan's dead.'

'Jónatan – dead?' echoed the young man.

'The poor boy was run over by a car,' said the woman. 'It's simply ghastly. And there's more – he was in police custody at the time and this officer is claiming that Jónatan killed that girl – the one who was found behind the theatre. Isn't that madness? Isn't it absolutely preposterous?'

'He was a suspect,' corrected Flóvent.

'Jónatan?' gasped the young man incredulously.

'Isn't it utter madness?' said the woman again. 'I've never heard such outrageous nonsense. That he met her in the Shadow District and . . . and mistreated her . . .'

The young man looked at Flóvent. 'Is that true?'

Flóvent nodded.

'I . . . don't believe it.'

'Did you know him well, sir?' asked Flóvent.

The young man seemed distracted, and Flóvent had to repeat the question.

'I . . . we were pals,' he said. 'Is he really dead? Jónatan, dead! And you actually believe that he . . . ?'

'Assaulted the girl? Yes, I'm afraid so,' said Flóvent. 'Unfortunately the evidence is compelling. He was about to take us to the scene of the crime when he escaped and met with this tragic accident.'

43

They stood silently in the drawing room as the unbelievable news Flóvent had brought them started to sink in: Jónatan, a young man they knew well, was not only dead but actually suspected of Rósamunda's murder, and several months earlier he had allegedly assaulted her somewhere in the Shadow District. The MP and his wife seemed shattered by the news, while their son Hólmbert seemed unable to take it in. After giving them a little time to recover their composure, Flóvent began tentatively asking questions. They answered readily, volunteering information, until the woman suddenly announced that she could bear it no longer and asked her husband to take her outside.

'I haven't seen Jónatan for quite a while,' she said. 'But he used to come round occasionally, and he was a good boy, I can assure you of that, whatever else you may think of him.'

'Talk to Hólmbert,' said the MP as he escorted his wife out of the room. 'He knew Jónatan best. Hólmbert, old man,' he added to his son, 'you'll tell him all you know in case it can help the police get to the bottom of this dreadful affair.'

Hólmbert nodded distractedly, apparently still digesting the news. He took out a packet of cigarettes and lit one with a pre-occupied air, then offered the packet to Flóvent, who declined.

'I'm absolutely flabbergasted,' he said. 'Jónatan? Who would have believed it?'

'It's particularly hard when it involves someone you thought you knew well,' said Flóvent.

Hólmbert looked at him. 'Perhaps it's . . .'

'Sir?'

'Perhaps it's inappropriate of me to bring this up in the circumstances but . . .'

'Bring up what, sir?'

'At least, I didn't like to say anything while my mother was present.' Hólmbert went over to the door to check that it was definitely shut. 'But to be honest I was on the verge of contacting the police about Jónatan.'

'Oh?' said Flóvent. 'Why was that?'

'He . . . it must have been about three days ago. He asked if we could meet up because he had something on his mind. I ran into him at the university – I'm reading law there, though actually it bores me silly. Anyway, he seemed rather weighed down by something, so I said all right. I went round to his digs that evening and immediately got the feeling he was very anxious, and when I asked what was wrong he started talking about the girl you mentioned. Rósamunda, wasn't it? I'd read about her in the papers, of course. I found him strangely evasive, as if he had a bad conscience.'

'What exactly did he say, sir?'

'Not much. Just that he'd met her at a university dance a few months ago and they'd gone for a walk out to Seltjarnarnes, then intended to go to her place afterwards. He was reluctant to say much more. He'd recognised her from a shop where he'd taken some clothes to be mended.'

'The Stitch?'

'I'm afraid I don't remember the name.'

'What happened?'

'Well, it wasn't very coherent but my understanding was that he'd tried to . . . to take advantage of her. She'd seemed willing at first, then . . . then begged him to stop. But he didn't.'

'And he told you the girl in question was Rósamunda?'

Hólmbert nodded. 'There was a struggle which left her in a bit of a mess, so he told her to say she'd had a run-in with the *huldufólk*. That was Jónatan's area – he was obsessed with the elves and that kind of thing. He said he'd make her rue the day if she went to the police.'

'And he told you all this?'

'Well, I drew it out of him. I'd never have believed he was capable of such a thing. He was quite distraught – after the event. If it's true, then naturally his behaviour was reprehensible.'

'Was Jónatan aware that she'd been carrying his child and had an abortion?'

'I very much doubt that,' said Hólmbert. 'At all events, he didn't breathe a word about it.'

'Did he openly admit to having killed her?'

'He more or less came right out and said so.'

'Whatever for?'

'I think she'd threatened to report him. I was getting ready to pass all of this on to the police but couldn't bring myself to do it straight away because . . . I knew Jónatan quite well. It was painful, and I could hardly believe it.'

'He's a relation of your mother's?'

'I suppose that was part of it,' said Hólmbert, looking a little shamefaced. 'Of course I urged Jónatan to come clean of his own accord because frankly I found the whole thing deeply shocking. And, as I said, I could tell he was suffering. I haven't breathed a word of this to another soul, by the way; not even to my family.'

'Not even to your father?'

'No. Not to a soul.'

'Did Jónatan happen to mention another girl, called Hrund?'

Hólmbert frowned pensively, then shook his head. He had a thin face, fair, prematurely receding hair, and a small mouth with lips so thin they formed a single line above his chin. His nose was narrow and finely sculpted and his whole appearance conveyed an air of sensitivity.

'She lived in Öxarfjördur,' said Flóvent. 'Jónatan was working on the roads there when she disappeared.'

'No, he only mentioned the one girl.'

'What made him do it, do you think?'

Hólmbert stubbed out his cigarette. 'As far as I could work out, it was the promiscuity that got to him. The Situation. He loathed it – the way women and girls were making sluts of themselves, running after the soldiers and the way the soldiers used them. He thought it was disgraceful. That came as no surprise to me because he'd often ranted about it. About how debauched and squalid the Situation was. It really got to him.'

'And Rósamunda was forced to pay the price?'

'Well, I don't know if it was exactly like that, but those were his views,' said Hólmbert. 'Look, I'd be grateful if you could leave my name out of this. I feel rather a heel for telling you, as if I . . . Of course, I should have alerted you earlier. But we were good pals, you see, Jónatan and I.'

At that moment the door opened and the member of parliament reappeared and closed it carefully behind him.

'Please forgive me,' he said to Flóvent. 'Has Hólmbert been able to provide any assistance? It's shattering news you've brought us. I've already made arrangements to get in touch with his parents. In the circumstances I imagine they'd rather this whole affair was kept quiet. That the poor boy's funeral should be conducted in private. There's nothing standing in the way of that, is there?'

'I don't believe so,' said Flóvent. 'They're free to collect his body for burial whenever they like, although the inquiry's still in progress.'

'Still in progress? Why's that?'

'Because we still need to interview his parents, piece the story together, verify the odd detail here and there. Your son has already been extremely helpful in that regard.'

'I do appreciate that you're only doing your job, officer, but don't you think his parents will suffer enough without your interrogating them about this whole unfortunate business? From what you've told us, it sounds like an open and shut case. If you like, I could have a word with your superiors about winding it up.'

'Well, sir, with all due respect, that —'

'This matter impinges more or less directly on my family,' continued the MP, his voice taking on an authoritative edge. 'I do hope you understand my position. It's unfortunate and could become very awkward if we don't take steps to limit the damage. The boy was here in Reykjavík under our protection, thanks to my wife's generosity and the family connection, but I'd be sorry if we were all dragged through the mud because of him. Merely because we offered him a helping hand. Naturally we feel a great deal of pity for the poor boy and the way he was led astray, and, it goes without saying, for the unfortunate girl, but that's not the issue. The issue is how to prevent the damage from spreading any further than it already has. The situation is regrettable enough as it is. Do you follow me?'

The MP and his wife had used their time well, Flóvent reflected; he suspected that this had been their real reason for leaving the room.

'You can count on me to act with discretion, sir,' he said, 'and you're welcome to talk to my superiors, should you so wish. I appreciate that this is going to be an ordeal for all concerned, and I'll bear that in mind.'

'That's all I wanted to hear,' said the MP. 'This is an extremely sensitive matter. Best to draw a tactful veil over it in the circumstances.'

44

Konrád sat in his kitchen in Árbær, sipping red wine and contemplating his visit to Magnús in Borgarnes. Helena Eyjólfsdóttir was crooning 'The City Is Sleeping' on the stereo, and as the old hit played on, he could feel a sense of calm spreading through his body. He was dog-tired from the drive, from struggling to make sense of what he had unearthed, but at the same time he felt satisfied with the progress he had made. Sensed that he was tantalisingly close to a breakthrough. Tomorrow he would go and see the other brother, Hólmbert, in defiance of Magnús's warning that it would be a waste of time. He was convinced that Thorson had tried to make contact with Hólmbert, that it was one of the last things he had done. And Konrád wanted to know if he had succeeded.

He reviewed the evidence so far: Rósamunda had been assaulted, possibly at the member of parliament's house, and refused to run any more errands there for her boss. The member of parliament in question had been on a visit up north at the time of Hrund's disappearance. Both girls were around the same age and both had blamed, or been ordered to blame, the *huldufólk* for their assaults. Was it conceivable that the MP himself had been involved? Was that the conclusion Thorson had reached? If so, why had the significance only belatedly struck him now, rather than at the time, in 1944? And what had precipitated his recent enquiries relating to the case? He had apparently been badly shaken when he learnt of Rósamunda's refusal to set foot in the MP's house. Some aspect of the original investigation must have triggered that reaction. He must have had a revelation.

Konrád didn't know much about the MP beyond the date of his death, so he went online again to refresh his memory of the man's career. Shortly after the inauguration of the republic in 1944, he had retired from politics and acquired an import company that was not only still in business but had grown to become one of the largest of its kind in Iceland. He was rumoured to have exploited his political connections during the years when currency was hard to come by and imports were tightly controlled. Despite withdrawing from mainstream politics, he had remained active behind the scenes of his party and died at a grand old age in the 1970s. The company had passed down to his son, Hólmbert, whom the MP had allegedly favoured over his other children.

They had made their fortune and enjoyed the rewards, thought Konrád as he went into the sitting room to put another Helena Eyjólfsdóttir record on the turntable. While he was up, he opened a second bottle of wine, then sat down again in the kitchen letting the dulcet tones wash over him. He sat in his usual spot, watching the sun set over the city, and thought about the disputes that tore families apart. Money – such a paltry reason to fall out with your kin. Magnús and Hólmbert, the MP's only surviving children, hadn't spoken for decades because of it. Even after Hólmbert became seriously ill, Magnús couldn't bring himself to visit him, hiding behind the excuse that it was too late.

Konrád had also searched for Hólmbert's name and learnt that he had run the firm creditably at his father's side, expanding and diversifying the business so that its share portfolio now included fisheries, an airline and a large building supplies chain. In the last months of the war, after abandoning his law degree at the University of Iceland, Hólmbert had sailed to America, where he made deals and established business connections that were to prove invaluable for the company. His wife, who was still alive, had also sat on the board and was well known for her charity work with organisations such as the Red Cross and Icelandic Church Aid. Hólmbert had ventured into politics like his father, becoming a member of parliament, then a cabinet minister in two governments, before retiring to devote himself entirely to running the firm. He was an honorary member of various business associations and had been decorated by the president for services to his country.

The couple's son had taken over as managing director of the company at the start of the millennium. By then Hólmbert would have been getting on a bit, and, Konrád guessed, the first signs of Alzheimer's might have begun to impair the old man's judgement.

He returned to puzzling over what Magnús had said about his father's presence in the Öxarfjördur area at the time of Hrund's alleged suicide, and he suddenly thought of another question he should have asked. He checked the clock. Perhaps it wasn't too late.

He looked up the number and took out his mobile phone. But as he was waiting for Magnús to pick up, he checked the clock again and realised that the old man had probably gone to bed; his question could easily wait until morning. He was about to hang up when Magnús answered.

'Hello?' he heard him say.

'I'm sorry to ring so late, Magnús. I do hope I didn't wake you.'

'Who is this?'

'Konrád – I visited you earlier today. Were you asleep? It can wait till morning.'

'What . . . why are you ringing?'

'Because of a tiny detail that's been bothering me ever since I left you.'

'What's that?'

'You told me your father had been on a visit to the north of the country around the time the girl went missing.'

'Yes?'

'Did he tell you or your family anything else about the incident, any details he picked up locally about the girl, for example?'

'No, it . . . probably only the bit about the *huldufólk*.'

'Did you hear that from him?'

'Yes, or my brother.'

'Your brother?'

'Yes, Hólmbert.'

'How did he know about it?'

'Oh, because he was travelling up there with our father when it happened. We heard the story from them. And of course I heard more about it later when I went there myself and . . .'

'You're saying Hólmbert was also there at the time of the girl's disappearance?'

'Yes, that's right. Hólmbert was quite the favourite with our father, so he used to take him along on his trips. You were . . .'

The connection deteriorated and Konráð missed what Magnús said.

'Sorry, I didn't catch that, my battery's running low, could you – ?'

'. . . and a man called me recently, enquiring about exactly the same thing,' Magnús was saying. 'About Hólmbert and my father's trip up north. You were telling me earlier about a man you thought might have visited me, but I didn't know what you were talking about. Well, I think it must have been him. The one who phoned. It had completely slipped my mind.'

'Do you mean Thorson? Stefán, that is. Did he ring you?'

'Yes, it must have been the Stefán you mentioned. He said he'd been reminiscing with someone about Öxarfjördur and odd, unexplained incidents that had happened in the area, and the subject of the girl had come up, and I told him . . . he was particularly interested in Hólmbert – I couldn't work out why.'

'What did you tell him?'

'What I told you, that Hólmbert had been visiting the area with our father. Look, I wasn't quite straight with you when you started asking about the Rósamunda affair. The truth is, we were familiar with the incident because a family friend, a relative of ours really, a young man called Jónatan, was involved in some way that was never properly explained to me. It wasn't talked about. I suppose it was a skeleton in our family's closet, so to speak.'

'So you decided to keep quiet about it?'

'I'm not in the habit of discussing private matters like that with strangers.'

'Who was this Jónatan?'

'He was a student at the university.'

'Did you say student?' Konrád remembered Petra saying that Thorson had muttered something about a student as he left. He thought of the notes describing an interview with an unnamed university student. *What happened was a tragedy.*

'Yes, apparently he died after being hit by a car. I didn't know him very well. But my brother Hólmbert and he were friends. And really, that's all I've got to say on the matter. I'm ringing off now. Goodbye.'

45

Thorson picked his way slowly along the path, past graves marked by crosses and headstones which here and there had sunk into the ground, standing crooked, weather-beaten and mossy, their inscriptions nearly illegible. These were the old graves, bearing dates from early last century, from a vanished age. Yet, as Thorson contemplated them, he realised he was older than many of them. A few of the stones dated from the years around the Second World War, and it was to one of these that he made his way now. Since returning to Iceland he had often visited the cemetery and beaten a path to this particular grave. Nowadays the walk took him longer; he used to be quicker on his feet. The years had rolled by, one much the same as the next, for in Iceland he had found the quiet life that he had craved after the war was over. The only surprise was that he should have lived so long. Thorson came to a halt in front of the stone. His mood was lighter than it usually was when he made this pilgrimage. Finally he had news to impart, though he knew it came too late.

Although it had all happened a lifetime ago, Thorson had never quite been able to forget Jónatan or Rósamunda. The other day he had been sitting at the kitchen table, leafing through the papers, when his eye happened to fall on a page of obituaries for a woman who had worked at the dressmaker's where Rósamunda had once been employed. He remembered the woman's name and recognised her face from the accompanying photo. She had been a friend of Rósamunda's. He and Flóvent had interviewed her at the time; she was the girl with the raven-black hair who had told them about Rósamunda's rape. There couldn't be many people who remembered the events surrounding the girl's murder, and their numbers must be rapidly dwindling. He himself was living on borrowed time, and soon there would be no one left who knew or cared about Rósamunda's fate. Obeying a sudden whim, he decided to go along to the funeral.

The church was packed when Thorson arrived and he took a seat towards the back. The minister chanted out of tune and a choir sang the funeral hymn, after which the congregation was invited to attend a reception in the church hall. There Thorson ran into an old engineering acquaintance. They had both been involved in bridging the rivers on the vast glacial sands east of Vík í Mýrdal, which had led to the long-awaited completion of the Ring Road in 1974. Their conversation came round to the deceased who, it turned out, had worked in the engineer's office, and Thorson explained that he had met her because she'd once worked for a dressmaking company that had featured in an old murder investigation. The engineer was intrigued, so Thorson filled him in on the details of the Rósamunda case, at which point it emerged that the man knew a woman called Geirlaug, who was a family friend of the dressmaker in question and still in touch with her daughter. But the engineer couldn't remember the dressmaker's name.

'Really?' said Thorson. 'She had a daughter?'

'An only child, I believe,' said the engineer. 'Wasn't there something a bit fishy about that theatre case? Geirlaug was talking about it once.'

'Fishy? How do you mean?'

'Oh, I forget what it was.'

'Something linked to the dressmaker?'

'Yes, I expect that was it.'

'Had this Geirlaug been talking to her then?' asked Thorson.

'Yes, or to her daughter, I think.'

A couple of days later, unable to shake off his curiosity, Thorson rang the engineer's friend Geirlaug and asked her for the daughter's name. She was happy to oblige, informing him that the dressmaker's daughter was called Petra. When it came to actually contacting her, though, Thorson dithered a little before finally going ahead. He needn't have worried. Petra was friendly and invited him round. She was the one who provided him with the missing piece: Rósamunda had refused to take any deliveries to the Reykjavík home of the very member of parliament who, together with his son Hólmbert, had been instrumental in implicating Jónatan and persuading Flóvent to drop the investigation.

Rósamunda's case had haunted Thorson ever since that rainy day when he said farewell to Flóvent on the Reykjavík docks, and all through the fighting that followed and the subsequent years of peace. After his demobilisation, Thorson had headed home to Canada to finish his degree. He had realised his dream of qualifying as a structural engineer, and when his father died after a brief spell in hospital, Thorson decided he had nothing to lose. He sent a speculative letter to Iceland, which resulted in the offer of an engineering contract. He had only intended to spend a few years there, while he tried to achieve some sort of equilibrium after the turmoil of his wartime service. His mother had noticed the change in him since he came home from the fighting in Europe, noticed a tendency to depression, anxiety and tension that was quite unlike her son. Thorson never spoke much about his part in the war, merely commenting that it was nothing to be proud of. Despite being decorated by the Canadian Army for his bravery, he insisted that he was no hero; the real heroes were the comrades he had lost and still missed.

'What are you going to do in Iceland?' asked his mother. If anything, she had tried to discourage him from going.

'Living there agreed with me.'

'Are you planning to come home again?'

'Oh, I think so. But I need to go back. To try and recapture the peace of mind I found there. Take a step back. I think it might do me good.'

'Won't you give it a little more thought?' asked his mother as she watched him pack his suitcase.

'I don't think so,' said Thorson. 'Iceland's been on my mind a lot since I left. I'd like to see it again.'

'Is it that murder you told me about? A sense of unfinished business? Is that why you want to go back?'

One evening, when his spirits had been particularly low and he had wanted a break from his futile habit of reliving episodes from the war, Thorson had found himself opening up to his mother about the Rósamunda case. He had often thought back to his time with the military police in Reykjavík, to his collaboration with

Flóvent and the way their last investigation had ended. He had brooded over the inquiry and its outcome, wondering whether there was anything they could have done better or at least differently. He had been unable to put the matter to one side and move on, because he blamed himself for what happened. He should have kept a closer eye on Jónatan. Should have taken his mental state into account. He knew the pangs of conscience Flóvent had suffered were, if anything, even worse. There had been no need to put their feelings into words.

Two days after Jónatan's tragic demise they had met on the docks. Thorson was embarking for England and Flóvent had come to see him off. He described his visit to Jónatan's relatives and expressed his doubts that the case would be taken any further. Thorson could think of nothing to say. Flóvent was clearly shattered by the accident. The MP had pleaded his cause with senior figures in the police, assuring them that no charges would be brought by Jónatan's family. Flóvent would not be reprimanded for professional misconduct, but Thorson could tell that it made no difference to him.

A freezing shower of Icelandic rain broke over their heads as they shook hands, vowing to meet up again once the war was over. The harbour was grey with naval vessels. Flóvent and Thorson could hardly hear each other over the shouting, the throbbing of engines, the pounding of boots as the troops marched past to the waiting ships.

'No,' Thorson told his mother, closing his suitcase. 'I need to get . . . I need a change of scene. I feel restless here. It's hard to explain but, strangely enough, in the heat of battle, when men were dying all around me, my thoughts went there. To the stillness. There's such an incredible clarity and silence in the Icelandic wilderness. And I promised myself that if I lived through the war, I'd go back there one day and experience it again.'

One of the first things Thorson did on arriving in Iceland was look Flóvent up. He remembered the way to his house in the west of town, so one day he went round and knocked on the door, and immediately recognised the man who answered it as Flóvent's father. After they had exchanged greetings, the old man invited him in, remembering him as a colleague of his son's. He said that he was fit for nothing these days; he'd had to give up his job on the docks and was struggling to make ends meet on the dole, an indignity that seemed to him no better than receiving charity.

'You two weren't in touch at all?' asked the old man, when Thorson had explained why he was there.

'No, I'm afraid not. We were planning to meet up again after the war but it's taken longer than I intended. I meant to write to him but never got round to it.'

'So you haven't heard the news?'

'News?'

'I'm sorry you should have to find out like this but my son's dead. He passed away two years ago.'

'He's dead?'

'Yes. He left the police shortly after that last case of yours and took a desk job with the civil service – the tax office, in fact – and worked there right up until he went into hospital.'

'I'm very sorry to hear that. How . . . ?'

'He'd been suffering from stomach pains for a long time but hadn't done anything about it. Turned out he had cancer.' The old man passed a hand over his eyes. 'He died a miserable death, a wretched death, the poor lad. You can find him in the graveyard near here on Sudurgata. Close to his mother and sister.'

'I didn't know,' said Thorson. 'Please accept my condolences.'

'Thank you. Well, it can't be helped. The poor lad.'

'I . . . to be honest, that was the last thing I was expecting to hear.'

'Yes, well, none of us knows how long we've got.'

Thorson couldn't think of a reply to this, and Flóvent's father seemed lost in his recollections. They sat for a while in a silence broken only by the tiny plinks from a dripping kitchen tap.

'Did he ever talk to you about the case of the girl behind the theatre?' asked Thorson at last.

'No, very seldom. Deliberately avoided bringing it up, it seemed to me. Didn't want to remember. I got the feeling it had never been properly cleared up, but he didn't know what to do about it.'

'What hadn't been cleared up?'

'I don't know. But I got the feeling he wasn't happy about the way it ended. I expect it was because of the accident with your prisoner.'

'Of course, it didn't end well.'

'No, that's what he said. My son seemed to grow old before his time, and I blame it on that damned business.'

'It was a difficult investigation.'

'It hit him very hard. I don't believe Flóvent was ever satisfied with the way the case was closed. In fact, I think he may have wanted to reopen it before he died. Of course, you never got his letter.'

'His letter?'

'He wrote to you but the letter was returned.'

'Which letter?'

'He didn't know where to address it, so he tried sending it to your regiment but they sent it back. It should be around here somewhere. I found it among his papers after he died.'

The old man went into his bedroom and came out again with an envelope addressed to Thorson, which he handed over. Thorson opened it carefully and read the enclosed letter.

Reykjavík, 13 December 1947

My dear Thorson,

I hope this note will reach you. I don't know if you made it through the war alive, but I wanted to try to find out.

Over the last couple of years I've often found myself thinking of you and our work together. I don't know if I ever thanked you properly for all your assistance, cooperation and support, so I wanted to make amends for that now.

I can only begin to imagine the horrors you must have endured during the fighting. I've read a great deal about the Normandy landings and believe I have some idea, if only superficially, of the devastating bloodbath you must have witnessed first-hand.

Our final case is never far from my thoughts. I believe we came to the right conclusion, yet sometimes I feel a creeping suspicion that we could have done better. Pursued a different line of inquiry, perhaps. But this is probably only my uneasy conscience speaking, because of what happened to the boy. I have found it hard to come to terms with the way it ended. Naturally his family up north were shattered when they heard the news, but they didn't blame us for what happened once they were apprised of all the facts.

Our principal witness and helper in all this was the MP's

son, Hólmbert. He confirmed all our suspicions about
Jónatan, and this should have set my mind at rest, but for
some reason the matter won't give me any peace.

Well, my dear friend, I'd be grateful if you would send
word, even if only a few short lines, to let me know how you
are. I should be greatly reassured.

Yours, Flóvent

Thorson stood contemplating his old friend's grave for a while,
then made the sign of the cross and said a short prayer. Flóvent's
father was lying near at hand, and beyond his stone was one of the
mass graves that had been dug at the height of the Spanish flu,
where Flóvent's mother and sister lay beneath the turf, side by side
with other victims of the epidemic.

Rest in peace read the inscription on the headstone, and Thorson
knew that if ever that prayer was appropriate for someone, it was
for Flóvent.

46

With a little detective work, Thorson had discovered that Hólmbert was in a nursing home in Reykjavík, and it was there that he headed after his visit to the graveyard. He didn't know the man from Adam, had never met him, though he had been a familiar face in the press over the course of his political career. His name had lingered in Thorson's memory because Flóvent had made a point of noting how very helpful Hólmbert had been.

Thorson took the bus. Conveniently enough, it stopped close to the cemetery and its route also went right past the nursing home. He had given up driving. The fast-paced roads, the impatience of the other drivers, the heavy congestion these days: it had all become too much for him. Taking the bus was a far more pleasant way to travel, except in bad weather when it was easier to take a cab.

There were few other passengers to distract him, so he fell to thinking about his visit to the dressmaker's daughter, Petra, and what she had told him about Rósamunda's refusal to set foot in the MP's house; about Hólmbert's role in the whole affair, and his own recent telephone conversation with Magnús in Borgarnes, during which he had learnt for the first time about the presence of Magnús's father and brother up north at the time of Hrund's disappearance. Little by little the pieces of the puzzle were falling into place. Pieces he'd known nothing about until now. Pieces that had been deliberately withheld from him and Flóvent, because certain people had thought they were best swept under the carpet. The words of Flóvent's letter were running through his mind as he walked in through the doors of the nursing home: *for some reason the matter won't give me any peace.*

He asked for Hólmbert and was given his room number. He summoned the lift. Up to now he hadn't discussed his enquiries and suspicions with Birgitta for fear of worrying her. Besides, he wanted to wait and see what came to light before he started spreading gossip that might not actually be true.

Having located the right room, Thorson saw a man of about his own age lying in bed, surrounded by photographs of loved ones, children's drawings, and vases of flowers.

'Hólmbert?' Thorson said, inching his way into the room. 'Is that you?'

The man didn't answer, or react in any way. He was lying flat on his back and one would have thought he was asleep were it not for the fact that his eyes were open, staring up at the ceiling.

'Excuse my barging in on you like this but –'

Thorson broke off when a nurse breezed in with a tray of medicines and a glass of water. Raising the patient up in bed, he helped him to swallow the pills.

'Am I in the right room?' asked Thorson. 'This is Hólmbert, isn't it?'

'Yes,' said the nurse. 'You are . . . ? Can I help you?'

'I haven't visited him before.'

'Were you trying to talk to him? Hólmbert's very far gone, I'm afraid. He's got Alzheimer's and hardly reacts at all to visitors.'

'Oh, I had no idea. Alzheimer's, you say?'

'Are you a relative?'

'An old acquaintance. I haven't . . . we haven't been in contact for many years. Does that mean there's no point talking to him?'

'You can talk all you like, but don't expect any answers,' the nurse said and continued on his rounds.

Thorson closed the door and sat down beside Hólmbert's bed. He pitied the man his wretched fate, yet, however futile the gesture, he felt a compulsion to share with him the reason for his visit.

'My name's Thorson,' he began. 'One-time friend and colleague of a man called Flóvent. We conducted a murder investigation here in Reykjavík during the war. The victim's name was Rósamunda and she worked for a dressmaker your family did business with. She used to take deliveries to your house until one day she flatly refused to go near the place again. Now it so happens that a few months before she died she was raped and her attacker told her to blame it on the *huldufólk*.'

Hólmbert lay motionless, staring at the ceiling with dull, colourless eyes.

'Three years earlier a girl from Öxarfjördur, called Hrund, came out with the same story about being attacked by one of the *huldufólk*. She was so distraught after her ordeal that she vanished shortly afterwards. Took her own life perhaps. Or had an accident. At all events her body was never found. Then again, it's possible that she was disposed of, and that the culprit was an important man from Reykjavík who just happened to be visiting the area at the time.'

Thorson shifted closer to Hólmbert.

'Can you tell me anything about that?'

Hólmbert didn't react.

'Had you left the area or were you still in Öxarfjördur when she disappeared?'

The man in the bed lay deathly still.

'The business of the *huldufólk* establishes a link between the two girls,' Thorson went on doggedly. 'Their stories were identical. Flóvent and I caught the man who killed Rósamunda. He as good as confessed to us. His name was Jónatan. A relative of yours, but not a blood relative. You helped us solve the case; you did your bit for the investigation and effectively incriminated your friend. Case closed. It didn't hurt that Flóvent and I were already receptive to the idea. We'd made a mistake – Jónatan died in our custody. Perhaps, deep down, we felt that if what you told us was true then he'd got his just deserts for what he did to Rósamunda and there was no need for us to feel so guilty. We latched on to your story. In fact, your testimony couldn't have come at a better time.'

Hólmbert began to stir and suddenly turned his head towards Thorson.

'You know what I believe?' said Thorson, looking him in the eye. 'I believe it was you. You murdered Rósamunda, and you ruined Hrund's life and maybe even killed her too. I still don't know if you'd left the area by the time she vanished but I'm going to find out. You got the idea about the elves from your friend

Jónatan. He was the expert. That's why we were so sure it was him. But it wasn't: it was you. You'd heard him talking about folklore, about encounters with the hidden people. That's what gave you the idea. Well, I'm going to make it public; let the world know your dirty secret. Jónatan was innocent when we arrested him. He was innocent, for God's sake!'

Hólmbert stared at Thorson. The corners of his mouth trembled, his pale eyes began to water and his face twitched as if he were about to speak. His bloodless lips formed a word but all that emerged was a sigh.

'What?' said Thorson. 'What?'

Hólmbert strained with all his might to articulate the word: 'Ró . . . samund . . .' he whispered.

At that moment there was a noise outside in the corridor, and the door opened.

47

Konrád drove up to the nursing home. He had called several such institutions in the capital area before finally discovering Hólmbert's whereabouts. Fortunately, there were no other Hólmberts of a similar age. During his brief phone conversation with one of the staff, Konrád had posed as a friend from the countryside hoping to visit. The woman, who was very chatty, knew a bit about Hólmbert's circumstances and explained that his condition was getting progressively worse. He had deteriorated, especially in the last few weeks, to the point where he was totally unaware of his surroundings and now required round-the-clock care. All the same, the woman encouraged Konrád to come and see him since visits were always appreciated, even if the patient himself was unaware of them. In most cases the relatives would be grateful. When Konrád asked if Hólmbert received many visitors, the woman said not really; most of his friends were dead and he didn't have a large family.

Entering the foyer, Konrád approached the reception desk, where he learnt that Hólmbert was on the third floor, and was directed to the lifts. The place reminded him of Vigga's nursing home. The same combination of bustling staff and shuffling patients; some walking unaided, others reliant on Zimmer frames; some fully clothed, others in their dressing gowns. Inside the rooms the elderly residents lay in bed, asleep, reading or listening to the radio; a few lifted their heads as Konrád walked past.

Hólmbert wasn't in his room, and when Konrád enquired after him, he was told the old man was in the lounge. He was wheeled there every morning and passed the time staring at the TV. Konrád asked if he was confined to a wheelchair and was told yes, almost entirely these days. In spite of this, he asked if Hólmbert could have left the nursing home at all recently and was assured that he hadn't gone anywhere for at least two months.

'I'm afraid his Alzheimer's is pretty advanced, poor old fellow,' said the nurse.

Konrád found Hólmbert in the lounge, where he was sitting slumped in his wheelchair, eyes glued to a cartoon. The volume was turned down but he seemed content to watch the flickering screen. He was wearing a warm, blue-checked dressing gown, below which bony, white shins were visible above his slippers. There was a white floss of hair on his head and he had several days' worth of stubble on his jaw. The eyes in his gaunt face were small and colourless like his hair; his lips invisible around a wrinkled, pursed mouth. He didn't so much as look round when Konrád drew up a chair beside him.

'Hólmbert?' said Konrád.

The man didn't answer or let this interruption distract him from the screen.

'Hólmbert?' Konrád repeated.

Unresponsive, Hólmbert continued to gawp at the cartoon characters.

Konrád had only a superficial understanding of Alzheimer's, though he had tried to read up on it before coming here. He knew it was a degenerative brain disease that affected the short-term memory but, in its early stages at least, had less impact on the long-term memory. The disease was incurable, despite the development of new drugs that inhibited its progress, and it led slowly but inexorably to utter dependency and loss of the power of speech, culminating in total dementia and death within ten years or so. The disease also had a devastating impact on the next of kin, who were forced to look on, helpless, as their previously fit and healthy loved one fell prey to a pitiless mental and physical decline.

'I wondered if I could ask you about something that happened a long time ago,' Konrád said, 'during the Second World War. It involved two girls, one called Rósamunda, the other Hrund.'

Still no reaction from Hólmbert.

'Do you remember those names?'

Hólmbert gazed at the television as if he were alone in the room.

'Hólmbert?'

The old man didn't answer.

'Do you remember Rósamunda? Do you remember a girl called Rósamunda who worked at a dressmaker's?'

As the cartoon finished and another began, Konrád caught a hint of movement through the glass in the door. A man, in his fifties at a guess, was hurrying along the corridor towards the lounge. A slim, handsome figure in a dark suit. Konrád watched his approach, assuming he would turn aside into one of the residents' rooms, but instead he burst into the lounge and brusquely demanded to know who Konrád was.

'I heard downstairs that he had a visitor,' the man said. 'May I ask who you are?'

'The name's Konrád.' He rose to his feet and held out a hand in greeting. The man shook it briefly.

'What business do you have with my father? How do you know him?'

'I don't actually,' said Konrád. 'You are . . . ?'

'I'm his son. My name's Benjamín. If you don't know him, what are you doing here?'

'I came to ask if he'd had a visitor recently, an old man called Thorson. He may have been using the name Stefán Thórdarson.'

'Thorson? Stefán Thórdarson?'

'Yes, but I gather your father won't be able to help me. My sympathies. It must be a harrowing illness.'

'Thank you. It is.'

'Do you know if this Thorson I mentioned came to see him?'

'Thorson? No, not that I'm aware. Though he may have visited without my knowledge. Dad had a lot of friends . . . *has* a lot of friends, and I haven't met them all.'

'No, of course not. The thing is, I'm investigating an old criminal case from the war years, and I thought he might be able to help me with some information. But I suppose that's out of the question.'

'There's no point asking him anything. No point even talking to him any more.'

'May I ask if you've heard of the case?'

'From the Second World War?'

'Yes. A girl was murdered. Her name was Rósamunda.'

'My family's familiar with that case,' said Benjamín. 'But I don't see what it has to do with you.'

'I used to be a detective, though I'm officially retired now. But CID asked me to dig around for information on this man Thorson, or Stefán. I assume you'll have seen the news – he was found dead in his flat and the police believe he was deliberately smothered.'

Benjamín nodded. 'I saw the news.'

'I've established that Thorson made a phone call to your Uncle Magnús in Borgarnes. What he learnt during their conversation would almost certainly have propelled him to visit your father next. This would have been only a couple of weeks ago. I'm almost sure Thorson came here to see him. Were you aware of the fact?'

'No, I wasn't.'

'What about you yourself?'

'Me?'

'Did you meet Thorson?'

'No.'

'Are you sure?'

'Sure? Are you calling me a liar?'

Konrád shrugged.

'May I ask on whose authority you're here?' demanded Benjamín.

'I'm assisting the police. If you'd like confirmation, you can ring CID and ask to speak to an inspector called Marta.'

'Well, you could try talking to the staff here,' said Benjamín, in a slightly more conciliatory tone. 'There's a chance they might remember the man, though I don't recall having met him. Magnús hasn't spoken to my father for decades, so I don't know how reliable an informant you'll find him. They broke off relations completely, you know, and I wouldn't put it past Magnús to blacken my father's name.'

'Are you implying that Magnús was lying about your father?'

'Frankly, I'd rather not discuss my family's private affairs with a total stranger,' said Benjamín. 'Now, if you don't mind, I'd like to be left in peace with my father.'

'Of course,' said Konrád, 'I'm sorry to intrude. Just one last thing. You knew at once which case I was referring to when I mentioned Rósamunda. May I ask how come?'

'If I tell you, will you leave us alone?'

'Of course.'

'Our immediate family was aware of the girl's fate, though it didn't spread much further,' Benjamín said, making no attempt to hide his impatience. 'The police were quick to track down her killer. His name was Jónatan and he was a friend of ours. The incident affected my family very badly, as you can imagine. To make matters worse, Jónatan died in police custody. Apparently he escaped and ran in front of a car. The whole business was very unfortunate. Both the fact that he killed the girl, obviously, and also the way he lost his life. My grandfather was an MP at the time and used his influence to hush the matter up. He spoke to the girl's parents and made them see the unpleasantness it could stir up. After all, the facts weren't in doubt; the perpetrator had been caught. In my grandfather's view there was no call for our family to be dragged into the scandal.'

As Konrád listened it became clear to him why there was no record of the case in the archives. The police must have been very confident they'd got the right man for them to have colluded in a cover-up. Either that or the MP had sufficient clout to go over their heads and supress the inquiry.

'I have reason to believe that Thorson had unearthed some new information about your father,' said Konrád. 'He was one of the investigating officers at the time, working with the military police, and could never forget the case, perhaps because he felt it had never been properly resolved. Are you by any chance familiar with the story of a girl called Hrund, who lived in the Öxarfjördur area?'

At that moment they heard a noise from the old man in the wheelchair and turned to look at him.

'. . . ósamu . . . ?'

They both stared at Hólmbert. His gaze remained fixed on the television, but it was clear that he was trying to say something. He appeared to be lost in a world of his own, completely oblivious to his son's presence, let alone Konrád's.

'. . . ós . . . am . . . un . . . ?' he whispered hoarsely at the TV screen.

'Dad, it's me Benjamín, your son.'

Hólmbert didn't react or shift his gaze from the television.

'Hólmbert?' tried Konrád. 'Can you hear me?'

The old man sat motionless as if the two visitors had nothing to do with him.

'What's he trying to say?' asked Konrád.

'I haven't the faintest idea. Look, you'd better go.'

'Didn't it sound to you like –?'

'It could've been anything,' interrupted Benjamín, his patience running out. 'I'm asking you to leave him alone. It's . . . I'm asking you to leave us alone.' He went over and stood by the door. 'Please, just go.'

Konrád decided to back down. 'OK, no problem, I'm sorry to inconvenience you. I really didn't mean to intrude.' He went out

317

into the corridor and heard the door swing to behind him. As he was leaving the nursing home, he took out his phone and rang Marta.

'What now?' she asked.

'Have you still got those recordings from the CCTV cameras in the vicinity of Stefán Thórdarson's flat?'

'Yes, a whole pile of them. All bloody useless.'

'Why useless?'

'Because I don't know what I'm looking for. They just show people coming and going, and I don't know who any of them are.'

'Let me have a look at them.'

'Why? What have you found out?'

'I'm not sure,' said Konrád. 'I'd need to check the CCTV footage. But, unlike you, at least I know what I'm looking for.'

'Hurry up then,' said Marta. 'I was just about to head home.'

48

It wasn't easy for Konrád to persuade Benjamín to meet him behind the National Theatre. Benjamín flatly refused at first, protesting that he didn't have time for such nonsense and insisting that Konrád leave him and his family alone. Meeting behind the theatre was an absurd idea. He had no interest in Konrád's melodramatic attempts to smear his family. What happened in the past belonged in the past. Rósamunda's murder had been solved by the police seventy years ago; her killer had been caught, so he saw absolutely no reason to waste his time on wild conjectures and rumours.

Konrád countered that the matter concerned not only Rósamunda's case but some new evidence that had come to light regarding Thorson's recent demise. He reiterated that he would wait for Benjamín behind the theatre. There were a few details he wanted to run by him. If Benjamín didn't show up, it would make no difference; the matter would progress to the next level, though Konrád's part in it was finished.

'Have you notified the police?' asked Benjamín, after a weighty pause.

'I've shared some of my findings,' said Konrád, 'but I've yet to give them my final report.'

At this, Benjamín retorted that he wanted nothing more to do with him and hung up. Konrád put his phone away. He sat in his car, peering into the doorway where Rósamunda had been found alone, discarded, back in the days when the world had been at war and the theatre had been an army depot. He was parked on Lindargata, a stone's throw from Skuggasund. The streets were quiet. A black cat slunk across the road and darted into a nearby garden. A pair of lovers walked hand in hand along the pavement and disappeared in the direction of Arnarhóll.

Konrád got out of his car, walked over to the theatre and gazed up its obsidian-dashed walls, studying the decorative features designed to resemble pillars of columnar basalt, with their allusions to the country's geology and centuries-old folklore. Within these thick, dark walls human dramas were staged for public entertainment; sorrow and joy were doled out in equal measure, just as they were in life itself. The difference being that when the curtain fell the performance was over and the audiences could go home. Whereas in the real world the drama never ended.

Three quarters of an hour later, Konrád decided to call it a day and head home, having given up all hope that Benjamín would put in an appearance. He opened the car door and was about to ease himself into the driver's seat when he noticed a figure standing motionless on the corner of Skuggasund, head turned in his direction.

'Benjamín?' Konrád called.

The man crossed the road towards him and Konrád saw that it

was indeed Benjamín. So Konrád had at least succeeded in whetting his curiosity.

'Why did you ask me to come down here?' asked Benjamín. 'What's all this in aid of?'

'Thank you for coming.'

'You didn't exactly give me much choice.'

'Do you find yourself drawn here at times? Because of what happened?'

'I sometimes go to the theatre, if that's what you're asking. Apart from that I have no reason to come here.'

'Are you sure about that?'

'I can't imagine why I should. I don't know what you're trying to insinuate. What happened here had absolutely nothing to do with me or my family.'

'Yet you came anyway.'

Benjamín didn't reply to this.

The theatre was illuminated by small floodlights that threw strange shapes on the walls as in a shadow play.

'I grew up around here,' said Konrád conversationally. 'In these streets. Among these buildings. It was here that I first heard about Rósamunda. About her being found in that doorway over there. The incident affected me directly, so maybe that's why I can't let it go. You see, a seance was held at my house for Rósamunda's parents. Disinterring bodies was in fashion at the time and phoney mediums saw a chance to get in on the act, though that's another story. I don't know how or why, but this particular medium told my father that alongside Rósamunda he'd sensed another girl, whose spirit could find no rest. Then, the other day, I learnt about the existence of a second girl, called Hrund, from an old neighbour of mine from the Shadow District. If I believed in seances,

321

which I don't, I'd have thought the girl the medium mentioned must have been this Hrund.'

'You said you had new evidence,' said Benjamín impatiently. 'Is that it? Is that all? A seance? Paranormal claptrap?'

Konráð smiled. 'You told me you hadn't met Thorson at the nursing home. I believe he went there after discovering that your father had been in the north when Hrund went missing. The news struck him as significant; he must have regretted that he didn't make that discovery at the time. That's why he urgently wanted to go and see your father and try to establish the truth.'

'You said something new had come to light. What's new about any of this? Don't tell me you dragged me all the way down here just for that?'

'Did you visit Thorson after he went to see your father?'

'No.'

'Did he tell you he was going to have the case reopened? Alert the press? Bring it to the attention of the public?'

'I never spoke to the man,' said Benjamín.

'What if I tell you that we have CCTV recordings from two locations close to Thorson's home, both of which show you in the area at the time of his death?'

'CCTV? What are you talking about?' asked Benjamín after a moment's silence.

'You hurried away across the school playground after your visit to Thorson,' said Konráð. 'And you passed the entrance to the bank on your way to his place, though naturally you weren't in such a hurry at that stage. The timing fits. You must have gone to see him at lunchtime. Somehow you managed to trick him. To allay his suspicions. Perhaps you pretended to leave. Left the door on the latch and crept back in after he'd gone for a rest. Somehow, I don't know exactly how, you managed to catch him unawares –'

'This is absolute bullshit,' protested Benjamín.

'You were careful to park some distance from his building. Had you already decided what you were going to do before you knocked on his door?'

'That's it,' snapped Benjamín. 'I have nothing more to say to you.'

'Your grandfather made a favourite of Hólmbert and left the family business to him, over all his other children. Did he know about his son? Did he know what kind of monster he was?'

'My father isn't a monster,' objected Benjamín. 'He's a desperately ill man who has a right to die in peace.'

'Unlike Thorson, you mean?'

Benjamín stared wildly at him.

'Are you aware of what your father did?' said Konrád. 'Do you know his story? You must do. Or you'd never have gone round to see Thorson in the first place.'

'This is a waste of time,' said Benjamín and, spinning on his heel, stormed off towards Skuggasund. Konrád remained where he was, watching him go. He had been toying with a theory that he wanted to try out on Benjamín. He didn't know if it was true, but he wanted to test it on the one man who might be able to confirm it.

'I don't believe it was necessarily your father who was the monster,' he called after Benjamín.

The other man didn't break his stride.

'Did you hear me? I don't believe your father was the monster.'

He saw Benjamín slow down and finally come to a halt on the far side of Lindargata. He stood motionless for a while, hands thrust into his coat pockets, head a little bowed, as if he were deep in thought. Konráð studied his figure from behind and tried to imagine the struggle that must be going on inside him. Finally Benjamín's shoulders sagged in defeat and slowly, reluctantly, he turned.

'What do you mean?'

'I believe your father may have been an innocent pawn in all this,' said Konráð.

'What . . . why . . . what makes you think that?'

'He's not the only possible suspect,' said Konráð. 'He may have been an accessory to the crime since he knew what had happened, but I'm not convinced he was the one who dumped Rósamunda here.'

Benjamín retraced his steps towards him.

'What are you talking about?'

'Family secrets. About your father. And your grandfather. The police didn't know they'd been travelling together up north when Hrund vanished. That information was never revealed. Thorson only found out about it recently. Nor did it ever come out that Rósamunda was frightened of your house. Had Thorson known that at the time, the case would have turned out very differently. I'm guessing he urgently wanted to find out the truth and bring it to the attention of the police before it was too late for him. That's why he went to see your father. And that's why you went to see Thorson.'

'You can't . . . you've got no . . . no . . .'

'Oh, I've got enough,' said Konráð. 'Enough to implicate you in Thorson's murder and enough to reopen the old inquiry into Rósamunda's death.'

'You can't . . .'

'Of course I can. It's over, and you know it. What you did may not have come naturally to you, but you did it all the same, and you need to confess. For your own sake.'

'I . . . we . . .'

Benjamín gazed imploringly at Konrád, as if begging for his understanding. Konrád saw that he was no longer angry. His defiance was
waning, giving way beneath the crushing weight of his guilt. He was
overwhelmed by the repercussions of what he had done – the fallout
from the act he had tried to justify and bury so deep in his conscious-
ness that it seemed almost to belong to someone else.

'Tell me what happened,' said Konrád. 'You didn't have to
shoulder this burden. You did it out of a sense of loyalty to your
family. I can understand that. I can understand what motivated
you, but you went too far. You simply went too far.'

'But the old man was going to expose the whole thing.'

'I know.'

'I couldn't allow it. Just couldn't. I couldn't . . . perhaps if it had
only been my grandfather . . . but my father was . . . my father was
no better . . . I caught the old man in my father's room and threw
him out . . . He started going on about Rósamunda and claiming
that Dad had . . . I didn't know what to do . . .'

Benjamín was incapable of continuing. For a long time he just
stood there, eyes lowered, until finally he drew an envelope from
his pocket and held it out to Konrád. 'I found this in his flat and
didn't dare leave it behind.'

Konrád took the letter. It was addressed to Thorson. Reading it,
he saw that it was from Thorson's old colleague Flóvent. It included
the information that Hólmbert had been the police's main informant in the case against Jónatan.

'I didn't dare leave it behind,' repeated Benjamín. 'After I'd . . .
I'd . . . what I'd done . . .'

49

Hearing a knock at the door, Thorson went and opened it, only to discover that Hólmbert's son had come to see him. It was just after lunch and Thorson had been about to go for a rest as was his habit at this time of day. But he had been half expecting this visit.

'I wanted to apologise for what happened at the nursing home earlier,' said the man, having introduced himself as Benjamín. He seemed perfectly calm now that he was standing on Thorson's landing. 'I had no right to speak to you like that, let alone threaten you,' he went on. 'I was brought up to respect my elders, so I do hope you won't hold it against me. What you told me came as a shock, but my behaviour ... it didn't do me any credit and I wanted to apologise.'

'I was only saying what I believe to be true,' said Thorson.

'Of course, I do see that. I hope you'll forgive me. Ideally, I'd like a chance to get to the bottom of this matter myself, but if you feel the need to involve the police, of course you have every right. And I'll give them all the assistance I can.'

'I'm glad to hear that.'

'To be honest, it came as a horrible shock . . . Look, could I possibly come in for a minute? I feel awkward discussing this on the landing.'

'Please do.'

'Thank you.' Benjamín followed Thorson into the sitting room.

'Unfortunately, I have good grounds for believing that what I told you earlier is true,' said Thorson. 'Although nobody else remembers the events any more, I do, and if my suspicion proves correct, the case will have to be reopened.'

'Yes, of course, I can see that now I've had time to think,' said Benjamín. 'Of course the whole incident needs re-examining. I couldn't agree more. I take it you've already spoken to the police?'

'I'm planning to do so shortly. I know this will be unwelcome news for you. Presumably you'll want to discuss it with your brothers and sisters, and your mother?'

'Yes, naturally. My father's seriously ill. He won't be aware of what's going on even if the case does become a police matter. On health grounds, I very much doubt he'll be forced to stand trial. He hasn't got long to live. I was wondering . . .'

'Yes?'

'I was wondering if I could appeal to your sense of compassion,' said Benjamín. 'If what you say is true, don't you think that justice has already been done? He's suffered. My mother's suffering. It's been incredibly painful for me to see someone who was always so strong and vigorous reduced to an unrecognisable husk by this horrific disease.'

'I suppose that's not really the kind of justice I was talking about,' said Thorson. 'What you say is quite right: your father's a very sick man. But, strange as it may seem to you, he's the least of my concerns. What concerns me is a young man called Jónatan and a detective I once worked with, whose name was Flóvent. I owe it to Jónatan to see that the truth comes out. And Flóvent would have wanted me to clear the boy's name. We abandoned the inquiry just when it should have been getting going. I left the country. Flóvent was badly hit by Jónatan's death. We both were. It's not too late . . .'

'For the truth to come out?'

'Yes.'

'Is there nothing I can do to change your mind?'

'I'm afraid not.'

'Well, in my view what you claim is outrageous,' said Benjamín. 'I still can't understand how you've come to such a conclusion. But that's your business. All I beg is that you shield my father, shield those of us in his family who are still alive . . .'

'I can only do what's right,' said Thorson. 'However badly it may affect you.'

'What do you mean by "right"? Do you really think it's right to destroy my family?' Benjamín hesitated a moment, then continued. 'I'm a wealthy man. If you'd like me to make a donation to some charity or organisation . . . some pension fund . . . either now or in the event you ever find yourself in need . . .'

Thorson shook his head.

'Incidentally, that's in no way intended as an admission,' said Benjamín. 'Only that I know that the moment this becomes public – assuming the police make it public – the rumour mill will start up and it'll be almost impossible to reverse the damage. I run a large company. We're prominent members of society.

Allegations of this kind would be a serious blow to our reputation.'

Thorson didn't know how to respond to this.

'Are you quite sure it was my father who did this to the girls?' asked Benjamín.

'I'm convinced, and I believe a proper investigation will confirm my findings. At least in Rósamunda's case. Hrund is more difficult. Her body was never found, so there's no way of knowing exactly what happened.'

'I see. Fine. Then I'll expect a call from the police shortly. Again, please excuse my behaviour earlier – I lost my temper when you started coming out with those allegations. I hope you won't hold it against me.'

'Thank you for coming to see me,' said Thorson. 'And for your understanding. I believe it's best for everyone concerned to have this matter cleared up once and for all.'

'Yes, maybe you're right.'

Thorson made to rise and show his visitor to the door, but Benjamín told him not to inconvenience himself; he could see himself out. They shook hands in parting.

'You're dead set on this?' said Benjamín.

'Yes, I'm afraid so.'

'All right, goodbye then,' Benjamín said, his voice dropping to a whisper, and he left the room.

Thorson heard the door close behind him and sat for a while, thinking over the visit and wondering if he was doing the right thing by rescuing the case from oblivion and trying to have the investigation reopened. He was feeling more tired than usual after his trip to the nursing home and Benjamín's subsequent visit; the whole business must have affected him more than he'd realised.

He thought about how convenient Jónatan's death had been for Hólmbert. How he had seized the chance to pull the wool over the eyes of the police, blaming Jónatan for the sole purpose of deflecting suspicion from himself.

Gazing unseeing out of the window overlooking the garden, Thorson made up his mind once and for all to take his discoveries to the police without further delay.

He went into the bedroom, opened the drawer of his bedside table and took out the photo of his lover that he'd kept by his side all these years. It brought up painful memories of the lengths to which they'd had to go to keep their relationship a secret, the social stigma that used to be attached to people like them. Although times had changed for the better, out of habit he still kept the picture discreetly tucked away in a drawer. It reminded him of the trials they'd had to endure, the prejudice they'd faced. He took it out almost every day, seeing again that direct gaze, that inscrutable smile, and remembered the time they'd had together, the love they'd shared, the love he had lost and grieved for ever since.

Feeling bone weary, Thorson replaced the photo in the drawer and stretched out on the bed. A succession of images passed through his mind: Rósamunda; Benjamín trying to bribe him with money; Benjamín's father, Hólmbert, the former cabinet minister and his grandfather, the MP. And as always his mind presented him with a picture of Jónatan lying in a pool of blood on Laugavegur, the tiny snowflakes settling on his eyes.

The MP and his son . . . Had the MP been aware of his son's crimes? Had he protected him? Or had the son been protecting his father?

Thorson began to drift off to sleep.

Had the son been protecting his father?

He awoke to find himself struggling to breathe. Even in the midst of his struggle, his mind latched on to the MP, and he knew suddenly that Hólmbert was not the only suspect in Rósamunda's killing. There was his father the MP, whose house it was that Rósamunda had refused to visit; who had been on a trip up north with his son when Hrund was assaulted; who had been of sufficiently high rank, in a sufficiently elevated position, that the girls wouldn't have dared to expose him.

Waking up properly, Thorson found that he really couldn't breathe; his head was being pressed down into the bed by a deadly weight. He struggled to open his mouth and draw breath but was overcome by a terrible sense of suffocation. As he frantically fought for oxygen the realisation hit him that he was being overpowered by someone stronger than himself . . .

50

Benjamín stared without speaking into the dark corner where Rósamunda had been found.

'My father was an accessory,' he said at last. 'He didn't kill Rósamunda. But he walked in on his father standing over her body, and helped him dispose of it. To that extent my father's as culpable as my grandfather was. He was confronted with an impossible dilemma when the police came to see them. Either to come clean and point the finger at his father, or lie and frame his friend, who was already dead.'

'He chose to lie.'

'What would you have done? What would you have done in his place?'

Avoiding Konrád's eye, Benjamín kept his gaze fixed on the doorway, as if he could see Rósamunda's cold, lifeless body.

'He discovered what his father had done and had to live with that knowledge for the rest of his life. Had to take care that the truth never came out. Could never be free of the guilt.'

'How did you know?'

'It was his illness.'

'His illness? You mean his Alzheimer's?'

'Yes. My father kept it secret right up until he developed dementia. The disease made him lose control of the memories he'd been keeping locked away inside him. They slipped out, one by one, including the most painful ones. He started talking about episodes from his past that he'd never spoken of before, hardly seemed to realise he was doing it. Naturally I knew – we all did – about Jónatan, but my family never really discussed him or what had happened. It was never really talked of. But then my father started rambling on about Jónatan and always seemed very disturbed when he mentioned him. He kept saying that my grandfather had picked up some ideas from him about the *huldufólk* and used them to do something unspeakable. He kept crying – a man who'd never shown his feelings. Naturally I was curious, and in the end I got the truth out of him. I found myself confronted by a family tragedy – the ugly truth about my father and grandfather. And of course the other, much greater tragedy involving the deaths of Rósamunda and Hrund and later of Jónatan. I had no idea what to do with the information. It was just too much for me. I felt I had to contain it at all costs. I felt responsible. All of a sudden I found myself in the same position as my father. He had been wrestling with his conscience all these years. Then one day when I was visiting him at the nursing home I found a man his age sitting in his room with him. He'd dug up the truth, only he thought my father was responsible for what my grandfather had done, and he was talking about going to the police. I went round to see him. Not to hurt him but to talk to him.'

'And the temptation was too great? If you got rid of him, you got rid of the whole problem?'

333

'I don't know what came over me,' said Benjamín, his voice suddenly breaking at the thought of what he had done. Konrád saw that he was fighting back tears, still staring fixedly into the doorway as if he wouldn't be able to meet anyone else's eye if his life depended on it. 'I thought . . . he was old, and I thought all I had to do was put him to sleep, then my problems would be over . . . but it doesn't work like that. I have horrible night-mares . . . Though he was frail, he fought back with all his strength, and I was going to stop but . . . but it was too late. It was over so quickly . . . so quickly . . .' Benjamín heaved a sigh. 'I . . . I want this to stop,' he said. 'I don't want to live with these secrets. I don't want my son to have to hide what I've done, to go through the same hell. I want it to stop here.'

'Did you say that Hólmbert had caught his father in the act?'

'As far as I can work out, Dad found him with Rósamunda's body. My grandmother was staying with relatives in Stykkishólmur at the time, and my grandfather was alone in the house apart from my dad. Rósamunda had turned up out of the blue, com-pletely hysterical, accusing my grandfather of getting her pregnant and saying she'd got rid of the baby. She was ranting about a girl up north who she was sure was another of his victims, and threat-ening to denounce him so everyone would know what kind of man he was. That was how Dad knew what my grandfather had done to her.'

'He'd raped her, you mean?'

'Yes. She'd come round one day a couple of months earlier to deliver some dresses and my grandfather had invited her in. Somehow he managed to lure her down to the laundry, then started slapping her around and finally raped her.'

'And your father insisted he hadn't known beforehand?'

'No, he didn't find out about the rape until later. My grandfather admitted the whole thing when Dad caught him with Rósamunda's body. By the time my father walked in it was all over. He said it was a horrible shock. The girl was lying on the floor of my grandfather's study. My grandfather had only meant to shut her up, but before he knew what he was doing he'd throttled her. He asked Dad to help him. Ordered him, rather. Said they had to stick together. The family honour was at stake. The girl had been out of control, and he'd acted in self-defence. But Dad immediately suspected that the same thing had happened three years earlier when they were up north. My grandfather had been in a strange mood one evening, and there were obvious cuts or scratches on his neck that he was trying to hide. When Dad asked about them, my grandfather wouldn't answer, but the incident lingered in Dad's mind, and he couldn't help wondering about the story of Hrund and her disappearance. It was only when he walked in on my grandfather with Rósamunda's body, though, that he found out the truth. He demanded to know what had happened to Hrund and eventually my grandfather confessed that he'd assaulted her too. He swore he hadn't killed her like Rósamunda but admitted he'd raped her.'

'I take it he intimidated her into keeping silent?'

'Yes. And he forbade my dad to report him – one minute pleading, the next furious. Dad took the decision to cover for him. And stuck by it. For my grandmother's sake. For the family.'

'What was all that business about the *huldufólk*?'

'My grandfather was familiar with stories about the elves – you know the kind of thing. It runs so deep, especially in the country-side. And Jónatan was forever talking about them. Apparently my grandfather got the impression that Hrund was very naive and gullible, and he took advantage of that. But Rósamunda was a different story.'

'So the two of them decided they would pin the whole thing on Jónatan?'

'The idea only occurred to my dad when the police came round to notify them of his death. Jónatan was their prime suspect, but my father sensed that they had their doubts. He simply made sure they were confident that they had the right man. All he had to do was fuel their suspicions about Jónatan. After all, Jónatan was dead. It couldn't hurt him. If you look at it like that.'

'Why did they bring her here, to the theatre?'

'My father was a bit vague about that. Perhaps because the National Theatre was supposed to resemble an elf castle, so it fitted the lie. And my grandfather knew that girls used to go there with soldiers. It would be very convenient if they could shift the blame onto them. My father watched from a distance. Stood on Skuggasund and waited until a soldier and his girl came across the body. Then he made himself scarce.'

'And was richly rewarded for his silence.'

'He inherited the family business,' said Benjamín flatly.

'And you? Weren't you faced with the same choice when you decided to dispose of Thorson?'

The other man didn't answer.

'You must have been thinking about the family honour – whatever that's worth?'

'I just couldn't face the idea of the past ever being exposed. Of anyone knowing that about us. About my father. My grandfather. The old man was intending to go to the police. I saw my chance and took it. There's no excuse for what I did. Absolutely no excuse.'

'You really thought you could keep it secret for the rest of your life?'

'I felt I'd been put in an impossible position. Just like my father before me. A completely impossible position.'

'Oh, I think you could both have found better solutions,' Konráð said and sensed that his words had touched a nerve. Taking Benjamín by the arm, he led him to the car and made him get into the passenger seat. Then he climbed behind the wheel and drove off down Lindargata, glancing over, as he always did, at his old house, on his way to keep his appointment with Marta, who was waiting for news at the station.

51

Thorson's funeral was attended by Konrád, Birgitta and a scattering of old engineering colleagues. It took place on a grey, rainy day at the chapel in Fossvogur Cemetery, where many years ago Thorson had bought a plot beside the grave of the man he had loved. The ceremony was brief: the minister delivered a blessing, they sang the old funeral hymn 'The One True Flower', then the undertakers shouldered the coffin and carried it out to the cemetery, where they lowered it into the ground.

One of the first things Konrád did after Benjamín's story had come to light was to share it with Birgitta, explaining how it was that her old neighbour had come to die at the hands of a murderer, how his death had been intended to protect a shameful family secret. He told her about Rósamunda's fate and about the girl from Öxarfjördur who had never been found and presumably never would be now.

'They're all guilty – three generations – each in their own way,'

338

commented Birgitta as they stood over Thorson's grave. 'The grandfather, son and grandson.'

'I don't suppose Benjamín knew what to do when Thorson suddenly turned up out of the blue, all set to expose his father and grandfather. He claims he didn't go to see Thorson with the intention of killing him. It was a spur-of-the-moment decision. A moment of madness. He thought the problem would go away if the old man did.'

'What about the grandfather?' asked Birgitta.

'Benjamín got the impression that his grandfather didn't have a lot of respect for women. It was a different era. Men saw nothing wrong in taking advantage of them. Then there was the social upheaval brought about by the war. Benjamín thought that perhaps in his grandfather's eyes the girl up north and Rósamunda had represented everything he despised about the Situation. Innocent though they were, they were made to pay the price for the behaviour of other women. Though at this remove it's impossible to know what was going through his head. For all Benjamín knows, there may have been other girls who landed in his clutches and never dared say a word.'

'Stefán never forgot the girls,' said Birgitta as they walked slowly back to the cemetery gates. 'Even after all these years.'

'No, he was never satisfied,' said Konrád. 'Never happy with the way it ended.'

Later that evening Beta dropped in on her brother, and he told her the whole story. She sat in the kitchen listening to Konrád's account without a word, and afterwards was silent and pensive for a long while.

'It must have come as a nasty shock for this Benjamín when his dad started rambling on about Rósamunda, and the horrific truth came out,' she said at last.

'He wouldn't have known which way to turn,' agreed Konrád. 'Then Thorson pops up, then me. The whole thing was blowing up in his face.'

'All his family's dirty laundry about to be exposed.'

'Yes.'

'And his dad a former cabinet minister and all.'

'He wanted to protect his reputation – his family's reputation.'

'Just like you're always trying to defend *your* dad?'

'I'm not "always" trying to defend him.'

'Odd that he should have been connected to all this,' said Beta.

'Yes, but then he was mixed up in a lot of things.'

'I'll never forget the moment when Mum told me the news. That he'd been stabbed outside the abattoir and no one knew who'd done it. Somehow I didn't care. I actually think I was relieved. I didn't miss him at all. He was despicable to Mum – to a lot of people. And Mum said he was well on the way to turning you into the same kind of good-for-nothing.'

'That's not true,' said Konrád. 'OK, he had his faults but he had his good moments too. I know how he treated Mum, how he drove her away.'

'It's called domestic violence, Konrád. She fled all the way east to Seydisfjördur. He only hung on to you to get even with her. That was typical. He was a nasty piece of work, Konrád. He drank, he was violent and he got sucked into crime.'

'I know all that. I was there, remember? It was ugly, and I've never forgiven him for what he did to Mum.'

'Yet you've always tried to defend him! You're always trying to find excuses for him. Like that Benjamín did, and his father before him.'

'That's not the same –'

'Yes, it is,' said Beta. 'You bloody men, you're all the same. Too bloody spineless to face up to the truth.'

'Calm down,' said Konrád.

'No, you calm down!' Beta got to her feet. Then, after a moment, she added in a less agitated tone: 'Do you think we'll ever find out what happened? By the abattoir?'

It was a question they used to ponder a great deal, but as time wore on the incident faded into the background, and these days they hardly ever discussed who could have stabbed their father to death and why. Beta was inclined to be more judgemental. She felt he had brought it on himself. But Konrád couldn't agree.

'No, I doubt it,' he said.

'It's unlikely at this stage?'

'Yes, not much chance now.'

52

Flóvent stood near the stage, watching the newly elected president of the Republic of Iceland deliver a speech to his countrymen who were huddled against the rain, having gathered in their thousands around the stands at Thingvellir, all the way up the Almannagjá ravine and down the River Öxará to the very shores of the lake. They had thronged here from all over the country to celebrate their new-found freedom as citizens of Europe's youngest republic. The King of Denmark had sent a congratulatory telegram despite his private dismay at being called on to surrender the colony in the middle of the war. The D-Day landings had recently taken place. News had reached them of catastrophic Allied losses on the beaches of Normandy. Flóvent often thought of Thorson and fervently hoped that he had survived the slaughter.

The new president's speech echoed across the historic assembly site with the rain, and Flóvent was proud that day of being an Icelander, despite his anxiety about the future and his sense of unease. He was living in treacherous times; the world was in turmoil, and there was still a foreign military power occupying the land.

As he stood by the stage, studying the ranks of parliamentarians massed behind the president, Flóvent spotted the cold profile of Hólmbert's father between upturned collar and hat. Their eyes met for an instant and the MP inclined his head.

Flóvent had tried not to dwell too much on Jónatan's tragic death, had tried to bury the memory he found so hard to endure. But it hadn't really worked. He stamped his feet and raised his eyes to gaze out over the lake into the wide blue yonder, and as he did so the shades of two girls came flying back to haunt him, one from the dark corner behind the National Theatre, the other from the cliffs of Dettifoss. As though they were begging him not to forget but to stand vigil over their memory, as though they were the only thing of true value in this newly independent land.

53

Deep in a remote cleft in the lava, too deep for the roar of the waterfall to reach, lies the realm of eternal cold and darkness. The cleft narrows as it deepens, its rugged walls sheer and perilous, its depths inaccessible even to raven and fox. The walls are overgrown with ferns and mosses, down which water seeps from the nearby springs, transforming the fissure into a fairy-tale palace in frosty weather. At the bottom a cold silence reigns, which neither the moaning of the wind nor the crying of birds can break, ensuring that the palace's only guest, the unfortunate elf maiden, never wakes from her long sleep.

Read on for a sample of the next
Reykjavík Wartime Mystery
by Arnaldur Indriðason.

1

The *Súd* steered a careful course around the frigates and mine-sweepers in the approaches to Reykjavík harbour before finally coming alongside the docks. Shortly afterwards the passengers began to disembark, one after the other, many of them shaky on their legs and relieved to have dry land underfoot once more. The voyage had been uneventful until they reached Faxaflói Bay, where the wind had veered to the south-west bringing squalls of rain and the ship had begun to roll. Most of the passengers stayed below decks, where a sour reek of wet clothes pervaded the cramped quarters. Several had been seasick during this last stage, Eyvindur among them.

He had boarded the ship at Ísafjördur, toting his two bat-tered suitcases, and slept for most of the way, worn out from trekking round the villages and farms of the West Fjords. The cases contained tins of polish: Meltonian for shoes and Poliflor for furniture. He was also lugging around a sample dinner service

349

that the wholesaler had imported from Holland just before the war.

Eyvindur had done quite well with the shoe and furniture polish, but in spite of his best efforts to sing the praises of the Dutch tableware, it seemed there was no market for such goods in these treacherous times. His heart really wasn't in it, and he hadn't even bothered to visit all the places that normally formed part of his route. Somehow he couldn't summon the powers of persuasion, that almost religious fervour which, according to the wholesaler, all successful salesmen required, and so he had returned clutching only a handful of orders. Eyvindur had rather a bad conscience about this. He felt he could have made more of an effort and knew that the few orders he had secured would make little impression on the wholesaler's mountain of stock.

The trouble was he had been in a bit of a state when he set out from Reykjavík a fortnight ago. That was one reason the trip hadn't gone as well as it should. Moments before he was due to leave he had made an accusation in his typically tactless way, which led to a row that had weighed on him throughout the trip. Vera had reacted furiously, calling him all kinds of ugly names, and he had started to regret his words as soon as the *Súd* sailed out of Reykjavík harbour. He'd had two weeks to brood and find excuses for his behaviour, though to be honest he still wasn't convinced that he had been the one in the wrong. Yet her outrage had struck him as genuine when she retorted that she couldn't believe he would accuse her of such a thing. She had burst into tears, locked herself in the bedroom and refused to speak to him. In danger of missing his boat, Eyvindur had snatched up the cases of polish and tableware and run out of the door, wishing with all his heart that he had a different job, one that didn't force him to spend long periods away from home while Vera got up to goodness knows what.

These thoughts were still rankling as he leapt ashore and half ran towards the centre of town, hurrying as fast as his legs would carry him, plump, a little splay-footed and out of condition in spite of his age, clad in his trench coat, a case in either hand. The rain was coming down more heavily now and water trickled from the brim of his hat, getting in his eyes and soaking his feet. He took refuge under the porch of the Reykjavík Pharmacy and peered round the corner into Austurvöllur Square. A small troop of soldiers was marching past Parliament House. The Americans were in the process of taking over from the British, and you could hardly move these days for Yanks, army trucks and jeeps, artillery and sandbags – all the trappings of military occupation. The quiet little town was unrecognisable.

There was a time when Vera used to meet him off the ship and they would walk home together, she chatting about what she had been up to in his absence, he telling her about his latest trip, the characters he'd met and the goods he'd managed to shift. He had admitted that he wasn't sure how long he would last in this job. He wasn't really cut out to be a salesman. Didn't have the necessary gift of the gab. Wasn't that comfortable in social situations unlike, say, Felix, who positively radiated self-confidence.

That was true of Runki too. He sometimes sailed on the *Súd*, his cases crammed full of headgear from Luton. How Eyvindur envied Runki his nerve; he was always self-assured, even cocky, never had any trouble getting people's attention. He was a born salesman. It was all about confidence. While Eyvindur was getting his tongue in a twist over the Dutch dinner service, all over town people were donning Runki's new hats, smug in the belief that they had got themselves a bargain.

351

Too impatient to wait for the weather to let up, Eyvindur grabbed his cases again, ducked his head and ran across the square into the wind and rain, that cold, late-summer rain that hung like a low canopy over the town. He and Vera lived in the west end, in a small flat that belonged to his father's brother. Rents were astronomical these days with all the people flooding in from the countryside to the towns, especially Reykjavík, lured by the prospect of working for the army, for hard cash and a better life. His uncle, who owned several properties in town, was raking in the profits, though he charged Eyvindur a fair rent. Even so, Eyvindur found it steep enough and occasionally had to ask for more time when his self-confidence was at its lowest ebb and he failed to bring home enough in commission.

The flat was on the ground floor of a three-storey concrete building. He unlocked the front door, then the door to the flat, before hastily retrieving his cases from the step outside and carrying them in. As he did so he called out to his girlfriend, who he assumed was waiting for him inside.

'Vera? Vera darling?'

There was no answer. He closed the door, switched on the light and took a moment to catch his breath. He needn't have bothered to hurry over the last stretch: Vera wasn't home. She must have gone out, which meant he would have to wait a little longer before he could beg her forgiveness for his crass accusations. He'd been rehearsing what he was going to say – would have to say – if he was going to make things right again.

His outer clothes were sopping wet, so he took off his hat and laid his overcoat across a chair in the living room, then hung his jacket in the wardrobe by the door. Opening one of the cases, he took out a pound of genuine coffee that he had managed to get hold of in the West Fjords, hoping to give Vera a nice surprise. He was just about to go into the kitchen when he paused. Something wasn't right.

Turning back, Eyvindur opened the wardrobe again. His jacket was hanging there, along with a second, longer jacket of his and another coat. It was what was missing that brought him up short: Vera's clothes had gone. The shoes she kept in the bottom weren't there. Nor were her two coats. He stood for a moment, staring blankly into the cupboard, then walked into the bedroom. There was another, larger wardrobe there with drawers for socks and underwear and a rail for dresses and shirts. Eyvindur opened it and pulled out the drawers, to be confronted by the astonishing fact that all Vera's clothes had disappeared. His own things were still in their usual place but there wasn't a single feminine garment left.

He couldn't believe his eyes. In a daze, he went over to Vera's dressing table and opened the drawers and compartments: it was the same story. Had she left him? Moved out?

He sank down on the bed, his thoughts miles away, recalling what Runki had said about Vera when Runki thought he couldn't hear. The day he caught the boat to the West Fjords they had bumped into each other at Hot and Cold, a restaurant popular with soldiers. Runki had been there with a friend, shovelling down fish and chips, and as soon as he thought Eyvindur was safely out of earshot he had dropped that remark about Vera.

An absurd lie – he should have gone back and rammed the words down the bastard's throat.

The lie that had made Vera so angry, so hurt when he was stupid enough to fling it in her face.

Eyvindur stared into the empty drawers and thumped his fist

on the bed. Deep down he had been afraid of this. He was no longer so sure Runki's remark had been an outrageous lie – that Vera was mixed up in the Situation.

And then there was all that nonsense his old classmate, that dirty rat Felix, had been rambling on about when they ran into each other in Ísafjördur. Was there any truth to it? All that stuff about the school and those experiments. Or was he simply out to humiliate Eyvindur because he was drunk, and hateful, just like he used to be in the old days when Eyvindur had laboured under the foolish belief that they were friends?

2

Flóvent surveyed the flat but could see no signs of a struggle, despite the aftermath of violence confronting him in all its horror. On the floor lay the body of a man, shot through the head. It looked like an execution pure and simple; no sign that the victim had tried to run. No chairs had been overturned. No tables knocked aside. The pictures were hanging perfectly straight on the walls. The windows were intact and fastened shut, so it could hardly have been a break-in. The door of the flat was undamaged too and locked. The man now lying on the floor with a bullet hole in the back of his head must have opened the door to his assailant or left it open, unaware that it would be the last thing he did. It looked as though the victim had just walked in when the attack took place, since he was still in his overcoat, the front-door key clutched in his hand. At first glance Flóvent couldn't see that anything had been stolen. The visitor must have come here to kill, and had carried out this intention with such brutality that the first police officers to arrive at the scene were still in shock. One had thrown up in the living room. The other was standing outside, protesting that there was no way he was going in there again.

The first thing Flóvent had done was shoo away those who had no direct role in the investigation: the policemen who had trampled all over the scene; the witness who had raised the alarm; the nosy neighbours who, when informed that a gun had been fired in the flat, were unable to say for certain if they'd heard a shot. The only people left inside were Flóvent himself and the district medical officer who had come to confirm the man's death.

'Of course he'll have died instantly,' said the doctor, a short, scrawny man whose prominent teeth were clamped on a pipe that he hardly ever removed from his mouth. 'The shot was fired at such close quarters that it could only end one way,' he continued, exhaling smoke with every word. 'The bullet has exited through his eye here, causing this God-awful mess.' He contemplated the congealed pool of blood that had spread out over the floorboards. One of the policemen had carelessly stepped in the dark puddle, slipped and almost fallen. You could see the skid mark of his shoe in the blood. There were splashes on the furniture and walls. Lumps of brain on the curtains. The killer had shot through a thick cushion to muffle the noise, then tossed it back on the sofa. The exposed side of the victim's face had been almost entirely blown away.

Flóvent focused on trying to remember the protocol for examining a crime scene. Murders didn't happen every day in Reykjavík and he was relatively new to the job, so he didn't want to make any mistakes. He had only been with Reykjavík's Criminal Investigation Department for a few years, but he had also done a six-month stint with the Edinburgh CID, where he had learnt a lot about the theory and practice of detective work. The victim appeared to be in his twenties. He had thinning hair; his suit and coat were threadbare, his shoes cheap. He appeared to have been forced down on his knees, then fallen forward when he took the bullet to the back of the head. A single shot in exactly the right place. But for some reason this had not been enough. After the execution, the killer had stuck a finger in the wound and daubed the dead man's forehead with blood. What possible motive could he have had? Was it a signature of some sort? A comment that the perpetrator regarded as important, though its significance was lost on Flóvent? Was it a justification? An explanation? Second thoughts? Remorse? All of these? Or none? Or a challenge, intended to convey the message that the person who did this had no regrets? Flóvent shook his head. The clumsily smeared mark meant nothing to him.

The bullet itself proved easy to find since it was buried in a floorboard. Flóvent marked the spot before prising the bullet out with his pocket knife and examining it in his palm. He recognised the make, as ballistics was a special interest of his. This was one of the innovations in forensic detection that he was keen to introduce to Iceland. Fingerprinting too. And the practice of systematically photographing felons and the scenes of major crimes. Whenever necessary, he called out a photographer he knew who had a studio in town. Bit by bit his department was building up an archive, though it was still very rudimentary and incomplete.

'The person who fired the shot must have been standing behind him, presumably holding the gun at arm's length,' said the doctor, removing his pipe for a moment before clamping it between his teeth again. 'So you ought to be able to get a rough idea of his height.'

357

'Yes,' said Flóvent. 'I was wondering about that. We can't assume the murderer was a man. It could have been a woman.'

'Well, I don't know. Would a woman be capable of this? Somehow I doubt it.'

'I wouldn't rule it out.'

'It was clearly an execution,' said the doctor, exhaling smoke. 'I've never seen anything like it. Forced to kneel on the floor of his own home and shot like a dog. You'd have to be a cold-blooded bastard to do a thing like that.'

'And smear his forehead with blood?'

'Again, I don't know . . . I've no idea what that's supposed to mean.'

'When do you reckon it happened?'

'Not that long ago,' said the doctor, looking at the congealed blood on the floor. 'Twelve hours, give or take. The post-mortem will give us a better estimate.'

'Yesterday evening, then?' said Flóvent.

At this point the photographer arrived, armed with his tripod and the Speed Graphic camera he had acquired before the war. Having greeted Flóvent and the doctor, he looked around the room, dispassionately appraising the scene, then went about his business methodically, setting up the tripod, removing the camera from its case, fixing it up and inserting the film holder in the back. Each holder contained two pieces of film. The photographer had come equipped with a number of these holders and extra flashbulbs as well.

'How many shots do you want?' he asked.

'Take several,' said Flóvent.

'Was it a soldier?' the photographer asked as he paused to replace the film holder then fixed the camera to the tripod again and changed the bulb.

'What makes you think that?'

'Doesn't it look like the work of a soldier?' The photographer was a world-weary man of about sixty. Flóvent had never seen him smile.

'Maybe,' said Flóvent distractedly. He was searching for clues to the identity of the gunman: any evidence he might have left behind such as footprints, clothing, cigarette ash. It looked as if the tenant had been in the kitchen fairly recently, fixing himself a snack. There was a half-eaten slice of stale bread and cheese on the table. Beside it was a cup of tea, partially drunk. Flóvent had fumbled in the victim's pockets for his wallet but couldn't find one on his body or anywhere else in the flat.

'I can't believe anyone but a soldier would be capable of a clean job like that,' said the photographer.

The room was briefly illuminated by his flash, then he recommenced the laborious process of setting the heavy camera up in another spot and inserting new film.

'It's possible,' said Flóvent. 'I couldn't say. You might know better.'

'An officer, maybe?' continued the photographer thoughtfully. 'Someone in authority? It looks like an execution, doesn't it? Betrays a kind of arrogance.'

'You two seem to be thinking along very different lines,' commented the doctor, tamping down his pipe. 'Flóvent thinks a woman did it.'

'No,' said the photographer flatly, studying the man on the floor for a while before snapping another picture. 'No, out of the question.'

'Perhaps he was robbed,' suggested Flóvent. 'I can't find his wallet.'

From his inspection of the flat, he concluded that the man had lived alone. It was a typical bachelor's apartment, small and spartan, largely free from ornament, but clean and tidy. The only extraneous object was the cushion used to muffle the shot. Apart from that the flat was sparsely furnished, and what furniture there was showed signs of wear: the sofa and armchair in the living room, the two old wooden chairs in the kitchen. On the sofa lay an open suitcase containing Lido cleaning products and several packs of Kolynos toothpaste. The merchandise was spattered with blood.

The flash lit up the sordid scene one last time, then the photographer began to pack away his equipment. The doctor paused in the doorway to relight his pipe. Flóvent glanced back at the man on the floor, unable to comprehend the sheer violence that must have lain behind his killing: the implacable hatred, the anger, the utter ruthlessness.

'Did you take a picture of that mark on his forehead?' he asked.

'Yes, what is it? What does it mean?'

'No idea,' said Flóvent. After his initial examination of the corpse, he had kept his eyes averted from the man's shattered face. 'I can't make any sense of it. Can't begin to guess what it means or why someone would have smeared blood on his forehead like that.'

'Have you identified him?' asked the photographer as he was leaving.

'Yes, his landlady told me who he was, and there are bills here in his name.'

'So, who was he?'

'I've never come across him before,' said Flóvent. 'His name was Felix. Felix Lunden.'